*The stain on my blouse spread
as the crimson liquid
began to steadily drip from
the balcony floorboards above me.*

I sprinted to the ladder leading to the balcony. At its base I hesitated. Did I really want to go up? Taking deep breaths, I climbed the ladder, questioning each step I took, wondering what I'd find. I pulled myself up the last rung. A wave of relief swept over me. I should have known. It was just some red paint leaking from a jar that had tipped over and broken.

I took a few trial steps forward, scanning the contents of the balcony for anything resembling drawings. What's wrong with this picture? I asked myself.

As I inched forward, I recognized the jacket. American. Ralph Lauren. The jacket Gino had worn yesterday. And to make matters worse, Gino was still in it—with one of Tony's walnut-handled palette knives skewering his throat.

TIGER'S PALETTE

TIGER'S PALETTE

A CAROLINE CANFIELD MYSTERY

JACQUELINE FIEDLER

POCKET BOOKS

New York   London   Toronto   Sydney   Tokyo   Singapore

An *Original* Publication of POCKET BOOKS

POCKET BOOKS, a division of Simon & Schuster Inc.
1230 Avenue of the Americas, New York, NY 10020

ISBN: 0-671-01559-1

First Pocket Books printing April 1998

10 9 8 7 6 5 4 3 2 1

POCKET and colophon are registered trademarks of
Simon & Schuster Inc.

Printed in the U.S.A.

In loving memory of my parents . . .

Dad, who took me to the library and
pointed out the mysteries
and
Mom, who took me to the park and
pointed out the squirrels.

"A picture is something which requires as much knavery, trickery, and deceit as the perpetration of a crime. . . . The artist does not draw what he sees, but what he must make others see."

—EDGAR DEGAS

1

*THE LAST TIME I SAW TONY HE TOLD ME OF AN OLD BELIEF,
perhaps still held in some parts of the world, that the
whiskers of the tiger are deadly. When scalded in liquid
they are said to produce a lethal drink. Funny how the
myth became reality.*

I kept a comfortable distance from the coffin, but even
from the sidelines of the chapel, I could see Tony's
hands—clutching in death his closest companions in life.
He would embrace them for eternity, for he'd be buried
with three Winsor & Newton paintbrushes pressed to
his chest.

For six years I had worked with him daily, but for the
last three we had drifted apart. It is the fate of mentor
and protégé—the better the teacher, the more eager the
student is to fly. And Anthony Chirico had been as good
as mentors come.

A shiver rocked my shoulders. The air-conditioned
chapel was as cold as a tomb—just not as silent. A string
of Italian expletives erupted from the alcove to my left

like a siren going off. The shrill voice—once heard, never forgotten—belonged to Tony's ex-wife, Antoinetta.

"Bastarda!" she screamed. "You have shown your hand! Get out! *Bastarda!"*

The room fell silent as a dark-haired figure fled from the alcove. I strained to get a better look at the object of Antoinetta's wrath, but even three-inch heels didn't offer a view beyond the high-rise hairdo of the woman next to me.

A curtain rang down across the alcove's doorway. Antoinetta had made a full-time career of driving off Tony's girlfriends, and this was probably just one more episode. Conversation in the room resumed, until another shriek ripped the air.

The visitors once again fell silent, their attention riveted on the draperied alcove as though anticipating Act Two. The curtain billowed several times, then through it—low to the ground like a streak of oily exhaust—shot a tiny, black-shrouded figure, emitting a whine like an untuned outboard motor. No one made an entrance like Antoinetta.

She torpedoed forward, her target apparent. Those of us in her trajectory moved quickly aside. In the widow's wake rushed two matronly figures, also dressed in black.

Antoinetta flung herself at the casket, her fists pummeling its side. "You bring shame to this family!" She brandished a fist in front of Tony's face. "I warn you. What you didn't pay in this life, you will pay in the next!"

"And if anyone can collect, it's Antoinetta," someone behind me muttered.

Surrounding the widow, relatives struggled to separate her from the casket, but she had clamped her hands like wrenches around the coffin's brass handrail. The two stout matrons pried her fingers loose and escorted her back to the private room. Once again the curtain fell across the alcove.

Glad at least that Tony hadn't witnessed that scene, I exhaled in relief, then drew another breath for courage. Slowly, I wended my way through the sea of women toward the coffin. Women had adored Tony, and the floozy faction was out in full force that day at the chapel in St. Charles, Illinois. We were forty miles west of the Loop, but there was enough hair spray in the room to fuel the great Chicago fire all over again. Fortunately, Mrs. O'Leary and her cow weren't among the mourners.

With each step I forced myself closer. *You can't leave. There's so much more I need to know—about painting—about life.* No more discussions of Old Masters over glasses of Frascati, no more quarrels about the status of women in art, no more help when I struggled with a painting. *This is it—the last time I'll ever see you. I really am on my own.* I shrank back, but the movement of the crowd propelled me forward until I stood at Tony's side.

My eyes shifted nervously in search of a haven to rest—anyplace but his face. Behind the casket glowed a back-lit photo of mountains and a lake. I'd seen one like it before—only with a beer logo over the snowy peak. The prosaic landscape, softened by sheer draperies, seemed a deliberate slap in the face to the master landscape muralist lying in state. At least it was consistent with the warped tape of "Rock of Ages" that throbbed over the sound system. My eyes went back to Tony's hands, wandered to the paintbrushes, hesitated on the knot in his necktie, but then reluctantly drifted to his face.

To look at him, one would never suspect the turbulence of his life. Even at sixty-eight, few lines marked the tight skin of his square face. His curly, light gray hair contrasted with bristly dark brows and steely mustache. A lump lodged in my throat. Tony's image blurred. Though the room was packed, I was quite alone with him for just a moment. *Good-bye, dear teacher. Good-bye, dear friend.*

"Get up closer, would'ja? I only brought my readin' glasses," a creaky voice said.

"Hold yer garters, Gert. You're steppin' on my corn," another answered.

Opposing odors of lilac/cedar closet clashed with gardenia/mothball and met head on under my nose. I glanced left, then right. I felt like I had just stepped into a Paris music hall scene painted by Toulouse-Lautrec. Two geriatric bimbos flanked me, blocking my retreat. I closed my eyes, but the sight was too much for even the untrained eye to forget.

The woman to my left had acid-yellow hair swept up into a beehive. Four violent tints of eye shadow, refusing to blend, stained the fleshy pockets of her eyes, like the washes of a garish watercolor. "Just look at him," she said. "He don't look like hisself."

Not to be outdone, the woman to my right sported winged hair the color of tangerines. Her makeup was heavy enough to have been applied with a palette knife. The tangerine reached into the coffin and rearranged Tony's hair as she clucked disapproval. "His hair used to be thicker. And why's his face so yellow?"

I bent forward to peer at Tony. His hair was thinner than I remembered, and his Sicilian complexion leaned more to chartreuse than olive, as well.

"Guess he won't be needing the lotion I bought him for that dry skin." The beehive perched her claw on Tony's wrist. "He was just so handsome. Like that A-rab movie actor, Homar Sheriff." Her joints crackled as she bent to kiss Tony's cheek.

Seeking comfort in each other, the two women merged in front of me. I stepped back. Like air to a vacuum, women surged forward to claim the space I'd surrendered. They scratched and clawed at Tony like tigers over a kill.

I retreated to the side of the chapel, pausing to view a large spray of unusual and delicate flowers. Curious as to their sender, I reached for the memorial card attached to a spiky stem. The sweet floral scent made me lightheaded. Or perhaps it was the glimpse I caught of the man next to me—just when I thought I'd given up on men.

From the corner of my eye, I judged him to be in his late thirties. While my hand fished for the card, I turned my head for a discrete look. Deep tan, longish thick brown hair. The light gray sport coat he wore over sharply creased jeans struck me as being formal for him.

When he glanced up from the bouquet and made eye contact, I instinctively smiled and held his gaze as my hand, fishing for the memorial card, continued to make circles inside the bouquet. Then with a sudden look of urgency on his face, the man lunged at me. I flinched, letting out a shrill cry. His hands shot past me to the vase, which was wobbling precariously. He planted it firmly back on its pedestal. For a moment it looked like he might speak, but he only smiled as though amused and turned away.

Glancing in embarrassment around the room, I happened to spot Tony's son. Even from behind, Vince was easy to identify in a crowd. His stiff posture and square shoulders always made me wonder if the hanger was still in his suit coat.

Before founding Chirico Construction, Vince had worked with me at Tony's art studio. All that summer father and son rubbed each other the wrong way. In the end Vince snapped his brushes in half, slashed a canvas and stormed out, swearing never to return. Tony cursed at him and threw a paint pot at the slammed door. And me? I got to clean it all up.

Keeping Vince in sight, I sliced my way through the wall-to-wall female bodies. Like a baby in the birth canal, I squeezed my shoulders together for the final passage, emerging right on target. My face plowed into the back of his silk suit.

He turned and steadied me, gripping my shoulders. "Caroline. Still tripping through life, I see."

"I'm thinking of just having 'excuse me' tattooed across my forehead." I said.

"Forget it. I'm used to women falling all over me. It's the Chirico curse." His hug enveloped me in a vapor of Pierre Cardin cologne as my lips brushed his cheek. Brush strokes of premature gray swept through the wiry black hair at his temples. Like his father, his dark good looks would only improve with age.

"Vince, I'm so very sorry."

"No harm done." Vince adjusted the turquoise hanky in his breast pocket. "Really."

"I meant I'm sorry about your dad."

"Oh, that."

That?

He poked out his chin and straightened his tie. "The old man had a full life doing his thing. Not everyone's that lucky."

"You are, aren't you?"

"Finally." Vince turned away to stare at the coffin. His shoulders slumped ever so slightly. "But he never forgave me for not following in his footsteps. He couldn't understand my idea of art was in building three-dimensional structures, not two-dimensional paintings."

"He knew somebody needed to build the walls before he could paint his murals."

"Yeah, well, the old man built plenty of walls himself." He crossed his arms. Diamond-studded cuff links peeked out from his coat sleeve. Vince's downcast gaze drifted to my fingers bundled in white gauze. "What the hell happened to you?"

I flipped my hand back and forth. "Sadistic staple gun. I was stretching a canvas and—"

"How the hell do you survive? You're a walking accident."

He had a point. As a kid, whatever wasn't bandaged was bruised. My mother had constantly warned me, "Watch where you're going, not where you've been." But I never outgrew the tendency. My eyes simply won't be confined to the road ahead. The sights around me remain too fascinating.

"Smart move you made giving up mural work," Vince added.

"After I nearly fell . . . I mean, if Tony hadn't grabbed me . . ." I sighed. "Anyway, afterwards I told him that was it for me. No more scaffolds. A drawing board and easel are more my speed."

"No shit. What did the old man say when you laid it on the line?"

"Nothing much. He was . . . disappointed in me." In many ways that had hurt more. "Since I've always loved painting animals, I opened my own studio. It's called 'It's a Wild Life.' "

Vince chuckled. "The old man put wildlife art in the same class as paintings of Elvis on black velvet."

"And yet Tony loved animals. When I asked him once about the inconsistency, he said he loved fruit, bread and wine too, but he wouldn't be caught dead painting a still life." Realizing my tactless comment, I quickly added, "That's why I was so surprised when he took the zoo commission."

"Wait'll you see Asia World." Vince's eyes sparkled. "Chirico Construction built the whole exhibit. It'll knock your socks off."

"I can't wait to see it. How did you ever get Tony to agree to paint wildlife murals?"

"Aw, there's a few animals in 'em, but they're basically landscapes—backdrops for the exhibits. Landscape was always his first love." Vince's eyes darkened, shadowed by heavy brows. "Maybe his only love." All Tony had told me was that he viewed the series of zoo murals as a chance to reunite his family. Apparently the reconciliation hadn't occurred. "How in hell did you put up with him all those years?" Vince asked.

"He was an artist, not a diplomat. He just wanted me to be the best painter I could be." I had overlooked behavior and comments from Tony I wouldn't have taken from anyone else. When I weighed my hurt feelings against what he'd taught me, the scales always tipped in his favor. I stared into Vince's umber eyes. "You look more and more like him." I knew the words were a mistake as soon as they left my mouth.

His eyes flashed. "I'm nothing like my father. I put my family first."

I shifted my eyes and shoulder bag simultaneously. "Where are Sara and the kids?"

Vince's lips tightened. "My wife hasn't been well since the miscarriage last year. I felt today might be too stressful for her. What about you? Still single?"

I merely nodded. After hitting thirty last year, I'd stopped offering explanations. I looked back at the coffin. "How could this happen, Vince?"

Vince shrugged. "He always said he'd die with his boots on. Shit happens."

The frown I felt inside must have appeared on my face.

His eyes searched mine. "Look, I know you lost your dad as a kid. You never had time to get to know your father the way I got to know mine. Maybe you were lucky."

My eyes tightened on his. "I'll just forget you said that."

Across the room, Antoinetta's steady whine turned to a wail. My eyes followed Vince's nervous over-the-shoulder glance toward the curtained alcove. Ashen-faced relatives barricaded the portal. One woman made the sign of the cross.

Vince gritted his perfectly aligned white teeth. "The son of a . . . even denied my mother the comfort of her priest by stipulating no religious funeral service."

I sensed the solace Antoinetta sought wasn't religion—unless it involved black magic.

"I'd better check on Mother." Vince squeezed my hand. "There'll be a small reception at the house about two o'clock. Stop by, okay?" He walked toward the alcove with the enthusiasm of a Christian on the way to the Colosseum.

I made my way down the side of the room to the rear. As I passed the doorway to the lobby, voices drew my attention. Planted at the mortuary's outside entrance stood a barrel-chested giant of a man wallowing in the onslaught of reporters and Minicams just outside the door. I recognized the media magnet in the bulging, tan safari suit as Miles Crandall, head of the Fox Valley Zoo.

A woman reporter, an up-and-comer on one of the Chicago nightly TV newscasts, jabbed a mike at him. "Tell me, Mr. Crandall—"

"*Doctor* Crandall," he corrected.

"Yes, well, how do you reply to rumors that Tony Chirico's fall could result in the closing of the zoo? If Fox Valley is held liable—"

Miles waved a giant arm in dismissal. Clearing his throat, he squared off with the Minicam. "Fox Valley Zoo has been totally absolved in this unfortunate accident. The scaffolding was inspected thoroughly and found to be faultless."

The reporter persisted. "Marcia Wilhelm and other animal rights activists say they will block the opening of the new exhibit one way or—"

"Nonsense. Asia World will open as scheduled. Mark your calendars, people, for October. We have a spectacular media event lined up . . ." With raised arms the zoo director stepped into the cluster of reporters outside, surrendering to the power of the press like a chocoholic to a double-fudge cake. The door closed behind him.

I found a chair and sat down, but Tony's lifeless form at the front of the room held my focus. *You always loved being in the news. But did you have to go to this extreme to do it?* Pulling out the obituary torn from Sunday's *Trib*, I read it again.

CONTROVERSIAL MURALIST PLUNGES TO DEATH AT ZOO

ANTHONY CHIRICO, 68, renowned painter and muralist, died Thursday following an accidental fall from his painting scaffolds at the Fox Valley Zoo, where he had recently been commissioned to paint the interior murals for the zoo's new exhibit, Asia World.

Chirico, a native of Sicily, was known for incorporating subliminal messages into his murals. His *Sunset on Tobacco Fields* caused the most controversy in recent years. In it he employed a technique called anamorphism, used most notably by Hans Holbein in his painting *The Ambassadors.* Viewed head on, the mural appears to be a traditional landscape. But when viewed from an acute side angle, the shadows cast by clouds over the tobacco field take on the shape of a skull and crossbones. The mural caused extreme embarrassment for the tobacco conglomerate that unwittingly used it for the cover of its annual report.

Litigation against the artist was rarely successful. Anthony Chirico was often quoted as saying, "I paint the truth. It is all I can see, it is what I must make others see."

I had the eerie feeling someone was watching me, so I glanced up. Through the crowd a statuesque woman advanced toward me.

The blond fashion plate brushed off the chair beside me before she sat down. "You're Caroline Canfield, aren't you?" Her sculpted, gold-highlighted eyes traveled over me. Worse yet, they took the back roads, not the interstate.

I squirmed with all the self-confidence of an eight-year-old with bubble gum in my hair and scabs on my knees. "That's right, I am." I sat up straighter and gave the woman some of her own medicine. I let my eyes travel, comparing her platinum, precisely clipped coif with the split ends of my long dark brown hair; her red Armani suit with my J. C. Penney basic black dress; and her manicured nails with my bandaged hand. My dark hose hid leg bruises. She didn't even have a snag in hers. I slumped a little.

I never outgrew the plunge in self-esteem that came from comparing myself to women who made a career out of looking perfect. After all, I'd lived with one—the "glamorous Vera Anders." For years I thought glamorous was Mom's first name.

The woman raised her brows. "You're prettier than I

expected. Good bone structure. Proportionate figure. Nice complexion." She ran through the checklist like a pilot before takeoff. "But you're dating yourself with that hair."

"My mother will be happy to hear I'm at least dating *someone*," I replied.

Her assessment continued. "A little unpolished, perhaps—awkward, even—but then it must be liberating to be so unencumbered by what is in fashion. Still, with a little work on your carriage and that Midwestern twang, you could be attractive."

"Gee, thanks. And you are—"

"Claudia B." She offered her hand like a pup, palm down. When I only stared at it, she tipped it back as though she had merely been inspecting her nails.

"You don't have to tell me what the 'B' stands for," I said.

"So you've heard of my exclusive holistic salon."

"Not really. I'm too busy dating myself."

"I can see you think I'm being forward," she said. "But Anthony spoke of you so often, I feel I know you. In fact I've been rather *jealous* of you, which seems silly now." She stared ahead at the coffin. "But you see, you shared with Anthony the one thing I couldn't. Oh, I took painting classes, I tried, but . . ." With her thumb she slowly rotated the large emerald on her finger. "Anthony spoke of the soul of art and the agony of creation. He knew how romantic that concept was to women."

Tony had danced through relationships with as much agility as he displayed on his painting scaffolds. Most women got in and got out before they made the mistake of taking him seriously. By the bitterness in her voice, I identified Claudia as one who had failed to do that.

"Tony could be very charming," I said.

"When he wanted something." She glanced down at her left hand. The diamond baguettes surrounding the emerald glimmered. The ring's heavy antique gold setting seemed old-fashioned and almost garish for someone so sleek and stylish.

"Like what?" He couldn't have wanted that ring.

"The mural commission for the zoo. I'm president of the executive board. He courted me, strung me along, and once he got what he wanted, he tossed me aside like some . . ." Her eyes accused me. ". . . bimbo."

I twisted around to confront her. "Tony and I had a professional relationship." I enunciated carefully.

"No doubt many of the . . . females . . . here had a *professional* relationship with him." She enunciated pretty well too.

"Tony was my mentor, not my lover."

Claudia seemed uninterested in the distinction. "Fine. Stay in denial." She glared at the coffin, eyes narrowed so that lines like little daggers formed in the corners. Beneath her chin was a tiny scar left, I suspected, by a pricey North Shore scalpel. At first I had estimated her to be forty. Now I guessed fifty or up. I pretended I saw someone I knew and started to rise.

She grabbed my arm. "He never even mentioned my name to you, did he?"

I plopped back down. "Tony didn't discuss his personal life with me."

She surveyed the estrogen-heavy room, then laughed the way you do when a politician promises to cut taxes. "And I thought I was special to him. The reality was he and I were both in love with the same man—himself."

"If you feel that way, why are you here?" I asked.

"My inner child needs closure to enter the healing stage."

Claudia wasn't as well put together on the inside as she appeared on the outside. I pictured her at home among chrome and glass bookcases overloaded with self-help books. It seemed she wanted to justify herself to someone. Why me? I wasn't her therapist.

"You know what I resent most?" Claudia's grip tightened on my arm. "He just wasted my time." She sighed as though she had just set down a heavy package—undoubtedly from Neiman Marcus. "I'll be damned if I give him one minute more." Like a dirty towel, she tossed my arm back into my lap and rose abruptly. "You have potential, but that hair is so . . ." She pulled a business card from her alligator-skin bag and handed it to me. The logo was a photo of her in a full-length mink. "Work with us but make sure you take the full-day appointment."

"Sorry, but animal skin doesn't fit into my fashion plan."

"Don't be silly. It's all faux. I know what's politically correct. My real furs are in storage." As quickly as she had appeared, she disappeared into the crowd.

I slipped her card into my purse—destined for my file of tastelessly bad art.

"C-C-Caroline?"

I felt a hand on my shoulder and glanced up. Ben Rudolph, Tony's attorney, stood over me. Tony had always been on one end of a lawsuit or the other, so Ben's face had quickly become a familiar one at Tony's studio. With his sad button eyes, bow tie, and pudgy body, he reminded me of my favorite childhood teddy bear. I squeezed his hand.

He glanced toward the casket. "Sh-shocking, isn't it?" He sat down in front of me. A bald spot peeked through long strands of gray hair wound into a nest on the top of his head.

"You and Tony go way back, don't you?" I asked.

He nodded and draped his arm over the adjacent chair. "I saved his butt more than once, that's for sure." As though gouged by a sculptor's tool, a deep crevice spanned his forehead. Above this facial equator lay pale, Arctic white skin, below it florid flesh scorched by the summer sun. Law was his love, but golf was his passion. "I'll never forget the first time I met him," Ben said. "Did he ever tell you the story?"

When I shook my head, a grin broke out on Ben's face. I leaned forward.

"Tony started out by p-p-painting advertising billboards," Ben began. "You know the type. Gal on a davenport in what my generation considered a compromising position, the guy handing her a m-m-martini. Inset into the corner of the ad was the product—a bottle of gin.

"Now this b-b-billboard was one of those that's painted in sections in a warehouse and then assembled on site. The client approved the finished painting at the warehouse, and it was disassembled and carted off to be installed. Except Tony had painted one extra panel. He switched it for one of the approved panels before the truck left the warehouse."

"Uh-oh."

Ben smiled. "The headline for the liquor ad was supposed to read 'Lovers, Beware!' But when the billboard went up, an 'i' had replaced the 'o' in the headline."

Picturing it, I cupped my hand over my eyes, then looked back at Ben with a grin. "But he was hardly a teetotaler," I said.

"You knew T-T-Tony. It was his idea of fun, a way of thumbing his nose at pretension. As the years passed he just got more subtle."

"What happened with the billboard?"

"It was fixed immediately, but not before AP sent the ph-ph-photo out over its wires."

"So where did you come in?"

"I was a young attorney on staff for the billboard company. When the liquor company filed suit, I came up with the idea to claim the misspelling was an innocent mistake—Tony's immigrant background and all. That got *him* personally off the hook, but our employer was held entirely liable. Tony and I were both f-f-fired."

"So that's how it all began."

"As it turned out, it was the best thing that could have happened. I opened my own f-f-firm, and with the whole truth in advertising trend just beginning, Tony became a minor folk hero." Ben faced the coffin.

We were both silent, united by the memories and stories that anyone who knew Tony could tell. For a moment I lost touch with the present. When I looked up,

I realized Ben was still talking. His eyes searched my face for an answer, but I'd missed the question.

"What?" I asked.

He shifted in his seat as if he were sitting on a porcupine. "I realize it's a shock, but I thought it best to tell you here—in person. So you can be prepared. The f-f-family could get emotional when they find out." He reached into his inside suit pocket and then slipped his card into the palm of my hand as he rose. "Call me. We'll discuss it at a better time. Don't worry. I'll help you." He gave me a limp handshake—the kind that made me hope that grip wouldn't be the only thing between me and the bottom of a cliff.

"Help me with what?" I gripped his doughy hand like a shredding lifeline.

"Weren't you listening?" He looked around the room, then leaned closer to whisper. "You're Tony's sole b-b-beneficiary."

2

UNABLE TO FACE THE TRIP TO THE CEMETERY, I SAT alone in the deserted chapel long after everyone else had left. My thumb and index finger pinched Ben Rudolph's card. Though I had bent its corners and twisted it into the beginnings of recycled pulp, its very existence grounded me in reality. Ben had been short on details, explaining only that he would meet with the Chirico family on Friday, and asked me to keep the news confidential until he broke it to them. I had no idea what

Tony's estate consisted of. For all I knew it could be a pile of debts. I only knew any inheritance was poor consolation for losing him.

Covering my ears, I bent forward and rocked myself. *Why did you leave me, Tony? And why did you leave me in the dark about the inheritance?*

My own father had left me in the dark, too, twenty years ago when I was only ten. He had kissed me at bedtime as he always did when he was home. The next morning he lay dead of a heart attack. For a long time I connected the two events. I believed—in a reversal of the Sleeping Beauty legend—that *my* kiss had killed him. I didn't need an analyst to tell me it left me with a fear that every man I loved would leave. And so far that had been a self-fulfilling prophecy. Tony became my father figure. I leaned on him, sought his approval and was devastated when he withheld it. I was no better than Antoinetta, Claudia or Vince—desperate for one last chance to prove my worth to him. But instead he'd left me forever indebted.

My nails dug deeply into my palms, but the chapel's frigid air had numbed them to pain. If only it could numb my heart.

In the absence of a stiff drink, I settled for a cup of strong coffee. I tossed my leather bag into the corner of a tattered booth at "Janey's Joint" across the street, then slid in beside it. A middle-aged waitress shuffled over. Her gray uniform had enough stains to pass for a drop cloth. Embroidered on the breast pocket was "Janev." The descender of the last letter had unraveled.

"Coffee, hon?" Stuck to her lower lip was a cigarette that bobbed up and down as she spoke. The ash plunged from its tip, hit the glass pot she held and scattered like, well, like ashes. *Ashes to ashes, dust to dust.*

I turned over a cup. Janey sloshed the brew into, over, and beyond its rim.

"You wanna see a menu?"

"This'll do, thanks."

She shrugged and shuffled away humming, her two stubby pigtails keeping time.

I flipped open my large carryall and pulled out a drawing pencil and sketchbook—my adult security blanket. Sketching always helped. I scanned the cafe for a likely subject. A woman with a single dark braid sat at the counter, but she had her back to me. I studied the profiles of two men at a right angle to her. The harsh fluorescent lighting made sharp shadow patterns on their faces—perfect.

Tony and I had often sketched together in public places. My pencil began an uncertain dance across the paper. *God, I'll miss you.* As though I had no control over it, the pencil picked up its pace. *As sole beneficiary, I'm probably going to have to go through your things.* The pencil shifted into high gear. The drawing blurred and the pencil came to an abrupt halt. The lead stabbed into the paper and gouged its way across the toothy surface. I slammed the sketchbook shut.

The yellow laminate tabletop stared back at me. Brown, red and green stains covered its surface. Playing "Rorschach" with the shapes, I slowly traced the pencil over their outlines, finally deciding they looked like a man wearing an upside-down hat. *Upside down. My whole life is upside down.*

"I hope I'm not intruding . . ." The voice caught me off guard.

For an instant I was back in third grade. Mrs. Bement had just caught me scratching "I love Bobby" into my desktop. The pencil leaped from my hand and bounced across the green tiled floor. I jerked my head up and saw, not Mrs. Bement, but a man in jeans and a gray jacket—the man who'd rescued the flowers in the chapel.

He signaled me to stay seated. "I'll get it."

Long, lean legs ending in shiny boots strode away from me. A marked improvement over Mrs. Bement's support hose. Before he turned around, I averted my eyes.

"Mind if I join you?" he asked.

"I'm probably not the best company today."

"That's okay." He slipped into the booth opposite me, motioning to Janey to bring more coffee. His eyes were cool, a bluish gray, Payne's gray. "Caroline Canfield, right?"

"How do you know my name?"

"I asked someone at the chapel."

"You could have asked me."

"It didn't seem like the best time." He glanced sheepishly down at the runaway pencil, rolled it between his fingers, then looked up. "My name's Jake." He studied the pencil once more before he handed it back to me. "Jake Statler." We shook hands. The scent of Polo galloped across the table. "I saw your show at the Vista Vue Gallery. Your paintings are very good."

"Thanks."

"I'm not exactly into art, but I like animals. And the ones in your paintings almost breathe."

If this guy was trying to win points, he knew the right buttons to push.

"I had a good teacher." My focus returned to the coffee splotches on the table. "Tony taught me to see— as an artist."

"How's that?"

"Well, for starters he made me paint upside down."

"Little tough keeping the paint on your palette, isn't it?" His straight face broke into a grin. The dimples in his cheeks were classics.

"The *subject*—a photo—was upside down."

"I give up. What was the point?" He reached for the sketchbook. "May I?"

I nodded. "It taught me to paint what I really saw— not what I knew. Not eyes or a nose, but abstract shapes of tone and color. It was a discovery that changed my life."

He paged through the spiral-bound book. "Forgers learn to copy signatures that way. Upside down." He looked up quickly. "Or so I've read. It's all related to that left side/right side brain business." He set down the sketchbook and motioned again for coffee.

"So how did you know Tony?"

"I interviewed him a few times—about his work."

"Interviewed? Are you a writer?"

"I write. I guess you could say now I'd like to finish the story."

In a haze of blue smoke, Janey puffed over. Before she poured, I pulled my sketchbook out of harm's way. Janey's aim was improving. The saucer caught the overflow. Our conversation ceased as we watched her waltz off, her hips responding to some inaudible tune.

"Seems Tony had a reputation for ticking people off," Jake said.

I studied his face, but I couldn't read it. "If you're looking for dirt, you won't get it from me."

"No dirt. Just pieces of the puzzle. For instance, you seem to be one of the few people who's genuinely upset that he's dead."

I looked past his dimples into his cool eyes. "If people didn't like Tony, it's because they didn't know him like I did. They didn't see the tears in his eyes when he talked about the death of his mother. They never saw him go out of his way like I did to help a kid lost in the park or to feed a stray cat. Tony respected kids and animals—maybe because they didn't judge him." In spite of my best efforts, I knew there were angry tears in my eyes.

He reached over and placed his hand on mine. "Tony was lucky to have such a loyal friend." His eyes, set into a clean-shaven, suntanned face, seemed sincere.

I was almost sorry when he let go of my hand and reached for the sugar.

Suspending the glass dispenser over his coffee cup, he poured sugar into his coffee as liberally as I poured turpentine into my brush washer. "Sometimes it helps to talk about the person you've lost."

"Maybe."

"Come on, tell me about working with Tony. It must have been exciting."

"It had its moments." I sipped my coffee. It was surprisingly good, and Jake was easy to talk to. "I remember the first mural I worked on with Tony. It was commissioned by Girdner Steel. Girdner had been under attack for toxic waste and pollution. Their employees were turning up with cancer in alarming numbers. So they paid a PR firm big bucks to tell the world they had cleaned up their act. Tony was hired to paint the mural for a lavish health club they built on the grounds for employees."

"Sounds pretty tame, so far," Jake said.

"Tony was directed to create a mural to instill pride in the steelworkers. The mural incorporated huge suspension bridges and roadways, all to the glory of steel. The sky at sunrise was a vivid blend of alizarin crimson and Prussian blue. At the horizon line, he'd used the warmer tones of cadmium red and chrome yellow. He'd taken an unglamorous object and transformed it into a thing of beauty. Girdner was thrilled. Until about six months later . . ."

"What happened then?" Jake turned his cup in slow revolutions as he listened.

"Some of the colors in the sky began to darken and every week the change became a little more obvious. Girdner accused Tony of not using lightfast colors. Tony challenged them to prove it. While insults and threats flew back and forth, the area of sky where the sun was rising in the painting continued to darken. In time the word 'pollution' emerged in huge cloud formations just above the horizon line."

"Didn't Girdner sue?"

"They filed suit, all right. Tony just laughed and said they wouldn't dare follow through. His attitude threw me. So I looked up the chemical properties of each of the colors in the mural's palette. The answer lay in two pigments—chrome yellow and flake white."

"They weren't lightfast?" Jake asked.

"Light had nothing to do with it. You see, chrome yellow and flake white are both lead chromates. They darken when exposed to heavy industrial environments. The continued pollution—the same atmosphere the employees were still breathing even in their new health club—caused the pigments to darken over a relatively short time."

"In other words, Girdner hadn't really cleaned up its act after all," Jake said. "And the mural acted as a litmus test."

"Exactly. The PR firm tried their best to hush the whole thing up. But the employees got the message. They brought a class action suit against Girdner for wrongful death."

"What about Tony?"

"Tony agreed to wash down the mural with hydrogen peroxide to restore its original colors. But he warned Girdner if they didn't drastically lower emissions, the painting would only discolor again."

"So the mural actually monitored the pollution level." Jake leaned forward, his elbows on the table. "Did Tony do that kind of thing often?"

"No one would have hired him if he did. But occasionally he would slip some subliminal messages into a mural. And after the Girdner episode, if there was a particular area of the painting Tony wouldn't let me touch, I had a good idea he was up to something."

"So Tony liked to literally make a statement with his murals?"

"What's your interest, anyway?"

"I've been following the progress on the zoo's new exhibit." He grinned and ran his fingers through his thick brown hair. "You see, I happened to be there one day and had a chance to watch Tony work. Beyond his obvious talent, I was impressed by how spry he was for a guy his age. Even went down the ladder frontwards. When I'd heard he'd fallen, it bothered me. I'm surprised it didn't bother you."

"Of course it bothered me," I shot back.

He glanced at his watch and slid three singles onto the table as he rose. "Sorry, I've got to go." He shrugged and turned toward the door. "Well, Tony was old, probably senile, maybe he was drinking, or just got careless and—"

"Look, Tony went up and down those ladders for over forty years." I grabbed my bag and followed him to the exit. "He practically lived on those scaffolds. He never—" I took a breath, trying to shake off the next logical thought. "He couldn't possibly have fallen. The whole idea's ridiculous."

Jake was silent for a moment, then he turned to me. "I knew you'd eventually arrive at the same conclusion. You see, I don't think Tony's death was an accident either. I believe he was murdered."

3

MURDERED? HAD I HEARD RIGHT? MY HEART POUNDED in my ears. But before I could recover, he was gone. Just like a man. Barge into my life, drop a bombshell, then split.

Was murder a real possibility? The police hadn't seemed to think so. Then what information did this Jake Statler have? Whatever he knew, he was right about one thing. No way on earth could Tony have simply fallen. Had my grief blinded me to that until now?

I spent the next hour trying to walk off bouts of anxiety. It worked to some degree. The blister I developed on my left heel had my undivided attention as I limped up the sidewalk in my new black pumps to the Chirico house. The hot, humid air had further wilted my hair, so before leaving the car, I had hastily woven it into a French braid.

As the undisclosed heir, I surprised even myself to have the nerve to show up at this reception, like the fox having dinner with the chickens before raiding the henhouse. But the need to find out if anyone shared my doubts about Tony's death overruled my scruples.

The mansion sat arrogantly on a knoll high above the Fox River. The structure was a Frankenstein of architectural styles ranging from English Tudor to Psycho House. A "Frank Lloyd Wrong" addition jutted off the back. I gazed up at the schizophrenic three-story structure. Gargoyles leered knowingly from the top floor, taunting me to guess the family secrets that lay behind the windows.

I climbed the wide cement steps. The welcome mat would soon no longer apply to me. The front door was ajar, so I slipped in—literally. My heel skidded, scarring the polished hardwood floor. I grabbed the door frame to prevent my fall. High heels on me are a lethal weapon. But I wear them for the same reason Salvador Dalí had walked around with a sharp stone in his mouth. There's something about living with the threat of danger that keeps one's senses more alert. And my heel had just issued its first warning.

I entered the living room. The atmosphere, saturated with olive oil, garlic and cigar smoke, hung in a heavy haze. For a moment I thought I'd come to a costume party. In the power corner stood Miles Crandall in his signature safari suit. Next to him were two men in Western suits and boots, holding cowboy hats. The husky one had a black patch over one eye. The group's eyes—all five of them—checked out my body parts as I passed.

The room seemed to both warn and threaten me as I crossed its length. I consciously avoided passing beneath the crystal chandelier that dangled between facing red velvet love seats set back from the marble fireplace.

Family photographs occupied three of the four walls.

A huge family portrait owned the fourth wall. For the time being, however, I was more interested in the credenza, well stocked with liquor, beneath the painting. It had been a rough day, and something told me it was far from over. The credenza sat next to an open doorway. The dining room beyond was dark, except for the glow of warming candles under chafing dishes on a massive table.

Vince's voice came from the darkness. "All right, so it took a little longer than I planned."

When there was no response, I assumed he must be on the phone.

"The lawyer's coming Friday," Vince added. "I'll have the cash in a few weeks."

I cringed. So Vince had already spent part of his non-existent inheritance.

"What ees-a your play-shure?" an unfamiliar voice with a heavy Italian accent asked.

I spun around and gazed into a pair of blue eyes. The last time I'd seen eyes that color they were on a Siberian husky. A sleek, inky brow arched suggestively over one eye. The young bartender's dark Mediterranean complexion contrasted with bright white teeth. A lock of black hair posed seductively across his smooth forehead. The guy knew he was a woman's best fantasy and worst nightmare rolled into one.

"White wine, please." I shifted my eyes away, but like magnets they returned to his.

He nodded approval and raised a bottle of Bolla Soave. "Ah, *vino bianca*—the nectar of goddesses." His voice was operatic, a tenor. "You must be the Goddess of Love!"

"Yeah, but you're catching me on my day off," I said.

His tongue flicked at the corner of his mouth. He poured the wine into a crystal goblet, his motions as fluid as the liquid, but his laser eyes never left me.

I blinked and pulled mine away. Looming over the credenza was the life-size family portrait—its heavy, gilt frame softened by a velvet swag. Sipping my wine, I studied the painting. In it, a surprisingly beautiful and young Antoinetta, dressed in a flowing ivory gown, sat on a red velvet love seat. She cradled a spray of red roses, but she held them stiffly, almost unwillingly. On her right stood Vince, about ten years old, fingering a petal of the rose nearest him. On the other side his younger sister, Diana, sat in a lacy white dress. Behind Antoinetta stood Tony, his hand reaching down to the flowers, a look of pride on his face as if he had personally grown the roses. Tony had signed and dated the canvas over thirty years ago.

The bartender interrupted. "You belong in such a painting. I shall paint you just so." He squinted and framed me between his hands. I expected him to add the words, "in the nude," but instead he said, "sitting in a '64 Corvette, of course." He crossed his arms with an air of satisfaction. Dark chest hairs peeked from his half-unbuttoned white silk shirt.

"A '64 Corvette?"

Both eyebrows peaked, and a sly smile crossed his lips. "I collect classic American cars. What do you drive?"

Out of the dining room glided Barbara DiGenova, or Bebe, as Tony had nicknamed his niece, a tray of Italian pastries in one hand, a drink in the other. Her tall, graceful figure circled the room. Short auburn hair, swept back from her face, revealed a flawless, milky complexion. She favored her father's northern Italian family rather than the Chirico side from Sicily.

Barb had been my roommate our freshman year at the U. of I. at Chicago. After the first semester, she switched to Southern Illinois to study zoology and genetics, and I transferred to the Chicago Academy of Fine Arts. After graduation, we ran into each other one day at Marshall Field's. Barb had a job at Fox Valley Zoo. I was still job-hunting. She mentioned her uncle Tony needed an assistant in his art studio and arranged a meeting between us. The rest was history. The last time I'd seen her—at least five years ago—she had just been promoted to curator of mammals at the zoo. As she passed, I grabbed her sleeve.

Her eyes opened wide in surprise, and she blinked twice. "Caroline!" She set the pastry tray down and gave me a hug.

"I must have missed you at the chapel," I said.

She kept one arm around me, careful not to spill the drink she held. "I wanted to be there, but I just couldn't." Her voice cracked. "Besides, I was needed here to set all this up."

She smelled strongly of Scotch. I didn't remember her being a heavy drinker, but we each deal with death differently. Like me, she had lost her father at an early age. It was part of what united us—that and our love of animals.

Her eyes were dull, lines of tension and grief surrounding them. She studied her empty glass, then pushed it at the bartender. "Another, Gino. This time in a glass *without* a chip."

Without a flicker of flirtation, he swept a fresh drink in front of her, then retreated to the end of the bar. Barb's perfectionism sometimes put people off. I reached for my wineglass.

"Wine?" Barb's eyebrows went up. "Don't tell me you've given up Manhattans."

"Just too early. But it was your uncle Tony, you know, who first introduced me to C.C. Manhattans. He told me the initials stood for Caroline Canfield."

"And you fell for that?"

"By the time I found out it stood for Canadian Club, I was already hooked." I sipped the wine. Its warmth, along with the company of an old friend, persuaded me I had jumped to conclusions earlier. Who was Jake Statler, anyway? Some tabloid journalist? This was a time for reminiscing. "Remember how Tony always called us Bebe and Cece? He said we were so close alphabetically, we'd be friends for life."

She rolled her eyes. "I hated that nickname, and he knew it, but the more I protested, the more he teased.

He could really get on my nerves sometimes, but he was awfully generous. He paid my full tuition through grad school and saw that my mother had everything she needed until she passed away last year from cancer." She pinched the bridge of her nose. "And now he's gone, too. But that's nature's way, isn't it?" She looked up. "So, tell me something good. What's new? Dating anyone I should know about?"

"I'm not even dating anyone you *shouldn't* know about," I said.

"What happened to . . ." She made a circular motion with her free hand.

"David? A wife happened to David."

"He was married?"

"Nothing so cliché. No, he got married while we were going together—just didn't bother mentioning it." When I saw the look of horror on her face, I added, "But I'm over it."

"Good." She draped her arm over my shoulder. "You know what your problem is? You're too trusting, too accommodating. My advice? Use 'em, then lose 'em. Work, that's what's important. Gives you less time to meet the man of your nighmares." She leaned close. "Speaking of nightmares, have you met Miles Crandall?"

My stomach rumbled. "Not formally." I reached for a black olive hors d'oeurvre.

Her fingers tweezed a stray hair off my shoulder. "Well, he wants to meet you. Where is that man?" She surveyed the room through squinted eyes.

I had never been able to decide if Barb's refusal to get glasses stemmed from vanity or an unwillingness to admit imperfection. "How can you miss him?" The man was a perfect subject for Chuck Close, the superrealist who painted portraits ten times larger than life.

"Right. Come on," she said.

I set down my wineglass. My heels squeaked as I followed her.

"Miles, you wanted to meet Caroline Canfield," Barb said.

Like a grizzly bear reared up on hind legs, he extended a massive paw. "Miss Canfield, a pleasure." His hand closed around mine like the jaws of a bear trap.

When he let go, I flexed my hand to get the blood flowing again.

"Tell me," he said, "have you visited our Fox Valley Zoo lately?"

"Not since I was a kid." I didn't mention that I remembered it being outdated and run-down even then.

"It's changed dramatically since then. Indeed, when I became director," Miles said, punching his finger at the air, "I put a basic market principle to work: Beat out the competition. Create an unforgettable experience—state-of-the-art exhibits the other two area zoos can't touch."

Sounded like Miles wanted to be to zoos what Walt Disney was to theme parks.

"I thought zoos cooperated with each other these days," I said.

"Of course we do, but make no mistake, we are all ultimately vying for the same dollar." He bared his teeth like a predator. "Fund raising. Publicity. Cash flow. That's what it takes. And the secret?" He was in my face. "Babies! People flock to the zoo for babies. Whenever there's a blessed event, I call in the press like that." He snapped his fingers in front of my eyes. "Result: membership soars, cash registers ring." The director sank his teeth into an Italian pastry.

Barb took advantage of the conversational lapse while he chewed. "Breeding is crucial, but we have to do it wisely. Mostly, we need to educate people about the importance of supporting research and conservation efforts."

Miles cleared his throat, like a Mack truck downshifting. "People come to the zoo to be entertained, not preached at, Barbara. Entertainment is the key, girls. Remember that." He tossed the pastry remnant into his mouth and swallowed.

Barb's mouth tightened into a rigid line.

"So, Barbara tells me you worked with Anthony Chirico," Miles said.

I focused on the whipped cream wedged into the corners of his mouth. "That was a few years ago."

"Let's talk, shall we?" He took me by the elbow and steered me to the only open corner of the room, like a wide-fin Cadillac looking for a parking spot among a line of Toyotas.

Over my shoulder I jerked my head for Barb to follow us.

"As you may be aware," Miles said, "we are the beneficiaries of an extremely large trust fund set up by the late Mrs. Worthington-Bentley. But with her bequest came the stipulation that the funds be spent in a total modernization of the zoo. If we do not accomplish our task according to her schedule, we forfeit the trust. You can appreciate that we can't let that happen. Indeed, if we do not complete phase one on time, we risk not only the loss of the trust fund, but other contributors' support as well—the domino effect, don't you know. In short, the entire future of our zoo is in jeopardy. Which brings me to you . . ." He smiled an ugly smile, his teeth bared like a tiger's. "The mural in our new tiger exhibit is unfinished. It must be completed by the end of October. As you are an authority on Chirico's painting technique—"

"I wouldn't say an authority." I glanced at Barb.

Miles moved his body between us, blocking me into the corner. "Indeed. Don't be so modest. I've been told you're quite the expeditious painter."

I didn't like the direction this was taking. "Expeditious isn't exactly the word I'd prefer to describe my—" I ducked under his arm to escape the corner. I used my eyes to send an SOS to Barb.

She lowered her eyes to her glass. "Excuse me, I need a refill." She headed to the bar.

"I'll be blunt," Miles said. "We need you, Miss Canfield, to complete that mural. And we need it by October thirty-one."

"I don't think this is the place to discuss . . ."

He waved his huge arm in the air. "Nonsense. Chirico has left us in the lurch."

It appeared Miles didn't consider death to be sufficient cause to break a commitment.

"I no longer do murals."

The man's nostrils flared. "As his protégé—"

"I work for myself now."

"—and a wildlife painter, you are the logical choice—"

"There's no way I'm going to—"

"—to pick up Chirico's brushes. Consider this an opportunity to make a final tribute to your mentor."

I scanned the room for a sign that said "exit." I tried to get Barb's attention, but she was deep in conversation with the bartender. "It's not that easy. Tony had a unique vision—"

"Who says you have to follow his vision? Make the mural your own. Paint whatever."

"With only two months to your deadline," I said, "there's no time to redesign it."

"Design? Paint some trees, paint some clouds. We just need it painted, for God's sake. It's not the Sistine Chapel." His voice filled the room. He swabbed his forehead with a handkerchief, but beads of perspiration hung on his upper lip. His nostrils pulsated.

Barb returned, carrying a fresh drink. "Have you forgotten, Miles, that Gino Tedesco has already offered his services?"

So Barb hadn't abandoned me after all. "Gino Tedesco?" I asked, hopefully.

Over her shoulder, she nodded at the bartender. "Tony's current assistant."

I glanced at Gino. "I didn't realize that's who he was." But I should have spotted it. He was just as flirtatious as Tony.

"We can't count on him," Miles said impatiently. "He's unreliable. Doesn't know a deadline from an immigration line." He looked at me as though staring down a rifle sight. "Miss Canfield is the logical choice."

"I won't work at those heights anymore," I said.

Barb turned to me. "I had no idea you suffered from a fear of heights."

"It's not *heights* that I'm afraid of. It's *falling* from heights that scares me," I said irritably. "Which, considering the circumstances, seems entirely appropriate."

"Oh, come now," Miles said. "It's not like you'll be climbing the Sears Tower. The topmost portion of the mural is already complete. I'm sure you won't be more than thirty feet off the ground."

"When your face is hitting concrete," I said, "you end up looking like a Jackson Pollock painting in either case."

Barb gasped. Horror was evident on her face from the mental picture I'd drawn.

"I'm sorry, Barb." What was the matter with me? But the comment had sparked a thought. Tony couldn't have fallen very far or there wouldn't have been an open casket.

Miles turned to Barb. "DiGenova, I expect you to use your influence on your friend to meet with us tomorrow. Or perhaps you'd prefer to go back to shoveling elephant dung."

Suddenly speechless, Barb and I exchanged glances. I knew I should have bought that book entitled, *Women Who Can't Say No to Men Ten Times Their Size.*

Miles rubbed his hands together. "It's settled then. Meeting. My office. Tomorrow. Oh-eight-hundred hours."

Confused whether to shake hands or salute, I flipped a palm at Miles. Good thing my fingers were bound in gauze, or I might have flipped him something else. But a meeting at the zoo would provide the perfect opportunity to get a glimpse of the unfinished mural.

Miles marched back to his cowboy friends. Barb and I moved back to the bar.

"Thanks for leading me into that ambush," I said.

"Sorry, but he made me promise to introduce you."

"And that smile of his . . ."

" 'Miles' is an anagram for 'smile,' " she said. "Or is it 'slime'?" She summoned Gino as if she were hailing a cab. "Scotch on the rocks."

The time had come. "C.C. Manhattan," I said, "straight up." Sensing the urgency, Gino went into action.

"Look at it this way," Barb said, "Miles is like a cockroach. You can't get rid of him, so you might as well learn to live with him."

Gino winked at me as he slid drinks in front of us.

"To the cockroach," Barb said, swinging her glass in the air. "Indestructible, adaptive and tenacious."

We clinked glasses. I downed the Manhattan in three swallows. "The good doctor makes me a little nervous," I said.

"Pphhh! I don't know what that doctorate of his is in, but it's not science." She swirled her drink in a circular motion. Ice cubes tinkled like wind chimes. "What he knows about zoology you could print on the side of an ice cube—a melted one."

"If he's so ignorant about animals, why did the zoo board hire him?"

"Desperation. We nearly shut down three years ago for insufficient funds. Miles brings money in hand over fist. You see those two guys he's talking to?" She jerked her head toward the men in Western attire. "Business associates of Vince—from Texas. No doubt our director is hitting them up for the annual contributors' fund. Nobody escapes the jaws of Miles." She imitated the two-note soundtrack from *Jaws*.

"If you dislike him, why not go somewhere else? You've got the credentials."

"And miss the chance of a lifetime? If the donations continue, we could build a research complex. Do you know that zoos are putting living cells of each species on ice, in case an animal becomes extinct in the wild?" Excitement was evident in Barb's voice. "I want our zoo to be a part of it. But it takes money. We can't afford to lose that trust fund, Carrie."

"Well, like you said, Gino can finish the mural," I whispered.

"It's too risky." She shifted closer to me. "With no green card, he could be on a boat back to Italy at any time." I could tell focusing was becoming a problem for her. "I don't think you appreciate the importance of this," she said to my nose. "It's not just us you'd be letting down. If the zoo loses the money, what happens to the animals? Have you thought about that?"

I had wondered how long it would take her to get around to the guilt trip. With all the talk about money, it appeared the stakes were high. Was there a relationship between Tony's death and the deadline to complete the mural?

"If accidents can happen once, Barb, they can happen again—and again and again, in my case." I held up my bandaged hand, trying to draw a smile from her.

"Fine! Forget the whole damn thing!" She shoved me away. "Forget everything that's at stake here. You're not a risk-taker. You never were, you never will be. Go back to your safe little drawing board. Never mind that the animals you exploit in your paintings today may be extinct tomorrow." Barb still knew which buttons to push.

"All right, I'll go to the meeting. But I'm not going back to mural painting. And while I'm there I want to study the mural."

"Study it?"

I hesitated. "This may sound crazy, but what if there's something in the mural?"

Her head bobbed up as though disoriented. "What are you suggesting?"

"What if someone didn't want Tony to finish it, for whatever reason?"

"Why would anyone . . . No one could have . . ." She glanced away.

I touched her arm. "Don't worry. With all the preliminary drawings Tony went through when he created a mural, if there's any message in it, I'll find it."

"Barbara, where is my Barbara?" Antoinetta's panicked voice echoed from the kitchen.

Barb straightened the collar on her stylish gray suit. "Duty calls." Steering slightly to the right, she wove toward the kitchen.

Left to myself, I turned to view the framed family photos on the wall. One was a snapshot of Vince as a boy standing in the snow with a small rifle aimed at a treetop. Captured by the shutter in that moment of time was a bird, its wings blurry, flying out of the branches. In the background next to a snowdrift stood an adolescent Barb, arms crossed and a scowl on her face.

Vince walked over. He looked at the photo I'd been studying. "Don't look at me that way." He gave the Boy Scout three-fingered salute. "I'm reformed. I haven't shot anything since I was a kid."

"Oh, really? What are those? Paperweights?" I pointed to the walnut-and-glass gun cabinet in the corner of the room.

"I'm a collector," Vince said. "Some of those antique guns are worth plenty. They haven't been fired for years. Every time Bebe visits, though, she threatens to get rid of them when I'm not looking, just like she did the BB gun Dad gave me that Christmas."

I smiled, remembering the story of how she'd acquired her nickname.

"I overheard Bebe tear into you," he said. "Don't take it personally. Since Dad's accident, her temperament has been as bad as Mother's."

That didn't surprise me. In college when her father died, Barb had put up a strong front. She didn't exhibit the obvious signs of grieving like crying or depression. Instead she had lashed out at everyone. Being her roommate had made me a steady target. Now she'd not only lost both parents, but Tony as well.

"Well, I really should be going. I'll just say good-bye to Barb," I said.

"Sure. She's in the kitchen. Come on."

As we passed the family portrait, I stopped. "By the way, where's your sister?"

"Diana?"

"Unless you have another one I don't know about," I said, with a laugh.

For a moment he seemed startled, then shook his head. "Diana said Dad never had time for her, so why should she make time for him now?" He raised his hands defensively. "I'm only quoting her."

My attention returned to the family portrait. "I don't mean to be critical, but this just isn't up to Tony's usual level. That bouquet of roses is almost phony-looking."

"Thanks."

"For what?"

"I painted them," he said. "Originally, Mother was holding wildflowers. She said they looked like weeds, and she wanted red roses. If it would make her happy, I thought, what the hell. So, shortly after the divorce, in my final act of committing art, I painted over them."

"I'm surprised she's let his picture continue to hang here."

"Hey, we're Italian. No matter how much she may hate him, he'll always be the head of our family. Go figure." He shook his head. "One thing's for sure—I won't ever let my family fall apart the way he did."

We crossed the darkened dining room. Ahead a glow emanated from the kitchen. Not a friendly warmth, though. More like the flames of hell. Vince held the door open for me. The scent of garlic, oregano, and fresh bread enticed me forward. Five or six women clustered around Antoinetta. Barb knelt in front of her, coaxing her to drink some water.

"Vincenzo, Vincenzo," the old woman cried, holding out her arms to her son. A stack of sympathy cards and a letter opener lay on the kitchen table next to her.

He rushed forward and took her hands.

"She needs to rest." Barb said in a weary voice. "Let's get her upstairs."

"I'll take care of it. Caroline wants to say good-bye," Vince said.

Antoinetta studied me. Her eyes narrowed. Lines of perpetual displeasure radiated from her mouth, accentuating her pursed lips. "How dare you invite her here! Isn't it bad enough she comes to the funeral?" She grabbed the letter opener. The cards tumbled to the floor. "Get out of my house! Get out!" She sprang from her chair, knocking Barb off balance. The glass of water shattered on the kitchen floor. Late afternoon sun caught the glistening bronze blade in her hand, throwing spots of light around the room.

I backed away.

"You try to steal my children's birthright." She jabbed the weapon at my wrapped hand. The gauze began to unravel. "You have shown your hand before! You cannot hide it! You are the devil. Take off your shoes. Show us your cloven hooves, as well."

She must already know the terms of the will, I thought. Vince placed himself between us, but she pursued me into the dining room. The huge table blocked my exit. She came straight at me. My hands shot up in defense, my fingers splayed, the gauze hanging limply from them. She stopped in her tracks. A puzzled look appeared on her face. Then she veered past me into the living room.

Too short to reach Tony's figure in the painting, she slashed the knife through the bouquet of roses in the portrait. The sound of shredding canvas sent a shiver through me.

Barb cradled Antoinetta in her arms, calming the old woman and gently removing the letter opener from her hands.

I grabbed the opportunity to head for the front door.

"Caroline!" Vince rushed after me. "I'm sorry. She just didn't recognize you. It's been a long time and her memory—"

"It's all right. It's been a difficult day for all of us." I crossed the front door's threshold, then turned around.

"Vince, you knew your father's work habits as well as I did. Don't you think it's odd he fell? I mean, could a heart attack or a stroke have caused it?"

"Dad was as healthy as a horse."

"It just isn't logical—" I nervously jingled my car keys.

"That's why it's called an accident. Do you know how much my company gets nailed for workmen's comp every month for accidents that shouldn't happen but somehow do?" He took me gently by the shoulders. "He's gone, Caroline. Accept it and move on." He bent, kissed me good-bye and closed the door.

I stood on the porch wondering if he'd be as philosophical when he found out he was disinherited. Did none of them question Tony's death? Or were they just covering up?

Adrenaline had sent the manhattan coursing through my bloodstream. I felt a little woozy. Turning a little too quickly on the doorstep, I snagged my heel in the mesh of the welcome mat. I tumbled forward down the front steps. The car keys flew from my hand.

At the bottom of the stairs, Gino reached up and caught them. Then he caught me. Over his silk shirt, he had donned a linen jacket, sleeves pushed up to the elbows.

"Thanks," I said as he set me back on my feet. My hands ran across the front of his jacket. "Nice threads. Italian?"

"American. Ralph Lauren," he said. A long blue cardboard tube was tucked under his arm. "There is something I must tell you. Perhaps you give me a lift?"

"No car? I thought you collected them."

He shrugged and smiled. "I didn't have a chance to collect one today."

"Where you going?"

"Toodeloop."

It took me a minute to figure out his destination. "I'm not going to the Loop. But I can take you as far as the train station."

"Which is your car?"

"That white Camaro over there."

"Hokay!" He wiggled the car keys between his fingers. I reached for them.

He pulled them away from my grasp. "Don't drive and drink," he said, putting the cart before the horse. "It can kill you."

I glanced back at the house. "Well, it'll just have to get in line."

4

GINO DROVE THE WAY I MIGHT HAVE GUESSED—LIKE A race car driver going for the checkered flag. My Camaro responded to his confident hands the same way a woman might—in total surrender.

"So what is it you wanted to tell me?" I asked, my eyes glued to the road.

"You must not take the zoo job."

"Why not?"

The middle-aged car squealed in orgasmic response as we rounded a corner, then panted up the incline ahead. "The scaffolds," he said. "No place for woman."

"Marie Antoinette would have agreed with you, even if I don't."

"*Chi?*" He threw his head back as though the strategically placed lock of hair on his forehead suddenly bothered him. Well trained, it fell back into the exact same place.

"I've worked on those scaffolds much longer than you have, Gino."

"Tony work forty years on scaffolds. And what happen? He die. No, this is man's work—*young* man's work."

I braced my feet against the floorboard and willed the car ahead to find another lane. "Were you there when Tony fell?"

"Sad to say, I was."

"What exactly happened?"

"*Uno momento*—painting, the next—*morte*." Gino swerved left and right looking for a break to pass the slow-moving car on the two-lane highway.

My shoulders swayed in opposing motion to the car. Great! Saved from a knife wound only to die in a car accident. We bounced over the curb as Gino made a two-fingered right turn onto Route 31.

I lurched and grabbed the wheel, guiding us back to the pavement. "Pull over! Let me drive." Now was a fine time to be wondering if he even had a driver's license.

"You need new shocks." He accelerated as he rapidly whistled "America the Beautiful."

"Slow down, for God's sake!" I shouted.

The tempo of his whistling changed to a slower beat. His head nodded in time. "You're right," he said. "That is better. No thumping."

I sighed and watched the road, prepared to grab the wheel again at any moment. "Had Tony been ill that day, disoriented, anything unusual?"

He thought about it. "No, he is fine, except his eyes. They are red, puffy."

Tony didn't suffer from any allergies that I knew of. "What made him fall?"

He shrugged again.

"You're overwhelming me with the details," I said.

He gave me a vague look.

"Tell me everything you remember about the accident, every nuance."

"Nuance?" He raised an eyebrow. "*Che cosa questo?*"

We were approaching traffic. I kept on eye on the road. "Think of it as though you are describing the back end of a '57 Chevy—every detail, every touch, every breath is important."

"Ah, you American women. Always talking in the dirt. I love that Jenny Jones."

My foot pounded the floorboard. "For God's sake, watch it!" I shouted. The Camaro almost mated with the Buick ahead, driven by a white-haired little old lady. In her demure pillbox hat she looked like—well, someone's grandmother, just not mine.

Gino leaned on the horn and accelerated around the sedan. I smiled apologetically out the window as we passed. The little old lady flipped me a white-gloved finger.

With the road clear ahead, the Camaro tore loose. The floor vibrated beneath my feet.

"Let's stop for coffee." Anything to get him to slow down.

"Soon." His eyes locked on mine. "I knew you want me from the moment we met our eyes."

"So that's how you collect cars." We ran a red light. I gasped as we just missed a truck crawling into the intersection. "What I want is for you to tell me about Tony's accident—before we have one."

"Ah, *si*, the accident. I can still picture him," Gino said, "painting the majestic tiger in the mural. He point his brush with his lips and with his maulstick as guide, he paint the whiskers of the tiger in very fine strokes. We laugh over an old tale—"

"About the whiskers being deadly?"

"Si."

"What happened then?"

"He complain about the white paint I just mixed up fresh. He say paint is too gru . . . how you say . . ." He rubbed his fingers together. "Too gr-r-r-ooty."

"Gritty?" I found myself rolling the "r."

"Gritty, *si*. So I go in back to mix up more. Then I hear the crash." He slapped his hands together and held them prayerlike in front of his mouth. *"Madonna."*

The car fishtailed. I grabbed the wheel. He broke my

grip and pushed my hands away. "You need a wheel alignment," he said.

"I need my head examined for letting you drive. How far did Tony fall?"

"Only one level. A pile of drop cloths and materials break his fall."

"Did you try to help him?"

"Of course. I run to him. He gasp for air. I do not know what to do. There is death in his eyes." There were tears in Gino's.

"But he was still conscious? What did he say?"

"He cannot talk. Breathing hard. Near his hand is drawing pencils. He pick one up. I think he want to write a last wish. I give him paper, but he just jab pencil in my arm. Look." Gino displayed graphite puncture marks above his wrist. "Then he stop breathing." Gino crossed himself. *"Morte."*

"Was anyone else in the building?"

"I don't see anyone. It is eight o'clock at night, almost dark. We are tired, but he want to finish the tiger."

"Did he eat or drink anything while he was painting that day?"

He turned toward me. Caution and a touch of apprehension had entered his eyes. "Not even a Hostess Twinkie. I love American snacks." He reached into his coat pocket. "Ho Ho?"

"No, thanks."

The car strayed indecisively as he tore the cellophane wrapper from the chocolate pie.

I steadied the wheel. "How did you come to work for Tony?"

He chewed, then swallowed. "He owe my dear dead papa in Italy an old favor. Papa say before I am born, Tony visit Firenze. He meet a young art student. They visit Papa's trattoria every night for dinner. The young girl, she get pregnant, but Tony—he is already married. When he go back to America alone, the girl she lives with my family until *bambino* is born. Then one night she disappear. Leave the child with Mama and Papa.

Papa say she kill herself." White Ho Ho filling clung to Gino's upper lip. His tongue rolled across it.

I inadvertently mimicked the action. "What happened to the baby?"

"Papa say he write to Tony. He return to Italy about six months later and take *bambino* to America. That is what Papa say. But I believe differently. I am that child."

"You? Ow!" I had literally bit my tongue. "His son?"

"Papa was a cook, Grandpapa was a barber, his papa was a farmer. But I, Giovanni Tedesco, am driven to be an artist. It is in my blood. Where else do I get this great talent? I am the son of Anthony Chirico."

"So how did you get to America?"

"When Papa die, I write to Tony. He agree to sponsor me."

"Did Tony recognize you as his son?"

"Does the night not know the moon? We are Italian. We feel—that is enough. I am the son of Anthony Chirico. I alone have his vision."

I squeezed my eyes shut as we left Route 31 and merged with traffic on I-90 heading east. When I opened one eye, we were already in the inside lane. At this rate we'd be in my home territory, River Ridge—speed limit 25—in fifteen minutes.

"You know, Tony never mentioned having a new assistant, let alone a second son." Not that he would have.

"Perhaps he thought you would be jealous. I think you have much fire beneath the ice." He massaged the crumbs from his lips and offered me his thumb. "Last chance. Want a taste?"

I shook my head. Gino licked his thumb, then lowered his hand. Fondling the blue cardboard tube lying between our bucket seats, he began to hum "The Star Spangled Banner."

"What's in the tube?" I shouted over the engine's thumping heartbeat.

"This?" He held up the navy-blue capped roll. "My permanent pass-a-port to America. Tonight I find out if

I have a buyer." His head waved from side to side as he sang, "Oh, say does that star-spangled—"

"Tony's vision for the mural wouldn't happen to be in that blue tube, would it?"

He clutched it to his thigh. "These are my ideas, my vision."

"Why don't you show me?"

He wagged his finger. "No, no, no, no, no."

"I'm sure you're extremely talented, but the powers that be at the zoo seem to think you don't have enough experience."

"Hah! I do most of work on other murals. But I am never allowed to express myself in this one." He clutched his fist in front of him, then jerked it to his chest. "Tony held me back. Gino, do this. Gino, do that. It was professional jealousy. My talent frightened him. It is so enormous, it sometimes frightens even me."

"No doubt," I said. Maybe Gino had wanted Tony out of the way professionally, except that Tony was Gino's ticket to citizenship. "Tell you what. If you show me your work, I'll put in a good word for you at the zoo."

"I don't need help from a woman."

"You might. Do you have proof you're Tony's son?"

"Can you look at me and not know it?"

"American courts usually require a little more. Without a sponsor or a job, you may have to go back to Italy. Isn't that the real reason you want the commission?"

He reached over and took my hand, stroking my knuckles. "I hear you earlier. You don't want it. I do. So? It is simple. I am only trying to, um, take you down off the hook."

"I don't need you to get me off the hook. Maybe I'm just playing hard to get with the zoo. Maybe I really want the job."

He smiled and shook his finger at me. "I love American women. You want to do everything man can do. You want to be, uh, on top, in the driver's seat." With a grin on his face, he squirmed in the bucket seat and accelerated.

Clearly, Gino couldn't take his mind off sex long enough to commit murder.

"Is all right," he said. "By tomorrow I will have the job stitched up."

"Get off—" I said, "at the next exit." The Camaro took the exit ramp like an O'Hare runway. We passed through the residential section of River Ridge as though we'd just robbed the corner 7-Eleven.

When the train station came into view, Gino found the brakes—possibly for the first time since he'd gotten behind the wheel. The Camaro, spent from its vigorous workout, skidded to a halt across the street from the station, in front of the Art Deco Nickleby Movie Theater in downtown River Ridge. Gino switched off the ignition, but the engine wouldn't quit. It whined, shuddered, almost died, then shuddered again several times. Finally it lay silent. Through the windshield I watched waves of heat rise from its hood.

Gino ran his hands lovingly over the dashboard. *"Bella."*

"I'm sure it was good for her too."

"You should take better care of your car, treat her like a delicate woman. And she needs more octane." He reached into his shirt pocket and pulled out a pack of Virginia Slims. "You must give her excruciating excitement. Bring her to the brink, but never mistreat her. Then you will see the wonderful things she will do for you."

"I'm not really into women, even if they are cars, but I won't rule out the future possibility." I tugged on the handle, gave the door a shoulder, and got out. The solid pavement beneath my feet reassured me.

Emerging from the car, Gino lit a cigarette.

I walked around to the driver's side. "You know, you could be right. Tony might have been holding you back. I remember when I worked for him. There were sometimes sections of the mural he wouldn't let me touch.

That he insisted on painting himself. Did that happen to you?"

"Of course. He paint all the landscape, and I paint all the animals. All except for the tiger. This tiger he keep for himself, like a man keeps a woman to himself. It is a special tiger. He say it need the Chirico touch." He took one last puff and crushed out the cigarette underfoot. "Thanks for the ride. See you later, irritator." Whistling the theme from *Rocky,* he jaywalked across the street with the cardboard tube under his arm.

"That's alligator," I called after him.

But I was really thinking about tigers. I knew all about the famous Chirico touch. Only this time I was afraid the Chirico touch had gotten Chirico murdered.

5

"RETURN THEM TO THE WILD! NO MORE ANIMAL PRISONS! Liberation is at hand!"

Circling the gates of Fox Valley Zoo just prior to opening the next morning were a dozen people chanting slogans and carrying signs. A trio resembling Peter, Paul and Mary sang, "Where have all the big cats gone? Long time passing." A man in a white belted robe with long white hair and beard marched past me in sandals with a two-sided sign, "Free the animals! No one should play God."

Conserving my energy for the meeting ahead, I slid past the protesters and entered a gate marked "Staff." The past night I had spent on the phone with friends, trying to take my mind off Tony's death. But as soon as I hung up all the doubts reappeared. My talk with Gino had convinced me that a message lurked in the tiger mural, just waiting to be found. Damn Tony and his need to rub people's noses in the truth. This time he had antagonized a killer.

The smells of popcorn and hot dogs mingled with gamier scents in the air. As I passed a concession stand, I wondered if the pumped-up gorillas and inflated silverized dolphins waved at me or warned me. An elephant bugled an alarm somewhere in the distance.

As I followed the signs to the zoo office, I reviewed my game plan. I'd appear to show interest in completing the mural, even though it was the last thing I intended to do. My little act of deception would buy me just enough time to study the mural, review Tony's drawings, figure out the hidden message, and go to the police with my findings. Let them take it from there. I could probably have it wrapped up by the end of the day, Monday at the latest. Gino could have the mural job with my blessing. And the best part of my plan? I'd do it all with my feet planted firmly on the ground. No way would I climb those scaffolds again. Yeah, that's what I'd do. Piece o' cake. The image of a double-layer cake lying splattered on the floor ran through my head.

I headed a little less confidently toward the large stone building. Entering the mausoleum-like administration building, I was quickly ushered into a conference room, where the receptionist asked me to wait.

I sat down at the conference table. In an effort to make the best use of time, I opened my portfolio and pulled out a file folder with my name on it. On my way to the zoo I had delivered three completed spot illustrations to my art rep. She'd handed me a new project: a one-page four-color ad for a wild animal park in Missouri. I had been in a hurry to get to the zoo appointment, so I had grabbed the job ticket and run. As I reviewed the contents of the folder, I wished I hadn't been so hasty.

The ad agency art director had provided a mounted marker-rendered layout with a note scribbled on the mat board: "Create a 'feel-good' montage." A note I assumed from the account executive to the art director read, "Susan—Client loved the concept, hated the photographs. Let's go with illustration. Think warm and fuzzy."

I opened an accompanying gray envelope on which someone had scrawled, "Photos for drawing reference only—inappropriate to use as is." I tipped the envelope, and the slides and prints tumbled out onto the table.

As I sorted through them, one in particular drew my attention—a photograph of a liger, the offspring of a tigress and a lion. A female, it had the striped body of its tigress mother, but the head of a lioness. The liger stared forlornly out of a chain link cage so small it couldn't even stand up, let alone turn around. On one paw an ugly sore festered. Flies feasted on a piece of raw meat on the floor of the cage. Anger welled up in me that my rep had accepted this project. Didn't she know me better? No way would I promote this place.

I shoved aside the photos, got up and walked over to a large coffee urn that was sitting on a side table. A mound of sweet rolls and doughnuts fermented on a sheet of wax paper. The zoo's animals might be on restricted diets, but their caretakers sure weren't. Reaching for a paper cup, I knocked a standing roll of wax paper onto the floor. I followed it as it unrolled across the length of the conference room, coming to an abrupt stop at the door. As I bent to pick it up, the door opened. Maybe it was the thump on the head I took from the door, or maybe the guy was really wearing hot-pink running shoes. As I stood up, my eyes skimmed over stone-washed jeans topped by a fluorescent pink and green Hawaiian shirt. The doorway framed a living Peter Max poster, straight out of the era of psychedelic art.

The tall man studied the length of paper at his feet. His muscular, darkly tanned arms crossed an equally well-developed chest. "I might not rate the red carpet treatment, but wax paper is a little tacky, don't you think?" He held out his hand. "Rob Bennett, zoo vet."

I introduced myself as he bent, gathered the carpet of wax paper at his feet and tossed it into the trash. Sandy-colored hair, thick on the sides, had receded considerably at his forehead.

Approaching voices signaled the arrival of others. Wearing a gray safari suit, Miles led the group, followed by two women I didn't know, and Barb in a crisp beige linen suit. She hurried toward me, took me by the arm and led me to a corner.

"Listen, I've been thinking about it," she whispered, "and I've decided the mere thought of you up on those scaffolds is as terrifying to me as I'm sure it is to you. I just want you to know you have my full support in declining this job."

"What about losing your funding?"

"We won't lose it. We'll find another artist. I'm already working on it."

"But what about you? Miles did threaten your job status."

"I can handle Miles. Don't let him bully you either. Just look him in the eye and tell him you're not interested."

"Well, I'm, uh, reconsidering . . ." I hated lying to her, but I'd seen enough detective shows on TV to know it was unwise to signal my real intentions to anyone, even a friend.

"Are you crazy?" she said a little too loudly. Realizing it, she returned to a whisper. "I don't want to see your accident-prone butt anywhere near those scaffolds. You hear me? Say no and be firm."

Miles staked out the head of the table with a stack of sweet rolls. He cleared his throat. "Ladies, if you're quite through with your little gossip and girl talk, shall we begin?"

Barb and I exchanged frowns and sat down next to each other. The two other women, one in a wheelchair, took places across the table from us.

Miles introduced me, then motioned to the thin-as-apaintbrush woman in the wheelchair. "This is our head of public relations, Yolanda Ramirez."

She extended a spindly arm. I took her hand loosely, afraid I might do damage, but her grip was surprisingly strong.

"And," Miles continued, "head keeper of our big cats, Ellen Riggs." The young woman across from me had the softest, prettiest brown eyes I'd ever seen, with the exception of Bambi's. The few extra pounds she carried suited her. Her glossy brown hair was drawn into a braid. She wore jeans and a yellow polo shirt. On the left pocket was a gold Egyptian-style cat pin.

"I take it you've already met Robert Bennett, our veterinarian," Miles said.

Rob glanced up from studying the photos I'd left on the table. "You can't hide a pretty woman from me, Miles, any more than they can hide a pastry tray from you." He gathered the photos into a neat pile. "These yours?"

"Just reference photos for an illustration—that I won't be doing."

"I'd put them away if I were you," he said. "So they don't get ruined."

I took them from his hand and set them in front of me on the table. A phone trilled. Rob reached into his back pocket and flipped open a cellular phone. He listened briefly, then said, "I asked you not to call me here." Flipping the phone closed, he noticed we'd all been listening. "Women," he said with a sigh. Then realizing his gender was outnumbered in the room four to two, he smiled. "I gotta love 'em. Well, can't keep my patients waiting. Their bite *is* worse than their bark." Reaching quickly for his coffee and doughnut, the back of his hand tipped over the steaming paper cup. Coffee flooded over the photos and slides. "Damn! I'm sorry." He swept the photos off the table so quickly I wondered if he had planned the action. "Tell you what, have a new set of prints made, and I'll cover the cost."

"I can't do that," I said. "I don't have the negatives. I've got to return those."

"Well, lots o'luck, they're totaled," he said. Coffee dripped from the photos in his hand. "I'll just get rid of them."

"Hold on." I grabbed them from his hand hovering over the garbage can. "I've spilled worse than coffee on photos. I'm an old pro at this."

Barb offered me a roll of paper towels. "Caroline not only knows the ten-step program for accident recovery, but she's its official poster girl."

"Very funny," I said, wiping off the photos and dabbing at the slides. "I'll just spread these out to dry on the table."

Rob looked perplexed.

"Don't feel bad," I said. "Accidents happen." Being a bystander at an accident, rather than an active participant, was a new experience for me.

Rob and his neon wardrobe left the room, and Barb shut the door behind him.

Miles bit into a sweet roll, then spat crumbs at Yolanda Ramirez as he said, "I trust you'll take care of those terrorists out front. Issue another statement about our ongoing improvements, but don't get into any debates. Alert me immediately if the press shows up again."

Yolanda brushed the crumbs off her pad and made a note.

"What are they protesting?" I asked.

"Protesting?" Miles shouted. "Harassing is more like it. Goddamn animal libbers!"

Barb touched my arm. "You see, in the course of renovating, we tore down three outdated facilities. We had to relocate a lot of animals. For years we've taken other zoos' overflow, but it's a one-way street. The last thing they want is these animals back. They're sometimes unflatteringly referred to as genetic trash."

"Which simply means their genes are overrepresented in the captive population," Yolanda, in her role as spin doctor, explained, "and they're of no further value for breeding purposes."

"In addition," Barb said, "because they were negligently bred in the first place, many have congenital health problems. That makes it even more difficult to find them new homes. Who wants a sick animal, when there aren't enough spaces for the healthy ones?"

"But these protesters," Yolanda said, "heard about our relocation problems and how we've also had to put a few animals down recently. Now they're demanding to see all our records on animal disposition."

"Fat chance!" Miles said. "We're a private zoo, not publicly funded. Marcia Wilhelm and her cohorts have no right to our records. Why, even the best of zoos have an annual attrition rate of . . . of . . . what is it?" He snapped his fingers in Yolanda's face.

"Fourteen to twenty percent per year," Yolanda said.

"That's right. Death is a fact of life at the zoo," Miles said. He paused to think about what he'd just said. "That's rather good, isn't it? You can use that, Yolanda."

"The community needs to know we're determined to be part of the new zoo culture of conservation," Barb said. "We're going to turn our reputation around, from a dumping ground for unwanted animals to a first-class accredited zoo."

"Not zoo," Yolanda corrected, "wildlife conservation park. The board voted for that name change."

Miles cleared his throat and rubbed his hands together. "Any fool knows it's only money that's going to change things. So let's get down to brass tacks, shall we?" He tapped his fingertips together in front of triangular lips. "Riggs, stop sitting there like a lump. Fill Canfield in on the new tiger exhibit."

Ellen Riggs reached under the table. She pulled out a blue cardboard tube—just like the one Gino had the day before. She pulled off the cap, slid out a roll of paper and stretched a blueprint across the table. "When you visit Asia World, you'll notice it's divided into four major habitats and several smaller ones." Ellen's index finger traced the path on the blueprint. "All the exhibits are finished except Tiger Forest." She circled a large area on the blueprint.

"The climax of the tour," Miles interjected.

"The architect and designer," Ellen continued, "took my suggestion to model our tiger exhibit on Ranthambhore National Park, a tiger reserve in India. I believe that if people see animals in their real surroundings, maybe they'll care more about preserving natural habitats."

"I'm afraid habitat destruction will continue whether we like it or not," Barb said.

"But that's the beauty of what's happened at Ranthambhore," Ellen said. "It was once the private hunting ground of the Maharajahs of Jaipur. But in the late 1970s it set a wonderful precedent. Twelve villages located inside the park were resettled outside its boundaries so the tigers could roam freely, undisturbed by man. Finally an example of man surrendering land to the animals, instead of the other way around."

"That's a nice story, Ellen," Barb said. "But those tigers are living in isolated pockets now. Inbreeding is inevitable in Ranthambhore. That weakens the gene pool and places the survival of the whole species at risk. That's why our work is so important. Where once we took animals from the wild to invigorate the strains of our captive population, we're reaching the point where we will have to use the gene pool from our captive population to strengthen those that remain in the wild."

Yolanda broke in. "I just wrote an article for our newsletter on how we hope to return healthy captives to the wild some day."

"That sounds good on paper," Barb said, "but the reality is, the wild is hardly a Garden of Eden for animals. Beyond loss of habitat, they face starvation, sickness, and predators, the worst of which is man."

Yolanda nodded. Her neck was so thin I thought it might snap. "Zoos—I'm sorry, conservation parks—have become Noah's arks. As long as we can provide everything an animal needs, it doesn't have to roam a huge

territory. It can be quite content in a confined space."
It was increasingly clear Yolanda was born for public
relations.

"Ladies, ladies, you're getting off the point." Another
pastry disappeared into the Bermuda Triangle of Miles's
mouth. He swallowed and brushed the crumbs off his
hands.

Ellen's brown eyes flashed. "It's the *whole* point, Dr.
Crandall. Do you realize how many trees are being cut
down in the time it takes you to . . . to . . . consume
one of those pastries? Do you know how many animals
are being robbed of their homes? At the rate it's going,
our grandchildren will never see any animals in the
wild."

Miles stopped chewing long enough to frown at her.
"So, they'll come to the zoo."

"Zoos are already the only chance for some species."
Barb's voice was cool and calm.

"You know," Yolanda broke in, "if we don't start
using the term 'wildlife conservation park,' instead of
'zoo,' how can we expect the public to?"

My head was beginning to spin from jerking it back
and forth between speakers. Clearly, I wasn't the only
one in the room with a private agenda. "I appreciate the
importance of everything you're telling me," I said, "but
I'd really like to see the mural."

The walkie-talkie on the table squawked. "Ellen, Rob
Bennett is here," a woman's voice said. "He wants to
take a blood sample from Kiara."

"Tell him to wait until I get there," Ellen replied into
the unit.

"Something wrong with Kiara?" Concern registered
on Barb's face.

Ellen shook her head. "I haven't noticed anything in
her behavior to—"

"Just because you don't want an animal to be ill,"
Barb said, "doesn't mean it isn't. These are precious
lives we hold in our hands, Ellen. I count on you to spot

health problems early, while we can treat them. It's only by our judgment that these animals live or die."

"That's why I want to be there when Rob examines her. So if I'm no longer needed, I'd like to get to work." Gathering up her papers and walkie-talkie, Ellen rose. Leaning over my shoulder, she whispered in my ear, "Welcome to the real jungle." She turned and walked out of the room.

"Who's Kiara?" I asked.

"Our white tiger. Our star boarder," Yolanda said.

"And the future occupant of Tiger Forest," Miles said. "Schedule, Ramirez!"

Yolanda Ramirez's spidery fingers crisscrossed color-coded flowcharts as she discussed the anticipated schedule for Asia World's grand opening. She underlined the date, October 31, with such force that the black marker squealed across the paper.

"Guarantee to meet our deadline, and you're hired." Miles leaned toward me, so close I felt his hot sugary breath on my face.

So far no one seemed particularly interested in my artistic skills, just my ability to meet the deadline.

"You will finish by the end of October," Miles said, issuing his proclamation.

"I really need to see the mural first, before I can make any promises," I said.

"We need to discuss this, Miles," Barb broke in. "And the board has to approve it."

"Nonsense." He slammed his fist on the table. "I have full authority."

Barb made saucerlike eyes at me. "I happen to know Caroline. She's notoriously late on everything. Aren't you, Caroline?"

I could tell she was afraid I was caving in to Miles. "I never miss a deadline," I said, almost enjoying pushing her buttons for a change.

She pursed her lips and glared at me.

I got up from my chair. "I can be more specific after I see the mural."

Yolanda's eyes rested on the photos drying on the table. She wheeled over to my side. "Not zoo shots, are they?"

I shook my head. "They're from one of those safari parks."

"Good, because I'd hate to be the one to have to explain these. There's been a lot of flak about this lately—zoos selling to unscrupulous dealers. That's why we've stated our policy on surplus animals clearly. Our dealers sign an assurance."

Barb walked over. "That's fine for newsletter drivel, but we don't do business with dealers. Having them sign a guarantee means nothing. That's why I personally check out a facility before I release an animal. It's the only way to be absolutely sure that the animal will be taken care of properly for the rest of its life. I think we owe our animals that." She glanced at the photos. "Good God," she said. A scowl crossed her face, the same one I'd seen in the childhood photo of her on the Chirico's living room wall. Maturity hadn't dulled her aversion to animal abuse.

"Never mind all that." Miles clapped me on the shoulder. "What say I give you a tour of the exhibit? Will you join us, Barbara?"

I looked her way, but she refused eye contact.

"No, I have some things to do that can't wait," she said.

"Why don't we have dinner later?" I suggested.

"I'm busy." She was letting me know that since I'd rejected her help, I was on my own in dealing with Miles.

Miles opened the door. "Shall we?"

I left the photos drying on the table and hurried to catch up with him, eager to get my first glimpse of the mural. When Tony painted a wall, sometimes it did talk. Maybe the one I was about to see would tell me who killed my friend and why.

6

As Miles and I passed the front gates of the zoo, one of the protesters pointed at him. "Check out the gray whale, man! Thar' he blows!" Derisive laughter followed.

Miles looked like he smelled something bad. He rushed at the demonstrators, who were handing out leaflets to arriving visitors. "Here now. Give me those—"

The circle of protesters scattered like a flock of pigeons. Miles grabbed the boxes of literature and threw them into a Dumpster.

"We're having a peaceful demonstration. You can't do that!" a woman yelled.

"How would you like to spend your life in a cage?" a man shouted, bombarding Miles with the ingredients of his vegetarian lunch. A tomato hit the director squarely on the chest.

"Goddamn bunny huggers! Get your ignorant asses outta here before I have you locked up for assault, not to mention littering!" Miles kicked at the discarded leaflets on the ground. He brushed off his jacket and rejoined me. "Publicity hounds! They create media events just to get free advertising."

That seemed like the cat calling the dog an animal.

As we neared the construction site, blue-green earthmovers bearing the Chirico Construction logo roamed the ground like mechanized dinosaurs. A turquoise crane lifted its brontosaurus-like neck in the air. Clearing away construction rubble, a bulldozer roared past.

When the dust settled, I had my first glimpse of Asia World. The rectangular building rose from a circular site. Cement block formed the walls, with slanted glass panels for the roof. Around the foundation of the building, landscapers sculpted exterior yards.

Miles surveyed the structure as though it were a temple. His eyes couldn't have taken in the scene more lovingly had the building consisted of stacks of hundred-dollar bills. I followed him up the cement ramp that snaked up one side of the building to the entrance on the second floor. Just inside the heavy metal doors hung a spotlighted portrait bearing a bronze plaque.

Mrs. Charles Worthington-Bentley.
May she rest peacefully
with the animals she so loved.

"Our patron," Miles said. I thought he might genuflect.

"It almost sounds like the woman's buried here," I said.

"As a matter of fact, her ashes were placed in the cornerstone at our groundbreaking."

"Quite an expensive headstone." Peering at the portrait, I recognized the artist's signature as belonging to a well-known Chicago portraitist. In a soft ivory gown, Mrs. Worthington-Bentley sat in a green velvet chair, her hands crossed in her lap. I did a double-take. On the ring finger of her right hand was a large emerald in an antique gold setting encrusted with diamond baguettes. Was it the same ring I'd seen on Claudia Baxter's hand at Tony's funeral? If so, I wondered how the ring had come to its current owner.

I glanced up. Miles had set off without me. I hurried to catch up, watching my step on the pathway. Jeep tire tracks and animal footprints were set into the concrete path—sort of a jungle Grauman's Chinese Theater.

Ahead of us lay a series of suspended serpentine bridges that crossed over the uncaged animal areas below. I must have looked unsure of the trail ahead.

Miles motioned me forward. "Come on. The bridges only appear to be constructed of wood and rope. Actually they're quite stable." Miles stomped his foot on the bridge. "Reinforced with steel, don't you know. The hemp and vines supply atmosphere."

The metal entrance door behind us scraped open. Ellen Riggs moved out of the shadow into the filtered light. "Dr. Crandall, you have some visitors from Texas waiting in your office. I can give Caroline the rest of the tour."

"See me in my office, Canfield, before you leave." His heavy footsteps thudded as he hurried out. Somewhere inside the building an elephant trumpeted.

"You mean the animals have already moved in?" I asked Ellen.

"Animals need time to adjust before we open to the public, and the keepers need time to train them to enter and exit the exhibits on command. As soon as Tiger Forest is complete, we'll move Kiara from her old quarters."

"How is she doing?"

At first Ellen seemed surprised by my question. Then she must have remembered I was present when she got the call. "We shifted her to a squeeze cage so Rob could draw blood."

"A squeeze cage?"

"It's a small cage with moveable walls that constrains the animal's movement long enough for us to give it an injection or draw blood without having to tranquilize. Anesthesia is particularly dangerous for white tigers. We haven't gotten the results back yet on the blood test, but I can read Kiara's moods. I know she's not sick."

"I hope you're right. So, what's the quickest way to the mural?"

"We might as well just take the public walkway through the building."

We entered a simulated bamboo forest. The sun had come out from behind the clouds, and light rays filtered down through the slanted glass ceiling. The mural consisted of a misty landscape of trees featuring a giant panda munching on a stalk of bamboo. The mural's size overwhelmed me. I'd never done anything on such a grand scale, even with Tony. If the tiger mural approached this one in size, I was glad my taking on the job was all an act.

"The mural is a little misleading," Ellen said.

"Why is that?"

"Miles wanted a giant panda, but they're just too scarce. They can't be taken from the wild, and they don't breed well in captivity. Instead, we'll show their smaller relative, the red panda, which is just as endangered, but a little easier to obtain." She leaned over the railing. "They must be in their dens. All the exhibits have been designed to stimulate activity. The trees and vines encourage them to climb. Exercise is just as important for them as it is for us."

"But it's comforting to know we also share the couch potato instinct." I pointed out a red panda sleeping high in a bamboo tree, its striped tail wrapped around its head like a turban. It looked like a raccoon with a henna rinse. Normally I would have been delighted by this private tour, but today I had other priorities. "The tiger mural?"

"This way." Ellen led me into the next environment. Tropic vegetation rose above the path, simulating a dense, steamy rain forest. Natural plants and trees blended almost magically with the two-dimensional foliage of the mural beyond. The illusion of depth of space was astounding. It reconfirmed for me the master muralist Tony had been. At the same time it convinced me that I had made the right decision in giving it up. My strength lay in the intimacy of a painting, rather than its magnitude.

"This is our orangutan exhibit. Only a few thousand orangs remain in Borneo and Sumatra," Ellen said. "But our female came to us only two weeks ago from Las Vegas."

I laughed, until I realized she was serious.

"It's more sad than funny. She was a performer, but most recently she and this out-of-work magician who owned her spent their time living on the street eating out of garbage cans. She's quarantined until we can be sure she's healthy. But it's going to be a struggle for Houdina to adjust to her new life here. She'll have to unlearn certain human behaviors—like wearing clothes and eating with utensils and sleeping on the floor instead of in trees. In time we hope to introduce a male."

"If she was trained, I'm surprised someone in Hollywood didn't snap her up."

"Mature orangutans can be quite a handful. They're very independent and extremely strong, sometimes impossible to control. That's when they get dumped, when they outlive their cuteness."

I suddenly realized we were no longer making forward progress on the walkway. "Please don't think I'm not interested," I said, "but I really need to see the tiger exhibit."

"We'll take a shortcut," she said. "I just thought you'd like to see everything."

I followed her through an emergency exit leading briefly outside. We swung back into the building on the opposite side. "India occupies the entire south end of the building," Ellen said. "This section is Tiger Forest."

Large scaffolds dominated the raw space we entered. Although I had tried to prepare myself for this moment, I trembled as my gaze fell across five stories of concrete wall and six staggered levels of scaffolding. *This is where Tony was killed.*

"What?" Ellen said.

I hadn't realized I'd said it out loud. "This is where he fell, isn't it?"

She frowned. "I didn't take you for the ghoulish sort."

"I'm not, but Tony mattered to me." I scanned the walls, curved at the corners, forming a three-sided di-

orama. Cerulean blue sky and billowy white clouds sparkled across the top of the walls. My eyes searched the
mural for the painted tiger, but I didn't see it. Color
ended abruptly at the horizon line where painting had
left off. Penciled drawing grids continued below. Each
grid contained a line drawing as a guide for the painter.

I recognized the classic grid approach to transferring
the drawing of the mural to the wall. A scaled-down
rendering of the mural is squared off into grids. A full-
size grid is applied to the wall using a snap line like the
kind surveyors use. The painting is then painstakingly
redrawn grid for grid to the wall's larger scale.

To minimize the times the scaffolding had to be
moved or rearranged, Tony worked section by section,
painting each grid to completion before moving on. That
was why every detail had to be worked out in compre-
hensive drawings prior to the final painting.

Even as a simple line drawing, I could tell Tony had
planned something spectacular for this mural. The scaffolding partially obscured my view, but a large lake, covered with duckweed and surrounded by tall grasses, lay
placidly in the center of the mural. Herds of sambar and
other deer clustered at its edge to drink. Ancient ruins
skirted the lake.

"That's the lake of Rajbagh—the Garden of the
Kings," Ellen said. "The palace was probably a summer
residence for the king. A real waterfall and a pool of
water in the foreground will lead into the lake in the
mural."

"A pool for cats?"

"Unlike most cats, tigers are wonderful swimmers.
They love water, although they don't like to get their
faces wet."

Some of the mural's plant forms I recognized. But on
the far right an unfamiliar tree was drawn, its snaky
upper branches intertwined. From the floor of the pit
rose large wire armatures, awaiting transformation into
rocks and trees by workmen with spray guns of liquid
concrete. Near the wall close to the walkway stood the

massive naked form of one such tree nearing completion. Its spindly fingers beckoned upward to the glass ceiling just as its exposed roots sought the ground. I noticed its similarity to the one drawn in the mural.

"That's a banyan tree," Ellen said. "Some of the banyans in Ranthambhore are eight hundred years old. We'll do our best to make it look real, but we have to construct everything so that the tigers can't use it to climb up to the public walkway."

"Good thinking," I said.

Ellen gestured toward several workmen in the pit. "They're installing robotic deer that will contain food for Kiara to find."

"When I was a kid, the keepers just slipped the food under the bars."

"For a while we had stopped feeding them while they were out in the exhibit. Hygienic reasons. Now we're going back to feeding them on display. It's called behavior enrichment. If an animal has to search out or work to find its food it makes their lives less boring." We leaned over the railing, watching the men work. "The whole exhibit will hook up to a central computer system. For instance, when Kiara claws the banyan tree's trunk, the action will initiate a monsoonlike storm. The skylights will darken by way of an electric charge in the glass, and the wind machines will be activated. Rain will pour down for about three minutes—everywhere except on the public path, of course. It's a way to give Kiara some control over her environment while also providing the public with what Miles calls entertainment."

"And what do you call it?" I asked, moving down the walkway closer to the side wall.

"Excess." She had to raise her voice to be heard above the sound of water now coursing over the man-made waterfall that the workmen were testing out.

My eyes continued to scan the walls as I walked closer. "So you don't buy Yolanda's argument that animals don't mind captivity as long as all their needs are met?"

"Would you give up your independence so easily?"

"I'd be tempted," I said, "but I like making my own decisions. And my own mistakes." I stopped in my tracks when I saw it—the painted tiger in the upper left corner of the mural. It sat atop some ancient ruins. The top scaffold had blocked my view previously.

Ellen noticed the direction of my gaze. "That's Ranthambhore Fort, nearly a thousand years old. Men battled on that site for centuries. Tigers reign there now."

"You must have worked closely with Tony to make the mural as authentic as possible."

"I gave him a lot of pictures and books about Ranthambhore to help him."

"Are you familiar with the myth of the tiger's whiskers?"

She nodded. "We're mixing trivia like that with facts about the tiger in the graphics and hands-on displays that will take up the whole back wall behind us."

I studied the tiger on the wall as she spoke. Its eyes glimmered in the light. Their yellow-green hue was perhaps the ugliest I'd ever seen, with the exception of a bridesmaid's dress that hung in my closet at home. They were painted flatly, with no roundness to the eyeballs. Something else was peculiar about the tiger, something untigerlike about its body, but I couldn't identify what it was.

From my new vantage point, however, I noticed something else. The pencil drawing of the banyan tree's lower trunk and exposed aerial roots had been smeared beyond recognition, as though someone had taken a sponge and washed it all away.

7

I STUDIED A WALL IN MILES CRANDALL'S OFFICE AS I waited. Framed press clippings and photos of him in grip-and-grin shots with presidents and other celebrities formed a border for the wall's centerpiece, an obscenely huge pink fish mounted on a slab of redwood.

Before leaving Asia World, I had checked Tony's supply closet, but there were no drawings, no sketches there—only paint, brushes and other tools. Until I could determine what had been obliterated from the mural, I'd have to string Miles along.

The door opened and the director entered. He motioned me to a straight-backed chair in front of his desk, then lowered himself into a plush leather bucket seat. His fists hit the desk between us. My chair reacted to the tremor.

"Now then. When can you start?" He leaned forward. His folded hands sat like a giant rump roast on the desk before him.

"Before I can begin, there are some things I'll need."

"Whatever you need, I can arrange. Just tell my secretary."

"And then there's the matter of my fee."

His nose shot into the air. "You'll get exactly what Mr. Chirico got."

I blinked. I didn't care for his choice of words.

With a smirk on his face, he opened a drawer and whipped a contract across the desk at me. The specified amount was more than I'd make in a year at my hourly rate working day and night. I just hoped the small print didn't mention a three-by-six pine box.

He handed me a fountain pen. "So, shall we consummate?"

The thought of that derailed me for a moment. "There's still one other problem," I said, "I have to find Tony's drawings."

His face turned into a ball of fire. "The drawing is on the wall, for God's sake! All you have to do is color it! It's as simple as paint by numbers! I could do it myself if I wasn't such a busy man!" Struggling to regain his composure, the director rose slowly from his plush throne. He glided around the desk and sat on its edge next to me. For a big man, he was as graceful as a dancer. "There are no problems," he crooned, "only opportunities. So, you'll start tomorrow then." He teetered forward like a huge boulder threatening to crush me in a landslide if I gave the wrong answer.

"I'd like the weekend to think it over."

His head jerked as his fists tightened. "I'll expect your answer no later than Monday morning. Oh-eight-hundred hours."

8

MY HEART POUNDED IN MY THROAT AS I RUMMAGED through my kitchen "Hell Drawer." I shoved aside credit card receipts, rubber bands, tools, batteries, expired coupons, and spare parts to God-knows-what. They had to be here; I knew I had kept them. A glint of metal gave them away, cowering in the back corner of the drawer—the keys to Tony's studio.

I hopped into my Camaro and shot along the Kennedy into Chicago. The studio was located on the top floor of a converted warehouse in Chicago's Printers' Row district. Once the hub of printing, the area had since gone trendy. The printing houses had departed for cheaper digs, and lofts had been converted into residences and upscale businesses.

Tony's was one of two apartments on the fifth floor. I crossed the lobby, passing beneath the engraved marble archway that read, "All Else Passes, Art Alone Endures." So much for art. The printer once housed here had specialized in "girlie" calendars.

I entered the elevator, an oversized shaft built to carry huge skids of paper. The ancient metal cage was still run by a troll at least as old. I had never ridden George's car without a hassle. With his green pants and dingy olive sweater, he looked like an old frog, perched on his stool, eyes closed, dozing.

He jumped awake when I bounced onto the car. "Like to give me whiplash!" He rubbed his stubbled chin.

"Sorry, George. Five, please."

He eyed me as though trying to decide if he knew me. "Ain't no point in goin' to five." White hair sprouted from his ears like the bristles of abused paintbrushes. "Ain't nobody up there. If you want the sculptor who's six months behind in his rent, he's de-leased. And if you want the painter, well sir, he's de-ceased." He choked on his laughter.

"I'm . . . uh, picking something up."

"Can't letcha take nothing out without no author'zation." He folded his arms.

"Come on, George, you remember me."

The elevator didn't budge. I wondered if he'd give me as hard a time if I weighed three hundred pounds, had bulging biceps, and answered to the name of Stosh.

"Are you taking me up or am I taking the stairs?"

"As head of security it's my duty to stop you." He crossed his arms, one palm out.

I reached into my bag. "All right, a buck a floor and you never saw me." I slapped a five-dollar bill into his palm.

"Five bucks a floor, and I never heard you neither."

I pulled out a twenty.

He snapped the bill from my fingers, like a frog snatching a fly out of the air with its tongue. "I know nothing. I see nothing."

"Let's go. I'm in a hurry."

He eyed me up and down. "Ooh . . . I'm trembling." His gnarled hands pushed the screeching metal door of his cage shut.

The car lurched, then creaked along at a mournful pace. Like it, I was eager and apprehensive at the same time. The elevator stopped close to five—about four and a quarter. George tried to level off several times and finally settled for four and three-quarters. I needed Air Jordans—not white tennies—for the leap up to the fifth floor, but I made it.

I headed down the hall to the studio, slipped the key in the door and opened it a crack. Peering around the dark walnut door frame, I almost expected Tony to be standing there. I pushed the door wide open. Something thudded, then crashed. I jumped backward. My heart banged in my chest. Then I remembered Tony used to balance a wardrobe pole between two open file drawers behind the door. I must have opened the door too far.

Leaving it ajar, I tiptoed in. The sticky sweet smell of linseed oil and turpentine greeted me. For a moment I stood there silently, transported back to happier times. Sunbeams streamed through the skylights, highlighting minute particles of dust in the air.

I glanced around. If I didn't know better, I would think the place had been ransacked. Tony's bookshelves had long since overflowed. Piles of art books and magazines created a landscape of free-form skyscrapers, with just enough room to pass between them. When I had complained once about having to work in such disorder, Tony had tapped his forehead and said, "Organization is up here."

I picked up the fallen end of the wardrobe pole holding sharply pressed suits and silk shirts and put it back in place. Tony lived in disorder, but was always immaculately dressed. I had teased him about being like Whistler, who had often painted in formal evening clothes.

I wandered past enormous paintings leaning against the walls. Rolled canvases, removed from their stretchers, stood on end in the corners. I ran my hand across the slick surface of one of the half-closed walnut pocket doors that separated the rooms.

I pushed the sliding door open and entered the room in which Tony had done much of his work. This was where each mural began. An unusually wide, custom-built, wooden easel stood ready to take on its next challenge. But there were no drawings displayed today, no work in progress. Yet drawings of what he had in mind for the tiger mural had to be here somewhere.

Committing a painting to a wall was merely the last step in the lengthy process of planning and designing a mural. The mural began as a mere seed in the artist's mind. Then came research: photos of tigers, Asian deer and foliage lay scattered across the studio floor. Next, Tony went through countless thumbnail sketches exploring composition. Horizon line and center of interest needed to be established. Larger, more detailed pencil sketches followed. When one was selected, numerous color sketches were done. Color choices were evaluated, reviewed and modified. Which blue to use? Ultramarine, cerulean, Prussian? Which red, which yellow? Then over months the mural would evolve through various rounds of revision to the final painting the public would see. In the last stages a scaled-down color comp on canvas or board was done. A grid would be applied, breaking it down into manageable square sections, so that the drawing could be transferred to the wall, and painting could begin.

I spent the next half hour searching corners and crevices. But all the canvases and sketches I unrolled related to other projects and had nothing to do with tigers. Had someone been here before me to destroy what I needed to find? As Tony's assistant, Gino probably had a key to the studio. Did anyone else?

In a wastebasket I found several discarded sketches of cats and my heart leaped. But when I realized they were only of domestic cats, disappointment settled in.

I wandered into the third studio, Tony's living quarters. His bed was unmade. I walked toward his mahogany desk on a raised platform behind an antique breakfront. Restacking the books from the chair onto the floor, I sat down behind the desk.

Layers of bills, junk mail and letters covered the desktop. The lilac and pink envelopes with ornamental borders screamed for attention. The one with roses along the edge reeked of stale perfume. Letters from his female admirers.

I sifted through stacks of receipts, invoices, magazine clippings, delinquent library notices and dozens of unpaid parking tickets. I tugged on the middle desk drawer, but it was jammed. I gave it an extra pull. An envelope fell on the floor at my feet. It was addressed to Tony in heavy black ink with the additional word PRIVATE! across its face. I was uneasy in my new role as a snooper, but this might be important. I unfolded the letter, also written in a thick felt-tip pen. My eyes froze on the message.

Our Baby died this afternoon thanks to you. But losing a baby or its mother has never particularly bothered you, has it? I hope you ROT IN HELL!

No signature. A chill traveled from my toes to my ears. My heartbeat went into a crazy rhythm. Had Tony gotten a woman pregnant recently? Claudia Baxter looked close to menopause. Could this message refer to an event further in the past?

Tony had scribbled notes all over the back of the envelope. It looked like "TAXES—Sept. 15th. S. Antoinetta," but I couldn't be sure. Even he couldn't always read his own writing. September 15 could refer to the quarterly estimated tax deadline for self-employed people like Tony and me. Since he frequently overlooked the date, the note might be a reminder. He often used shorthand, an "s" to mean "see." Maybe he needed to see his ex-wife Antoinetta for some reason, since he still claimed her as a dependent. Was the message on the outside related to the nasty note within?

Also inside the envelope was a well-worn, yellowed photo of a man and woman in an Italian piazza. At first I thought the swarthy man was Vince. But the photo was too old. Though the man's hair was dark, I recognized the physique, which hadn't changed much in thirty years. It was Tony. Next to him was a young, dark-haired woman. He had his arm around her and they appeared to be drinking wine at a cafe in the long shadows of the early evening. Nothing was written on the back, but the tired condition of the photo indicated someone had looked at it often over the years. I remembered Gino's story about the young girl who fell in love with Tony in Italy, the girl who had presumably killed herself. Was this a picture of Gino's parents? The letter didn't sound as though Gino could have written it, but maybe people didn't write with a noticeable accent.

I heard a creaking sound, like floorboards squeaking, possibly out in the hallway. The antique breakfront blocked my view. I stuffed the letter, photo and envelope into my bag and flew out of the chair. Tripping over the telephone cord, I crashed headfirst into the pile of books I had just moved. I lay there, facedown in *The Complete Paintings of Anders Zorn.* Mom said I always had my face in a book.

Using the wall to regain my balance, I pulled myself up and hurried to the front door. Careful not to disturb the wardrobe pole and its clothes, I opened the door a crack and peered down the dark expanse of hallway. No one.

As I stood by the door, something plopped onto the front of my blouse. I glanced at the red spot in alarm until I realized my nose was bleeding from the fall I'd taken. But the sight of my own blood reminded me I was dealing with a murderer. Was I nuts? I was here alone, with only George for backup. Where had I left my purse?

With my head back to stem the bleeding, I trotted back to the desk and picked up my bag. Feeling a need to restore Tony's privacy now that I had violated it, I yanked the room's sliding door shut behind me. As I did, I heard a crinkle of paper. I pushed the door partially open once again and craned my neck around the wood panel.

A tissued drawing was taped to the bedroom side of the door. It was a sketch of a tiger—actually several studies from different angles—and notations about physical characteristics. I picked at the taped corners and removed the drawing from the door panel.

Was the drawing meant to be concealed? Or had Tony merely tacked the drawing there as a convenience? Nothing unusual jumped off the page at me. Nevertheless, the subject of the sketch clearly related to the mural. I slipped it inside the sketchbook in my bag to keep it from ripping. I checked the other sliding doors, but found nothing else.

As I crossed the room and headed for the main door, a wet drop hit the top of my head. I glanced up at a knothole in the hardwood floor above me. The balcony. It ran the width of the loft. I'd forgotten to search there. I touched the wet spot on my head and looked at my fingertips. Dark red. Another drip hit my cheek. I wiped it off my face. The stain on my blouse spread as the crimson liquid began to steadily drip from the balcony floorboards above me.

My first instinct was to run. But what if someone was hurt up there? Moments could matter. I sprinted to the ladder leading to the balcony. At its base I hesitated. Did I really want to go up? Taking deep breaths, I climbed the ladder, questioning each step I took, wondering what I'd find. I pulled myself up the last rung, side-stepping an overturned gallon of turpentine. Tumbled boxes of supplies, more books and canvases lay across the floorboards. A wave of relief swept over me. I should have known. It was just some red paint leaking—too thin for oil, probably tempera—from a jar that had tipped over and broken.

I took a few trial steps forward, scanning the contents of the balcony for anything resembling drawings. My foot crunched down on a cast-off box of pastels. I edged along the rail of the balcony, past more overturned boxes. That's odd. Tony usually treated his materials and tools with more respect. And he'd never carelessly throw one of his jackets across the floor. What's wrong with this picture? I asked myself.

As I inched forward, I recognized the jacket. American. Ralph Lauren. The jacket Gino had worn yesterday. And to make matters worse, Gino was still in it—with one of Tony's walnut-handled palette knives skewering his throat.

9

I CLAMPED MY HANDS OVER MY MOUTH AND GASPED FOR
air. My fingers might have been sucked down my throat
except they were locked onto my face. I screamed and
backpedaled frantically. The floor went out from under
me. The walls went sideways. My butt bounced off the
cartons of paint behind me and hit the floor.

I lay in a pool of congealed blood. My formerly white
tennies had turned into scarlet blobs—covered in blood.
I raised up on my elbows, then pushed up on my palms.
The sticky red liquid oozed between my fingers.

Gino lay faceup, his complexion a waxy yellow. His
eyes, so blue twenty-four hours ago, gaped opaque black.
The stainless-steel palette knife had pierced his now ver-
milion throat just behind the Adam's apple, like a collar
pin behind a necktie. There was no chance he was still
alive. Next to him lay an empty champagne bottle. Its
bubbly contents must have quickly lost its effervescence
when it hit the blood.

The smell of urine permeated the air. My stomach
took the elevator to my throat. The doors to my mouth
parted, but nothing came out. I lay on the floor dry-
heaving.

I had to get to a phone but was in no condition to
climb down the ladder. Not the way my legs were shak-
ing. The only other time I'd seen death so raw, so grisly,
it had been roadkill. I crawled through the blood and

leaned my back against the loft's railing. I couldn't get up. I did my best to just breathe.

Shouting voices and a pounding came from somewhere below. "Police! Open up!" The sound of wood splintering.

I wanted to shout, but I could only croak, "Up here."

Heavy footsteps. The balcony shook.

"Jesus Christ!" a male voice boomed. "Don't move!"

"He's dead." I started to get up. Cold metal touched the side of my neck.

"No kidding, genius. I'm not talkin' to the stiff. Move and you're as dead as he is."

The balcony shook again, not as much this time. "Whad'ya got?" A woman's voice.

"Homicide."

Next to me feet shuffled closer.

"Holy shit!" the she-cop said.

"Got the perp right here, too," the he-cop said.

Big black Oxfords crushed my fingertips. I yanked away my bloody hand.

"Yeah, talk about red-handed!" The cops laughed.

I had lost my sense of humor.

I sat on a five-gallon drum of acrylic medium for what seemed like an eternity. Police radios squawked in my ear. A voice that sounded like mine explained in random order what had happened. I looked up. A guy in a brown suit was writing in a notebook like I was actually communicating.

Dark-uniformed bodies milled around me. Flashbulbs went off. A man laughed. Words like "lividity" and "postmortem" bounced off the plaster walls. My hands lay in my lap, their little red forms as alien to me as Martians. I looked around for something to wipe them clean.

Someone babbled in my ear about rights. A guy in a gray suit pulled me to my feet. "All right, let's take a little ride."

"Hell, I don't want all that blood on my back seat."

The brown cop plucked one of Tony's silk shirts and a pair of his pants from the garment pole. "Here, put these on and put what you're wearing in this bag." He looked around the room. "Where's the skirt?"

"I wasn't wearing a skirt," I said.

"Nah!" He swung around impatiently. "Luzinski!" he bellowed.

The woman cop approached.

He pushed me toward her. "Bag her clothes and search 'er."

The brown cop on my left arm carried my canvas bag under his arm like a football. He pressed the elevator call button. The gray suit to my right crossed his arms. I struggled to keep my head up, trying to get back my dignity, but I had a feeling the strip search was only the beginning of my ordeal.

Stepping into Tony's shoes had taken on an all-too-literal meaning. I had put on a pair of his Italian loafers as well as a silk shirt. I'd rolled the pant legs up so I wouldn't trip, but they were already working their way down. And with handcuffs on, I couldn't impede their progress.

George rose in his metal cage like Lazarus from the dead. Seeing him behind bars had always seemed appropriate. A mental picture of myself behind bars was another story.

Our trio stepped down into the car. I hoped this was just a bad dream. Maybe like Dorothy and Toto I would wake up and find myself back home in my warm little bed. I closed my eyes and clicked the heels of the loafers together. Nothing changed.

"You bring her up here?" the brown cop asked George.

"That's what they pay me for. I takes 'em up, I takes 'em down. Just like my pants." His cackle turned into a coughing fit.

"Leave your pants up and take *us* down," said the brown cop. "You the guy who reported this?"

"I reported a possible B and E." George turned around to face the cop. "I watch all them cop shows."

"I'm sure they'd be flattered to know it. You give our men a statement?"

"I gave 'em as many as they wanted." He snorted up phlegm and turned my way.

I curled my lip at him.

He swallowed. "Thought she was actin' a little shifty. Know what I mean?" He slapped the metal gate. "You run one of these babies, you get to know people."

"What time did she get here?" the gray cop asked.

George pushed the gates closed; they screeched in his caress. "High noon. Yessir. Bribed me, she did, to keep my mouth shut."

I leaned forward. "You lousy—"

The gray cop interrupted. "Did she tell you why she came?"

"Figured she come for a nooner with the I-talian hunk."

"So he was a regular visitor here?"

"Sure, Gino worked with Mr. Tony. Let hisself in all the time. Chicks comin' and goin' to that apartment all hours of the night." He winked at the cop and nodded at me. "One man-eater too many, huh?"

I lurched forward. "You pervert."

The gray cop pushed me back in the elevator. "Shuddup. What time did this Gino arrive?"

"Not today, and I been on since six this morning."

The brown cop shifted his weight. "What about last night? Who came in the building? You keep a log?"

"Is the pope buried in Grant's tomb? Course I don't. I ain't no KGB." George made a sandpapery sound as he scratched his chin. "But I can describe 'em. Yes sir, I'm a shrewd observer, like a scientist."

The brown cop smirked. "Okay, Einstein, who'd you see last night?"

"Let's see. If memory serves me . . ." George crossed his arms, again one palm out.

The brown cop looked at the gray cop. The gray cop kicked George's stool. "Speak, Fido," he ordered.

George bounced on the stool like a kernel of popcorn in a hot pot. "All right, don't have to get violent. First there was a nice-lookin' tall fella. Figured he was goin' to see Miz Hot-to-Trot on two. Then there was this real looker, legs up to here." He motioned to the level of the grease stain on his pants. "I think she was selling something. Before I had a chance to buy, somebody buzzed her up. Oh, yeah, and there was this other dark-haired mama. Forgit which floor she went to. She was wearing one of those big watches that beep at'cha, the kind that tell you everything 'cept when to take a piss."

"Those the only people who came by last night?"

"Wouldn't know if they come after 6 P.M. I'm off duty. Have to have a key to the stairs to get up then." He sucked up more phlegm and turned toward the brown cop.

The cop's smile faded. He backed away as though he was afraid George was going to use him for target practice. "Take us down, hotshot."

George stared at the cop.

"This thing does go up and down, doesn't it? Or do you need a gun to your head?"

George pushed the control lever. The car lurched. I fell sideways into the gray suit. It smelled like a giant nicotine filter. "Fasten your seat belt and keep your hands inside the car," George said. "Next stop . . . HELLLLLLLLLL!"

If Tony *was* there I had a few questions for him.

"Do I need an attorney?" I asked.

"I don't know. Do you need an attorney?" Mr. Brown said over his shoulder through the divider.

Mr. Gray caught my eye in the rear-view mirror. "Nah, you're wearing silver bracelets cuz it breaks our hearts to see a woman without jewelry." The cops laughed.

I was stuffed into the back of a patrol car. I hoped I

wasn't sitting in anything even remotely close to what I was smelling. Doing my best to take shallow breaths, I could feel my face swelling up from the fall I'd taken.

Mr. Brown leered at me. The afternoon sun cast deep shadows across his face, pockmarked like the surface of the moon. "Lemme put it to you this way, missssssss. We arrive on the scene and find the place ransacked, what looks like your fingerprints all over the place, a guy with a knife through his neck and you laying there in his blood."

"Some of it was my blood. I told you. I had a nose—"

"Yeah, right, a five-pint nosebleed. We find a handwritten death threat on you—"

"I didn't write that."

"A witness tells us you arrived about noon for, as he so poetically put it, a nooner."

"Yeah, well, he would think that, wouldn't he? The guy is a walking porno movie."

"Way we figure it is, the sex got a little rough. Your boyfriend pops you in the face. You bean him with the champagne bottle, grab a knife, and finish him off." He flipped back through his notebook, then flicked it shut. "We'd be home free, except the medical examiner's assistant says the guy bought it at least twelve to sixteen hours ago. I hope you're working on a good alibi for midnight last night."

A uniformed cop waited by the phone as I made the call. I just hoped Ben Rudolph was in his office downtown.

Ben showed up a half hour later. He brought with him proof that I was Tony's heir and had a legitimate, if not timely, reason for being at the studio. The initial estimated time of death satisfied the police I had at least not committed the murder that morning. They checked my phone records and confirmed I'd been talking to a friend in Denver at the time of the murder. Fortunately I hadn't touched either the palette knife or the champagne bottle. I told my story at least six times to various cops.

Finally I signed my statement, and they released me. They gave me back my bag but kept my clothes.

It was already dark when Ben dropped me back at my car, in front of Tony's studio. I wanted desperately to go home, shower and climb into bed. But I needed to talk to Ben even more. I followed him back to his office in my car and grabbed a meter on Wabash in front of his building.

I couldn't let go of the thought that Gino knew more about the mural than he'd let on. He'd said he had a business meeting downtown. The blue cardboard tube he had been carrying yesterday wasn't anywhere to be found today. The champagne seemed to indicate more than a business meeting. Had the lady-killer had a date with a killer lady? Or did it just indicate a celebration of some kind?

I was more convinced than ever that the mural held some secret. I had to work out a plan of action. After all, I was now dealing with someone who had murdered twice.

And in the process I'd violated one of Tony's cardinal rules of painting: planning. "Know where you're going before you get on the train!" he'd shout at me impatiently. Not only had I gotten on a train, destination unknown, but the damn thing was going too fast to get off. And I had a horrifying feeling the tunnel I'd just entered had only one track, and the light at the end of the tunnel was the headlight of an oncoming train.

10

I SANK INTO A BLACK LEATHER COUCH AT BEN RUDOLPH'S office. Like a warm friend it enveloped and comforted me. But I couldn't get Gino's face out of my mind.

"This'll make you feel better." Ben handed me a glass of brandy and poured one for himself. He turned and gazed out the office window at the night lights of the city. The elevated train made its grating ninety-degree turn on the tracks outside at Lake and Wabash. When the metal screeching subsided, the lawyer turned to me. His puffed cheeks deflated as he exhaled. "Didn't take a criminal attorney to know they couldn't hold you. But I know the right man to represent you if it goes any further." He sat down.

"You think it will?" I raised the brandy snifter to my lips.

Ben leaned back in his chair, his hands behind his head. "I doubt it, but the cops'll be around to question you again." In the security of his office, Ben had lost his stutter.

"I told them both Gino and Tony's murders were connected."

Ben rocketed forward in his chair. He braced his arms against the desk. "What are you talking about?"

"You can't believe Tony just fell," I said. "He was murdered."

His eyes were wide. "But who—"

"I don't know who, but I think Tony planned to reveal

something in the tiger mural and somebody stopped him from finishing it."

"You think Tony was up to his old t-t-tricks? Something about the zoo?" He considered for a moment. "Nah, that's crazy. There's no evidence, not even a hint."

"I'm pretty sure Gino had some drawings with him yesterday when I dropped him at the train station. They weren't there when I found him today."

Ben shrugged. "Maybe he left them somewhere else."

"He was taking them to a meeting. Gino Tedesco knew what was in the mural and was about to sell Tony's drawings to whomever the mural incriminated, but he was killed instead. I told the police, but they . . ."

"Aren't you jumping to conclusions?"

"There's something else about Gino. He claimed he was Tony's son."

Ben smiled and shook his head. "I warned Tony when he took Gino on. The kid was a character—and an illegal alien as well. He'd do or say anything to stay in America. What else did he tell you?"

"That he was there when Tony fell, but he couldn't tell me what caused it."

He looked at me without blinking. "I can tell you. Respiratory failure. Broken collar bone punctured his windpipe."

"Was there an inquest?"

"Every accident victim's death is reviewed by the coroner's office."

"What did they find?"

"Nothing. Death was ruled accidental."

"You and I were his best friends, Ben. There's got to be more. What caused the fall?"

Ben sighed and went to a file cabinet. He pulled out a folder, returned to his desk and glanced through some papers. "It appears Tony had conjunctivitis. It's listed as a contributing cause. I've had the condition myself. Probably impaired his vision, and he took a wrong step."

That was consistent with what Gino had told me about Tony's red, puffy eyes.

Ben closed the report and folded his hands over it. "I hate to be the one to tell you this, Caroline, but Tony knew he was going to die."

"He knew he would be murdered?"

"You're not listening to me. He knew he was dying. He didn't tell anyone, but his last physical wasn't good. The only reason I knew about it was he started getting all his papers in order."

"What was he dying from?"

"You know how he worked. He must have ingested a storehouse of poisons over the years by mixing his own pigments." He opened the folder again and scanned the list. "Cadmium, cobalt, lead. Shall I go on?" He filed the paper back into a folder.

"Can I see that?"

Ben frowned at me. Even his bald spot frowned at me. "It won't tell you anything more than I already have. I have no reason to withhold anything from you." He returned the documents to the file cabinet. "Personally, I think your nerves are shot. It's understandable. You're angry that Tony's gone. So am I, but we can't bring him back."

"Could the chemicals have caused his fall?"

"They were killing him, Caroline," he said. "Slowly, but surely. Maybe it was a blessing he went quickly."

I took a deep breath. Maybe I had gone off the deep end inventing this whole murder scenario. Maybe Tony had simply fallen after all. "Wait a minute," I said, "Gino is dead. Murdered. And there's no question about that." Gino had been hit over the head and stabbed. I flashed back to Antoinetta's rampage with the letter opener. "It must have been a snap decision on the murderer's part—stabbing him with a palette knife. Otherwise, why not use a real weapon? The killer must have hit him first with the champagne bottle, then—"

"Caroline, go home, get some sleep. It'll all seem less sinister in the morning."

"Maybe the murderer planned to meet Gino's demands in exchange for the drawings. Then something happened. Gino raised the stakes, demanded more, and the killer felt so threatened he or she picked up the first weapon at hand." Then it dawned on me. "During the meeting Gino realized Tony was murdered because of what was in the mural. He switched from just trying to sell some damaging drawings to blackmailing a murderer. The murderer snapped."

"Whoa, hold on. Now I know why they call people like you creative. Look, the police will investigate Gino's murder. But they're satisfied there was no foul play in Tony's death. Why can't you be?"

"I don't know. Something's not right. I think I owe it to Tony to find out the truth."

"How do you p-p-propose to do that?"

"The zoo wants me to finish the mural. Of course, I'm not going to go through with it, not in a million years, but if I can stall just long enough to figure out what's in the mural—"

"Well, if anyone can spot something, it'd be you."

"Funny, I thought the same of you. Would you take a look at it?"

Ben's forehead wrinkled. "With these old eyes?" He shook his head. "Besides, I'm color-blind. As your lawyer, I advise you to let sleeping dogs lie. As your friend, I beg you to let sleeping dogs lie."

"I can't do that, Ben. How can you?"

"Why open a can of worms? The first thing the police will consider is motive. Ask yourself, who stands to gain the most from Tony's death? Want a mirror?"

What I wanted was to see that autopsy report for myself. I had to get Ben out of the room so I could. "So how did the family take the news of their disinheritance?"

"Not good. Have you ever seen a pack of pit bulls?" He set his brandy on the desk.

Suddenly I knew how to get Ben out the room.

"Tell me about the estate," I said.

"Not tonight. It's late."

"Now."

He sighed, opened his locked briefcase and started pulling out papers. "On my advice Tony placed his assets in a trust. Here's a list." He handed me a packet of papers.

I extended my arm quickly across the desktop to take the papers. The thumb of my hand launched Ben's brandy glass toward him. He had pretty quick reflexes for a guy his age. He blocked both my hand and the glass with the fistful of papers. The brandy snifter did an about-face, pirouetted and landed in my lap instead.

"Jeez, Caroline, I'm sorry. I don't know how that happened," he said, hurrying to my side of the desk with a box of tissues. "There's a sink in the ladies' room just down the hall."

I was too clumsy to even make an accident go smoothly. Trying to hide my disgust with myself, I grabbed half the tissues. I stood up and blotted the front of Tony's baggy silk trousers I still wore. The rolled cuffs drooped and gathered at my ankles. "Forget it. These pants don't do anything for me, why should I do anything for them?"

Ben chuckled, returned to his chair and continued. "Now then, as you might have guessed, Tony left no life insurance. He didn't believe in it."

I picked up my brandy glass and circled behind Ben. Pacing came naturally in a lawyer's office.

"Frankly," Ben said, "Tony had little in the way of liquid assets."

"So then why is the family so upset?" I leaned over Ben's shoulder to read the document in front of him for myself. "What did he have? A few thousand in the bank?"

"How about upwards of three million dollars?"

"Three million dollars?" The brandy glass slipped from my hand to the lawyer's lap. He jumped out of his chair. Timid about dabbing at the front of his pants, I handed him the box of tissues. "Gosh, Ben, it really was an accident."

"Of course, it was. It's my own fault for mentioning liquid assets." He smiled.

"Three million dollars?"

"Tony had extensive real estate holdings, including that building his studio is in. As soon as you complete a few formalities, you'll own all the properties."

I'd relish my first official act—to fire one slimy elevator operator.

"They're all professionally managed, so you don't have to make any immediate decisions regarding them. Look, let's take care of the paperwork when you're fresh." Ben tossed the soggy tissues into the wastebasket.

"Surely the family will contest this." My mouth had gone dry.

"Wills are difficult enough to contest. To break a trust is almost unheard of. That's the beauty of it. It takes a long time to set up. The title to every asset that goes into it has to be changed. That amount of thought and effort works against the person trying to break it. The legal costs alone would be astronomical, not to mention the non-contest clause."

"What's that?"

"If one of the heirs should contest and lose the case, he'd be fully disinherited. It's a standard clause that's often inserted. So you see, Tony's wishes are pretty clear."

"But what has the family got to lose? Right now they get nothing."

"Not exactly." He smiled, sat down and flipped open a document. "This is Tony's will, separate from the trust." He read from the document. "I leave my former child bride Antoinetta $94.23—one penny for every day I was married to her. I leave her an additional five cents for all the joy she brought me."

He closed the document and slipped everything back into his briefcase. "Tony left his father's pocket watch to Vince and his mother's wedding ring to Diana. His Porsche goes to his sixteen-year-old grandson, but Tony stipulated the boy can't drive it until he's twenty-one."

"Why would he want to leave such bad feelings as his legacy?"

"I only advised Tony how to set up his estate, not the terms nor whom to leave it to. Don't feel sorry for his family. They were well taken care of in the divorce settlement."

Ben rotated the combination lock on his briefcase, pushed back from his desk and got up. He glanced at the front of his pants. "I better throw some water on this stain." The outer office door closed behind him. His footsteps echoed down the hallway.

I hurried to the file cabinet and extracted the manila folder with Tony's name. I flipped the pages frantically until I found the autopsy report. I scanned the sheet. The list of poisons in Tony's blood and tissue samples was staggering. Many of the names I recognized as ingredients of art materials. I was well aware of the dangers. Everything Ben had told me was true. I flipped to the next page. The edge of the paper sliced through my index finger.

Right next to the bloody fingerprint I left, I found something Ben had failed to mention. The report on the external body findings said a trace of lead was found in the white paint on Tony's lips. The blue line on his gums, the report went on, was consistent with lead poisoning.

Of course, there would be white paint on his lips. Gino had told me Tony had been painting the tiger's whiskers when he died. He had pointed the brush with his lips, like he always did. For years I tried to get Tony to switch to titanium white, but he preferred the consistency of flake white. It was thicker because it was loaded with lead. So there was no smoking gun in this autopsy report after all. And yet, something bothered me about that bit of information. What was it? A door slammed. I shoved the file folder into the cabinet, sat down and crossed my legs.

"Any questions before I see you to your car?"

"Just one. Why me, Ben? The last three years, Tony and I had dinner now and then, I'd stop by his studio when I was in the area, but we weren't as close as we once were."

He sighed. "There's s-s-something I haven't told you. Technically, you're the secondary beneficiary. The p-p-primary beneficiary was unable to accept the inheritance."

So I wasn't Tony's first choice, after all. "But who would turn down that amount of money?" I looked up at him. "I'm not listening again, am I? You said 'unable to accept.' Gino was the heir, wasn't he? Tony's son. And now that he's dead . . ." Except Gino was still alive when Ben initially told me of the inheritance. "Who was Tony's intended heir?"

"I can't reveal that information. Unlike a will, which is public information, the terms of a trust can be kept entirely private." He straightened the stapler and the penholder on the top of his desk. "Furthermore, should you not be able to fulfill the terms of the trust or not survive Tony by ninety days, the estate would pass to the third b-b-beneficiary."

Why was he suddenly stuttering again? "If I should not survive? I think I'd like to know who benefits if I should not survive."

"I can't tell you that either. Tony wanted the terms of the trust kept confidential."

"Ben, give me a break."

"I like you, Caroline, but I won't discuss it with you. It would be unethical. Now let's get you home." He took me by the shoulders and lifted me out of the chair.

We left the office and walked down the darkened hallway to the elevator. Our ride down was silent. Ben walked me out the door to my car.

I slid into the driver's seat. "Ben, you mentioned something about my fulfilling the terms of the trust. What terms? Is that why the first beneficiary didn't inherit?"

The lawyer braced his arms against the roof of the car. "Caroline, get some sleep. We'll go over all this when you're rested. Now get goin'." His palm pounded the roof.

"What terms, Ben? I'll keep you awake all night if you don't tell me."

The lawyer exhaled and leaned into the window. "There's one small stipulation that must be m-m-met before you inherit. And Tony was quite adamant about this."

"What's that?"

"You have to go back to m-m-m-"

I hated myself for the uncharitable thought, but for the first time since I'd known Ben, I wanted to hit him on the back, so he could spit it out.

He took a breath. "You have to go back to mural painting."

11

NIGHT. I STOOD ON A PRECIPICE, ON THE EDGE OF A VAST canyon. Tigers prowled the depths below, their roars echoing up the walls. Headlights bore down on me from behind. A net flew through the air and hovered over my head. I took a running start and leaped.

Jerking awake for the third time that night, I got out of bed, made coffee and waited for dawn. My blood raced every time I thought of climbing scaffolds again.

The fee Miles had offered, though tempting, hadn't persuaded me. Three million dollars was a different story.

Why was Tony trying to control me from beyond the grave? He may have been aware he was dying, but was he aware he might be murdered? Had he made me his heir for that reason? If the answer lay in the mural, and I believed it did, who else would figure out its message? Didn't I owe him that much?

I knew of only one other place to look for Tony's drawings. My call to Vince was a one-way conversation. Though neither of us brought up the inheritance, his warmth toward me had changed to a chill as abruptly as Chicago temperatures switch from summer to winter. I explained my dilemma about the missing drawings. Vince showed little interest in helping, until I mentioned that the mural's incompletion might delay further funds for construction. He agreed to meet me at four that afternoon.

By late Saturday morning I was on my way to the zoo. I'd been so preoccupied after my meeting with Miles— not to mention subsequent events—that I'd completely forgotten to retrieve my portfolio and the photos I'd left to dry on the conference table.

The administration building was virtually deserted, except for several docents sharing a few laughs. The photos were right where I'd left them, spread out over the table like an unfinished game of solitaire. I swept them into a ripple-edged pile and slipped them into my portfolio. I'd messenger them back to my rep on Monday.

Dangling from my arm, the portfolio scraped the cement steps as I left the zoo office. At the bottom of the stairs, the events of the last two days finally caught up with me. My knees started to buckle. I staggered to a park bench and sat down.

In the last forty-eight hours, I'd buried my mentor, inherited three million dollars on the condition I go back to a job I feared and hated, and last, but not least, I'd discovered a corpse.

The late summer locusts sizzled in the trees. "Hiss-scape! Hiss-scape!"

The pain behind my right eye was so intense it felt like someone had shoved an X-Acto knife through it. What was I getting into? What made me think I was going to uncover some murderous plot when everyone else, including the police, seemed perfectly satisfied that Tony's death was an accident? I had no proof Gino's murder was in any way related. This wasn't my territory. We were talking murder here. M-U-R-D-E-R. The letters flicked on and off like a neon sign in my brain.

The wind shifted, and a cool breeze blew the hair back from my face. The mural. It all came back to the mural. If I focused, it would guide me where I needed to go.

I donned my sunglasses and got up. Weekends were the busiest days at the zoo. People streamed past me. Several children brushed by, and a balloon bounced off my face. Off to the right an old red-brick building beckoned.

Taking a short cut through the area marked "Camel Rides $2," I walked against traffic like a zombie drawn to the arched entrance. An ornate terra-cotta bas-relief over the door featured frolicking lions and tigers. The artisans who had sculpted it were an endangered, perhaps even extinct, species themselves.

"The old lion house," a voice behind me said. "Except now there are no lions."

I spun around. A woman with closely cropped steel-gray hair faced me. I recognized her as one of the protesters.

"Sorry, I didn't mean to startle you." She carried a stack of brochures and photocopies. "My name's Marcia Wilhelm."

I was exhausted and not eager for a confrontation, but she might have some relevant information. I took a deep breath. The fresh air wasn't so fresh. I glanced down. A large camel pie protruded from the side of one of my new tennis shoes.

"I'm president of the local chapter of CCATZ," she

said. "Concerned Citizens Against Terrible Zoos. Perhaps you've heard of us."

I searched the ground for a stick to scrape my shoe. "What?" I found a twig on the grass.

"Marcia Wilhelm. CCATZ," she repeated. "We keep an eye on conditions at zoos and other public animal displays." She offered me several pieces of literature.

Instead I bent to scrape my shoe. "Odd name for a watchdog group."

"I hope some of our more strident members haven't turned you off to us," she said. "Every organization needs its radicals. Sometimes that's the only way things change."

"And what is it you want to change?"

"Attitudes. Our sister groups have opened the public's eyes to the atrocities of circuses and rodeos. Now it's time to target zoos."

I straightened up and accepted a crudely printed brochure, turning it over in my hand. "These pictures always look worse in black and white, but that's the whole idea, isn't it?" I offered her the stick in my hand by mistake, then realized my error and handed back the brochure. I tossed the stick into a trash container. "I spend a lot of time at zoos, sketching and taking pictures for reference. I like zoos."

"You like animal exploitation? Have you seen some of these?" She thrust copies of newspaper articles at me.

"Bad zoos deserve to be closed. But some of the most committed supporters and tireless workers for animal welfare I know work in zoos."

"Are you aware that Fox Valley Zoo is unaccredited? Unrecognized by other zoos?"

"They're working to change that by spending millions to improve conditions here."

"For the animals? Or for the public? Or for the staff?" Her eyes were as steely as her hair. "Nobody polices zoos like this. Except for us."

"Surely the government—"

"Look at these pictures. Does it look like the government cares? Oh, the Department of Agriculture has inspections, but the truth is, captive animals don't have much protection." She brushed a strand of gray hair from her eyes.

"What about the Endangered Species Act and other wildlife laws?"

She handed me another brochure. Did she have one on every subject? "Those laws are for just that—*wild*life. Most of the animals in zoos are captive bred. They aren't covered."

"But zoos protect endangered species. That's what they're all about."

She reached over and slid my sunglasses down to the tip of my nose. "Lose the rose-colored glasses, honey. Like most bureaucracies, zoos exist to perpetuate and protect themselves."

I glanced down at the brochure before she brought out pie charts. "Even you have to admit zoos have come a long way in the last ten years."

"So have nuclear weapons. It doesn't make them any more palatable."

I didn't feel like enlarging the argument to warheads. Still, I had to ask. "All right, so what do you have on Fox Valley Zoo? What are you accusing them of?"

"Nothing we can hang our hats on yet. But we're working on it. In the meantime, think about this. The zoo is overcrowded. You know what happens in animal shelters when they reach capacity? Think about that the next time you 'ooh and ahh' at a baby zoo animal. When those babies have lost their cuteness and their power to draw crowds and just become one more mouth to feed, what happens to them then? Are you aware how many animals this zoo has had to get rid of recently?"

"Relocated."

"Then why won't they give us names, dates, bills of sale, shipping records?" she said. "If they have nothing to hide, why are they unwilling to share their records with us?"

"I have nothing to hide from the IRS," I said, "but it

doesn't mean I'd march into their office and demand an audit."

"And your point is?"

She was getting on my nerves. "Look, unless you have something specific, some proof, you're just blowing smoke." I turned to enter the building.

"That's right, just turn and walk away. It's not your problem, right?"

Was she trying to recruit me? I glanced overhead expecting the net to fall. I had my own problems. Like losing the scent of camel poop, for starters.

"You can help us. Now that you're going to finish the mural—"

I faced her once again. "Who told you that?"

"We have our sources."

"What are you asking me to do?"

"Drag your feet."

I had to laugh. "Funny thing about me dragging my feet. I tend to trip and fall. Or is that what you have in mind? How far would you go—or have you gone—to close down this zoo? Is it worth the loss of human life?"

"Are you accusing us of—?"

"If the shoe stinks," I said. "Now, if you don't mind, I have other things to do."

"Fine. But I feel I must warn you, you're either with us or against us. When the walls of this rat hole come down, and they will, we're taking no prisoners."

"Are you threatening me?"

"Don't be ridiculous. We're just trying to get some answers." She turned and began to walk away. "If you're curious, try asking them whatever became of the liger."

12

I HURRIED INTO THE DREARY LION HOUSE. STUMBLING over the threshold, I caught my balance, only to trip over my portfolio. I sprawled facedown on the mosaic tile floor. Two little girls nearby giggled. The contents of my unzipped portfolio lay scattered across the floor.

A hand reached down to help me up. "Are you hurt?"

I glanced up into Ellen Rigg's warm brown eyes. "This is just God's little way of reminding me to increase my accident insurance."

She smiled and bent to pick up the photos, one by one, that had slid out of my portfolio. I got up and dusted myself off.

She handed me the prints. "I heard about Gino Tedesco. How awful for you."

I fought the picture but I lost. The scene replayed in my head. "How awful for Gino," was all I could say. The chattering of monkeys and squawking of birds inside was almost deafening. I recalled the bas-relief on the building's exterior. "Isn't this the lion house?"

"We relocated the lions when our renovation began. Now we're housing monkeys and small apes here along with some exotic birds until our next phase, Africa World, is built."

We passed under another arch into the building's cavernous main hall. People clustered around the cages where spider monkeys cavorted and screeched. Gibbons, marmosets, baboons and human primates joined the chorus. The echoes ricocheted off the brick walls.

"So you have no doubt the full renovation will go ahead as scheduled?" I asked.

"Why not? Or have you been talking to Marcia Wilhelm? I saw her prowling around."

"She sounds determined to shut down this zoo."

"To pull it down with her bare hands, if she has to. I'm afraid CCATZ is making inroads, little by little. For instance, we used to have names on all the cages. They picketed until we removed them. Pet names belittle the animals, they say, deny them their wild identities. It's true that people teasing them and calling out their names all day can irritate them. But it makes it easier and really safer for the keepers to use names which the animals generally respond to. We just don't advertise it to the public anymore. Come on, I want you to meet Kiara, or should I say, *Panthera tigris.*"

Crossing into a roped-off area, I followed Ellen to the far end of the building. Inside its cage the tigress paced restlessly. Light grayish brown stripes rippled across her immaculate, creamy white coat. Ellen made a funny noise. It sounded like the name she gave it—chuffing. Kiara made a similar sound and slowly padded to the front of the cage, her huge white paws plopping across the floor. She seemed pleased to see Ellen, only curious about me.

"I've only seen pictures of white tigers before," I said. "What causes an albino?"

"Kiara's not an albino. If she were, she'd have pink eyes and no stripes at all. She was born to a pair of normally colored tigers who carried the recessive gene for whiteness."

Kiara's eyes were a startling shade of cobalt blue, but something about them wasn't quite right. Her left eye stared directly at me. Her right eye had a mind of its own.

"Kiara's eyes are a little crossed," I observed.

"It's called strabismus—one of the problems in white

tigers. But it just makes me love her more." When Kiara ran a paw under the bottom rail, Ellen opened the side rail to get closer to the cage. "You see, all white tigers in zoos are descended from the same white male tiger, Mohan, captured by the Maharajah of Rewa. Mohan was bred to normally colored females, but no white tigers resulted. It wasn't until he was bred to one of his own daughters that several litters of white cats were born. One of the babies, Mohini, was bought from the Maharajah by a businessman during the fifties and presented to the National Zoo in Washington as a gift to the children of the United States. Kiara is one of Mohini's great-great-granddaughters." Kiara stood alert, her eyes facing me.

"But all the inbreeding has resulted in genetic problems like crossed eyes?"

"And worse, I'm afraid. In trying to offset it, zoos have bred white tigers, originally pure Bengals, to other subspecies. We can't correctly call white tigers Bengals at all anymore. Kiara's mother was predominantly Bengal, but her father was Siberian. In fact, Kiara's family tree is kind of a mess. I guess that's another reason I love her. We have a lot in common." Ellen motioned for me to join her behind the rail.

I approached the cage slowly, unable to take my eyes off the magnificent cat. "Is it okay if I sketch Kiara while we talk?"

"Sure. She's been a little sluggish since Rob took that blood sample yesterday. That's why I'm keeping her away from the public today. She probably just wore herself out. Like most animals, she goes berserk whenever she sees the vet coming." The beautiful cat circled its enclosure. Ellen rapped on the floor of the cage and Kiara came forward.

Pulling out my sketchbook along with several carbon pencils, I took another cautious step closer to Kiara. As she paced, I sketched rapidly with the soft blue-black lead of a 3B carbon pencil, held on its side to rough in the general form. Each time the tigress turned toward me, I worked to capture the details of her head.

"Kiara and I are old friends," Ellen said. "In fact, she arrived at the zoo the same week I started as a keeper in the lion house here, seven years ago."

Kiara's roar, more of a guttural sound, sent a vibration through the vaulted building that tingled my toes. People gathered near the roped-off area, but when they couldn't see into the cage, they moved on.

"Did you always want to work with animals?" I asked.

"One way or another. First I thought I wanted to be a veterinarian, but I wasn't the greatest student. I flunked out of pre-vet."

"You seem to have found your true calling. How long have you been head keeper?"

"Two years. They wanted to promote me after I went back for my master's in zoology and in chemistry, but I missed contact with the animals. The higher up you go, the further away from the animals you get."

"I think that was Darwin's theory."

Ellen laughed. I wished she did it more often. Kiara seemed to like her laugh as much as I did. The tiger's bright blue eyes looked steadily back at Ellen, as though in silent communication. I worked quickly to capture the details of the big cat's face. Kiara watched my movements. Her good eye studied me, and her jaw dropped open. She wrinkled her nose, stuck out her tongue at me and hissed. I backed away.

"Don't take it personally," Ellen said. "That's called the Flehmen response. It's a way for her to pull your scent up to a very sensitive gland, called the Jacobson's organ, in the roof of her mouth. It's kind of a cross between smelling you and tasting you." Ellen reached over the rail, took my hand, and pulled me forward. "Don't be nervous."

"I don't mind a sniff or two, but she's looking at me like I'm a bag of kibble."

"I'll be right back." Ellen disappeared through a door at the side of the cage. She returned with a large bone in her hands. "In the wild, a big cat may eat only once or twice a week, depending on availability of game. So once a week, our big cats fast. Today's Kiara's day, but she's been stressed. This bone might calm her nerves." Kiara saw the bone, opened her mouth and chuffed.

Ellen slid the bone under the bars at the corner of the cage. Kiara snatched the bone and carried it to the back of her enclosure where she plopped down, her back to us. Loud gnawing noises left no doubt that she was enjoying her treat. Ellen pulled the last two sheets off a slim roll of paper towels she had slipped under her arm. As she wiped her hands, I noticed something I hadn't before. The fourth and fifth fingers of her left hand were missing. I averted my eyes before she looked back at me.

Facing away from us, the white cat displayed the gray stripe pattern on her back that was unique to her. I sketched her in this new position, until she let out a roar. I jumped a foot back from the cage.

"For someone who paints animals, you're awfully nervous around them," Ellen said.

"Most of my wild models are in photographs. I guess I spend so much time studying an animal's appearance, I haven't had the time to learn about their habits or biology. Maybe by working here you'll help me change that. Then I won't be afraid either."

"I'm not fearless. I just respect the warning signs. Of the two species," Ellen said, "lions are the more unpredictable, more temperamental than tigers. They'll go after you for no good reason. But tigers are more levelheaded. As long as you don't move too quickly."

"Speaking of lions, I understand you used to have a liger here," I said as casually as I could, not liking myself for baiting her.

Perhaps it was the sudden change of subject that caused Ellen to wring the paper towel core into a twisted party favor. "She got sick."

"What happened?"

"She died. I don't want to talk about it." She walked down the row of cages and placed the mangled towel roll in a trash bin. She took her time returning. When she did, she said, "Did you know there are more tigers in captivity than are left in the wild?"

"No, I didn't know that."

"Well, it's true. You see, in the seventies zoos over-bred Siberians. When they ran out of room, breeding programs were drastically cut back. For the next ten years, very few Siberians were born. By the time zoos decided to resume active breeding, most of the captive population was too old. And the wild population had dwindled to an alarmingly small number."

"We were left with a vastly diminished gene pool." Barb stood in the doorway. "The whole species could have been lost because of our lack of foresight." She walked toward us. "Enter: the species survival pro-gram—the one good thing that came out of that dreadful experience. Now we record each endangered animal's genetic heritage in stud books, matching the right male to the right female, so something like that never hap-pens again."

Ellen disappeared into a back room.

"You've given a whole new meaning to designer genes," I said.

Barb smiled. The thing I'd always liked about her was that she got over her anger as quickly as it came upon her. She linked her arm through mine. "You know, if someone had designed your genes, you could have ended up a dancer, instead of a klutz."

"I'll have you know my mother sent me to ballet les-sons every Saturday," I said, "but each week Madame Cherovsky slipped me five bucks to go to the movies instead."

Barb laughed out loud. Then glancing into Kiara's cage, she frowned. "Ellen, did you give Kiara that bone?"

Ellen stuck her head out the door. "It's an extra treat."

"She needs to be kept on a strict diet, especially now.

You know she's susceptible to disease. Was Rob Bennett here today?"

"No, but I'm watching her."

"See that you do." Barb turned to me. "Come on, let's get out of here."

I called a good-bye to Ellen, but there was no answer. Barb and I strolled the length of the exhibit hall to the door where I'd entered.

"Are you all right?" she asked. "I couldn't believe what I heard on the news last night about Gino and how you found him. I've got to warn you. With Gino gone, Miles is going to put the screws to you now. You've got to stand up to him. We'll find another muralist. I don't want you to put yourself in jeopardy."

"So you think there's some connection between both deaths and the mural, too?"

"I don't know what to believe. That's up to the police. They were here earlier. But, don't worry, I told them that the last time we saw Gino alive was at the funeral reception."

"That's not exactly true, Barb."

Her eyes grew large. "You mean I unknowingly lied to them?"

I explained how I'd given Gino a ride and had a chance to talk to him. And how that talk had convinced me more than ever that Tony had left a message in the mural.

"Did Gino tell you what it was?"

"Not in so many words." I had a sudden brainstorm and grabbed her hand. "Come on."

Barb and I stood on the walkway in the same spot I'd stood yesterday morning when I'd first viewed the tiger in the mural with Ellen. Today, though, there were no workmen. Except for an occasional call of an animal in another part of the building, the place was silent.

"I think I know now what's so odd about that tiger in the mural," I said to Barb. "Look at the body proportions and the shape of the head. They're wrong. Not to mention the terrible color of those eyes. The cat does have stripes, but it's not a tiger at all. It's a liger, isn't it?"

She cocked her head as she studied it. "I suppose it could be, but so what?"

"What happened to the zoo's liger? Ellen said it died."

"I'm surprised she told you that much."

"You don't like Ellen, do you?"

"It's not a matter of liking her. She means well, but it sometimes clouds her judgment. About six months ago, I was promoted to director of research and conservation. Ellen was promoted to my former position, curator of mammals. Her first official duty was to supervise the movement of the animals to their new quarters here in Asia World. Everything went well, except for the big cats. She moved them prematurely, before their interior exhibit was complete. Since it was summer, she thought the tigers and leopards could simply move between their holding cages and their exterior yards. Except building and waste materials were lying all around. For whatever reason, the liger got sick and died. The necropsy Rob performed revealed it had been poisoned."

"And you blame Ellen?"

"I don't blame her for the liger's death—we never did determine how exactly it was poisoned—but I do blame her for faulty judgment. She was so eager for the animals to get into their new facilities and out of the old cramped ones that she didn't consult anyone else. Ellen's bright and committed, but she sometimes acts like these animals are her own personal property. I tried to back her up, but in the end it cost her the promotion. She was demoted back to head keeper. And in a sense I was demoted, too. Until we can find a new curator of mammals, I've got my hands full trying to do two jobs." She checked her watch. "I've really got to go."

"Remember the photo I had with me yesterday? The one of the liger?"

"Vaguely. I'm afraid I didn't look at it very long. It was so disgusting."

I slipped my arm into the portfolio and fished around for the photos. "Take another look." I shuffled quickly through the pile to find the one of the liger, then sorted through them a second time. The photo was missing.

13

VINCE WAS WAITING WHEN I DROVE AROUND TO THE staff's section of the zoo parking lot. He stood, arms folded, leaning against the driver's side of a new black Ferrari. Not exactly the family man's car. I had heard his marriage had been troubled even before his wife Sara's miscarriage. Money problems were probably placing an added strain on the relationship.

Vince had parked one space to the right of Tony's shiny red Porsche—right where Tony must have last parked it. I slid my battered white '79 Camaro to the left of the Porsche, got out and walked around to Vince.

"I appreciate your coming." I extended my hand.

He looked at it like it was a piece of dirt. "Just want you to get everything you've got coming." His fingers drummed on the Ferrari's roof, just above the window bearing a National Rifle Association decal.

"The terms of Tony's will were as big a surprise to me."

Vince held up his hands, palms toward me. "Spare me the speech, Princess Caroline. First your father croaks and leaves you set up for life, then your grandfather drops a small fortune on you. Now *my* father adds to your tidy bank account. Who's your next target? That shyster, Elmer Fudd, who set this whole thing up?"

"If it's any of your business, my father left only debts. And my—" I didn't owe him any explanations. But in truth, I was set up for life now if the figures Ben Rudolph had shown me were correct. "Maybe if you had taken the trouble to reconcile with him," I began. "That was the whole reason he took the zoo job. To bring his family together."

He pushed himself off the side of the car. "Let's get this over with, huh? I didn't come here to listen to you run your mouth. If that damn mural doesn't get finished on time, the zoo goes broke and takes me with it."

"Fine. You have the car keys?"

"Just remember the car belongs to my son."

I glanced at the right rear wheel, wearing the Denver boot. "Not until you get it out of hock." I held out my hand. "The keys?"

He glared as he handed them over.

I glanced in the side window of Tony's Porsche, but the inside appeared empty. Walking around to the back, I shoved the key in the lock, but the trunk was stuck.

"Can you give me a hand?" I asked.

Vince's hips leaned into the side of his car as he stared off into space.

"Dammit, I can't help what your father did. Maybe something can be worked out. I'm willing to talk about it." If Ben hadn't revealed the conditions to Vince, I wasn't going to tell him that I hadn't exactly inherited anything yet.

He spun around. "You like to talk, don't you?" His eyes turned into menacing slits. "I heard you've been nosing around since the funeral, suggesting maybe my father was murdered." He waited, but it was my turn to be silent. "Just watch what you say."

"Whatever I do is my business."

"You think you were something really special to my father, don't you, Princess Caroline?"

"Knock off the Princess routine."

"You think my father selected you as some exceptionally gifted student and took you under his wing, because he saw such promise. You want to know why you really got the job?"

"Let's not do this, Vince."

"Well, you're going to hear it. It's the price you have to pay."

I started to turn away.

Vince grabbed my arm and pulled me back. "When it was clear I wasn't an artistic genius, he latched on to Barb. He promised to pay her college tuition in full, if only she'd go into art, but she couldn't hack it either. So she found a replacement to get her off the hook—naive and impressionable Caroline Canfield. You know why my father liked you? Because he could order you around. You still act like he's some kind of god."

"Your father went out of his way to help me. I think that deserves a certain loyalty."

"Oh, he knew you were loyal, all right. You want to know what he used to say behind your back? He said you were loyal just like a dog—like a clumsy, dumb dog, Caroline."

Keys in hand, I pushed past him. "I came here to look for a few drawings, not to engage in a hate match with you." I tugged on the trunk's lid, applying all the rage I felt.

It popped open. The contents looked like a mini-version of the studio. Tucked over the right rear wheel were three rolls of vellum. My heart leaped. I unrolled them just to make sure, then slipped them under my arm. Feeling elated, I combed through the rest of the items in the trunk to make sure I hadn't missed anything. I didn't want to have to contact Vince again. I flipped through a black sketch book. "Mind if I take this, too? It has color notes for the mural."

The silence was not only deafening, it was earsplitting. I slammed the trunk shut and tossed the keys back to him. "Thanks for your help."

He tugged on his car door, bent down and reached inside. "You might as well have all of his artwork." He flung a long rolled-up canvas at me.

I caught it against my chest.

He reached back into the car. "What the hell, you might as well have this, too. God knows, I don't want it." He side-armed a small baggie at me.

It hit me in the face, then dropped to the ground. I bent to retrieve it from the pavement. The transparent bag appeared to contain items from a scavenger hunt. I looked back at Vince, already in the driver's seat.

He revved the Ferrari's engine. "That's what they found on my father's body. He never carried too much in his pockets. It ruined the line of his pants," he shouted out the window. "I gave the clothes he was wearing to the Salvation Army. If that violates the terms of the trust, sue me." He hit the gas, and the car rocketed backward. He shifted gears. The tires screeched as the car sped away. It took a moment to register. Someone had been sitting in the passenger seat. A young blonde. Vince was a family man, all right. He was dating a girl young enough to be his daughter.

I stared at the retreating car. When the dust settled, I unrolled the canvas just far enough. It was the slashed family portrait from the Chirico living-room wall.

14

I WAS EAGER TO LOOK AT THE DRAWINGS I'D RECOVERED, but equally intent on putting as much distance between me and Vince Chirico as possible. Forty minutes later I pulled into a gravel driveway that wound through towering trees until it ended beside a former country church.

I parked in front of the one-room red schoolhouse in back that I'd converted to an art studio two years ago. The evening sun reflected off the studio's large fan-shaped windows, which looked out on the Des Plaines River.

The small Lutheran church and school, built on a piece of farmland eighty years ago, had easily accommodated the twelve local farm families who had attended services there. But as the farms were subdivided and sold off for residential housing in the fifties, the congregation outgrew the structure and relocated to the wealthy side of River Ridge. The land reverted to the farmer who had allowed the church to be built on this half-acre. Perhaps because a tiny cemetery sat on the property, the lot had remained untouched except by time, until the farmer's grandchildren decided to liquidate. Buyers lost interest when they discovered the graveyard. But dead people didn't scare me half as much as some of the live ones I knew.

I bought the run-down property three years ago in a real estate auction at the urging of David Borden, the architect I was dating at the time. I had sunk most of my savings into the renovation. The relationship ended abruptly, as did the remodeling, six months ago. My current financial windfall would mean new life for the renovation, if not for the romance.

I turned the key in the door of the studio and went inside. Warm western light flooded the room's oak floor, enhancing the smell of linseed oil. I placed the mural drawings on top of my drawing board and unrolled them. Each panel was 24 by 19 inches and carried a letter and a number. The letters identified the panel's row, top to bottom. The numbers identified its location, left to right.

Shoving aside my taboret and chair, I lay the drawings out edge to edge, tacking them to the floor with masking tape to hold them flat. They stretched ten panels across and five down and covered most of the floor. The mural had been drawn to a two-inch scale. Every two-inch square of the drawing was equal to a square foot on the actual wall.

The pencil drawings on the floor appeared to match the enlarged drawing on the wall at the zoo. Matched it entirely too well, in fact. Panel C-9—the wall's smudged section—was missing entirely. Had Gino used it to blackmail the murderer? Was that what he had been carrying in the blue tube?

The tiger—or liger—in the upper left corner appeared identical to the one on the wall, except for the lack of color. With the liger photo missing, I couldn't compare it to the mural. Had that been the intention of whoever stole it? Anyone at the zoo could have taken it off the table. Rob Bennett had seemed pretty eager to get rid of the photos. I scoured each panel for further clues, but found nothing else. I'd study the drawings with a fresh eye again later, but it wouldn't help me discover what was in the missing section.

As I locked the studio door behind me, the last glimmer of daylight filtered through the oak and maple trees surrounding the church. I crossed the light-dappled ground and opened one of the church's double doors, painted bright red to contrast with the white frame exterior. Each time I came in the front door I still expected Buttons to be there, tail wagging. If only the pain of her absence would leave. No more pets for me. Too hard dealing with having them put to sleep.

Throwing my bag and car keys on a table in the narthex, I headed up the circular staircase to the choir loft. Pulling off my clothes, I tossed them onto the bed. After I took a shower, I slipped on the long T-shirt I intended to sleep in. Letting my hair air-dry, I decided to get dinner.

The Saturday night menu was really no different from the rest of the week: home delivery from Johnny's Cluck 'n' Moo. Before I could place my order, the phone rang. Maybe Johnny was checking up on me. I *was* a little later than usual.

"Eat yet?" the voice on the other end asked.

I tried to hide my surprise from Jake Statler. "Just about to."

"How 'bout some pizza? I know a great place."

"I don't think so." Emotionally I was flattened. Besides, I was ready for bed. With my hair still wet, I caught a glimpse in the bedroom mirror. Not a pretty sight. On the other hand, Jake knew something I didn't, and I needed to find out what it was.

"I can pick you up in twenty minutes," he coaxed.

Although I couldn't deny being attracted to Jake, his brain interested me more than his body at the moment. "Give me half an hour," I said, as though the extra ten minutes was going to make a difference. I gave him the address. "You can't miss it. It's the house with the steeple." I hung up before he could reply. I enjoyed seeing the first reaction when someone arrived. They often thought I was a preacher, or more often, a preacher's wife.

I ripped off my T-shirt and slipped on a fresh pair of jeans and a white silk blouse. With two pairs of tennies ruined in the last twenty-four hours, I was forced to wear heels.

Within thirty minutes I looked as good as I was going

to. I glanced out the choir loft window and saw Jake's car in the driveway. He sat in the driver's seat glancing back and forth between the big black numbers on the front door and a slip of paper in his hand. I applied a little mascara and some lipstick and dashed out the door.

15

JAKE PARKED THE CAR ON THE EAST SIDE OF THE RIVER, and we walked across a bridge. Ducks squawked a welcome as we descended a flight of stairs to Sven's, a riverfront restaurant. It sounded more like a ski shop than a pizza parlor, but maybe Sven skied the Italian Alps.

Sven's was stifling inside. Jake ordered a carafe of Chianti and two glasses at the bar and carried them to a table outside on the patio. We sat across from each other once again, as we had at Janey's Joint three days ago. Only this time I'd make him do the talking.

"So, when do you start work on the mural?" Jake asked, while I was still thinking about my first question.

"What makes you think I'm taking the job?"

He smiled. "Instinct. I figured you'd have to look into your friend's death." The sound of a pinball machine toting points punctuated his speech.

I refused to be the interviewee again. I crossed my arms. "I'm not saying one word more until you level with me. What do you know about all this?"

He raised the glass carafe. "Wine?"

I nodded and lifted my empty glass. The first sip of

Chianti sent tiny rivulets of perspiration running down my spine. "Aren't you hot in that jacket?"

"I'm fine," Jake said, perusing the menu.

The waitress took our order. "Sorry there's no air conditioning," she apologized.

"Think of it as saving the ozone layer," Jake said.

I liked that he took it in stride. David would have made an issue of it. The pinball machine registered more points.

"They keep promising a repair guy is on his way, but so far nothing." The waitress tapped the eraser end of her pencil on her order pad. "In the meantime some hawk has built her nest in back of the unit. Can you imagine? We're trying to get it out of there—"

Jake put down his glass. "Let me talk to the manager."

The girl looked startled. "Did I do something wrong?" She turned in appeal to me. "Is the wine bad?"

I shrugged at her.

"I mean it," Jake repeated. "Where's the manager?"

She turned on her heel and hurried away with a worried look on her face.

The wine tasted okay to me. "What's wrong?"

Jake shook his head.

One middle-aged manager jangled up to us. The heavy ring of keys on his belt had pulled his pants unglamorously south of the Mason-Dixon line. "Is there a problem?"

"Where's the air conditioner?" Jake demanded.

"It's broke."

"Show me."

What was this guy, a cool air addict or some kind of fluorocarbon fiend?

The manager hiked up his pants. "What the hell? Think you can fix it?"

Jake stood up. "Get the flashlight and show me where it's at."

The air conditioning unit extended from the outside wall just below the Shaker-style roof. Jake aimed a flashlight up at it. "Got a ladder?"

"I got a ladder if you're saying you know how to fix the air. Otherwise, who the hell you think you are?" The manager locked his hands onto his hips.

"Caroline, come over here."

Curious, I moved closer.

Jake squatted down. "Get on my shoulders."

"What?"

"Come on, just get on."

"I usually wait until the second date for that," I said.

He jerked his head toward his back. "Get on."

I swung a leg over each of his shoulders, and hung on to his head. He stood up and handed me the flashlight. "Tell me what you see up there."

"You're getting a bald spot," I said.

"Stop kidding around."

I directed the light beam to the top of the air conditioning unit and under the overhang of the roof. "It's pretty dark. I see a lot of straw and grass in the vent, and, oh, wait a minute, one, two . . . four eggs, and, uh-oh, one beady eye looking at me. It does look like a hawk."

"Are any of the eggs hatched?"

I eased the flashlight into the gap between the roof and the unit. My head followed. I leaned forward to peer over the edge of the nest. "They look intact."

The mother-to-be clearly objected to my presence. She snapped at my nose. A talon struck out at me. She fluttered and flapped her wings. Feathers flew up my nose.

All that flapping around my face made me start rapidly flapping my own limbs. "Get me down, get me down."

Jake lowered me quicker than I had anticipated. I think I might have kicked him in the ribs. My tailbone hit the ground first. It took me a moment to recover. I missed a chunk of conversation.

"What the hell?" the manager whined. "Who are you to tell me what to do?"

"I'm telling you, if you disturb that nest you're subject

to a $2,000 fine and a year in prison." Jake handed the manager the flashlight.

"What the hell . . . It's a crummy bird. We got a million birds around here." The manager waved the flashlight in the air, sending arcs of light through the night sky like a Hollywood premiere.

"It's probably a Cooper's hawk, a migratory bird protected by law, and if you move its nest, you'll be prosecuted by the federal government."

"Are you tellin' me—"

"I'm telling you the law."

The manager hiked up his pants again. The keys jangled. "Know how much business I'll lose with no air conditioning in August?"

"Until those eggs hatch, get yourself a big fan." Jake pulled me to my feet and steered me back to our table.

"What the hell—" The manager and his keys jingled off into obscurity behind us.

I was still a little dazed from the shock to my tailbone. When we got back to our table, our pizza was waiting. Fortunately there was no way it could have gotten cold.

"You were saying?" Jake said, as though the whole incident hadn't happened.

"Who are you? You know a lot about Tony and a lot about me, not to mention a lot about hawks. Just how do you know so much?"

"I happen to know the law. Is that a crime? Eat your pizza." Jake picked up a slice.

"I want to know why and how you think Tony was murdered. And why, if you're convinced he was, you've told me and not the police."

"I don't have enough to interest the cops yet, but our discussion at the coffee shop the other morning started me thinking. I'm thinking there's some message in that mural."

The pinball machine went ballistic.

"I'll get the drawings from the studio," I said, opening the front door. On the way home I'd told Jake about them. Maybe another set of eyes could find something in them I hadn't. "I don't have air conditioning, either. Just ceiling fans. You better take off your coat."

Jake started to remove his sport coat, then shrugged it back on. But not quickly enough. He knew I had seen the shoulder holster.

"You told me you were a writer. Writers don't carry guns."

"Bad writers might," he said.

"If you aren't going to be straight with me, I think you better leave."

"You're not being very friendly for a woman who had her legs wrapped around my neck a half hour ago." When I didn't smile, he looked at his watch. "Look, I can't explain it right now, but I will. I promise. If you're throwing me out, I'll just get on back to the zoo."

"The zoo? At this hour?"

"Some very interesting things happen there after dark. If you weren't such a screamer, I'd invite you along."

I opened the door for him in stone-faced silence.

On his way down the steps he looked up at the steeple. "Hey, you're not a nun, are you?"

16

I DRAGGED MYSELF OUT OF BED SUNDAY, DRESSED, THEN descended the stairs to the kitchen, the former vestry, where I made coffee. While two pairs of tennis shoes churned in the washer, I worked out with my personal trainer.

I'd bought the black Everlast punching bag more for relieving frustration than for physical fitness. Lately I'd been using it to work on my coordination. At first the bag had gotten in more punches than I had. But with practice I'd learned to avoid the rebound. The biceps I had developed were a bonus. Currently, I was concentrating on my footwork.

I went a few rounds with "Evvie" in the mudroom, where she hung by a chain from a beam, but it was clear I wasn't a contender today. When the tennies completed the spin cycle, I set them out to dry and left the house. Another stifling day lay ahead. I unlocked the studio and went inside. Humidity had warped illustration boards into wavy shapes. It had also loosened the tape I'd used to secure the drawings to the floorboards.

I turned on the air conditioner. The wall unit moaned in protest before blowing hot air in my face. The burst of air rearranged the drawings on the floor, sending several flying. Slipping the soundtrack from *Doctor Zhivago* into the CD player, I closed my eyes and envisioned the movie's ice castle scene. In a few moments I felt a little better.

A blank canvas rested on my easel. I hadn't painted since the day before Tony's funeral. If I took the mural commission, it would be months before I'd have time to pursue my own work again. An exhibit of my wildlife paintings currently hung at a gallery in Long Grove. The month was almost up, and I hadn't been informed of any sales.

Returning my attention to the scattered pile of drawings, I studied the panels above and below the missing one. An Indian cobra encircled the trunk of the banyan tree in panel B-9. Was this another clue or just part of the exotic landscape? In panel D-9, just below the missing one, a second tiger stalked the sambar in the tall grass by the lake. That panel now lay upside down, thanks to the air conditioner. I noticed something I hadn't when it was right side up. The contour of the shadow of the banyan tree, in which the tiger stood, appeared to be a skewed perspective of Texas. The tiger stood just below the panhandle. I remembered the two Texans at Tony's funeral that Miles had been talking to, business associates of Vince.

My speculations were interrupted by the phone.

"Miles Crandall here. You're on a conference call. Due to the recent turn of events, we've called an emergency board meeting today to discuss our options regarding the completion of the mural for Tiger Forest. With Gino Tedesco now, uh, indisposed, it seems our choices in muralists are rapidly diminishing and—"

"Caroline, this is Claudia Baxter." The icy voice cut to the chase. "Will you finish the mural or not?"

"Miles gave me until tomorrow to decide." I knew the answer. Why couldn't I say it?

"She claimed she needed time to find Mr. Chirico's drawings," Miles said, in an uncharacteristic whine. I had a new respect for Claudia if she could get Miles on the ropes that easily.

"We can't give you any more time," Claudia said. "Have you found the drawings?"

"She found 'em all right. I was there." Vince? What

was he doing at the board meeting? Not that he didn't have a big stake in the zoo's future.

"We must have your answer now," Claudia said.

"Caroline? This is Barb. We do have other options. In fact, I have another muralist holding on the other line." Barb was still trying to give me an out.

"That's right," Miles said, "and I'm prepared to give him the business."

"I want to talk to my attorney first," I said. Did my inheritance depend on my going back to mural painting forever or just this one mural? Of course, if I didn't survive this mural, the rest didn't matter.

"What does she need with an attorney?" Miles boomed.

"If you won't give us an answer now," Claudia said, "we'll take it as a no."

I raised my eyes heavenward. *God, I hope you've given Tony his wings, because I'm going to need a guardian angel fast.*

"Well? A simple yes or no."

My throat constricted. "A simple yes," I said. "I'll do it."

In the same instant my fax machine rang and began spitting out a sheet of paper. I knew God worked fast, but I didn't know he had a fax machine.

17

I SIGNED THE CONTRACT AND FAXED IT BACK IMMEDI-
ately, as Claudia had ordered.

I leaned back in my chair. My arms hung limply at
my side. I wanted to wrap them around something. I
had just been awarded a hefty commission. A three million dollar inheritance would also come my way as a
result. So why wasn't I thrilled? Maybe because I was
also about to inherit a murderer? I wrapped my arms
around myself.

I checked my watch. Mom and I always talked on
Sundays at noon. It was already half past. I longed to
hear her voice—not for what it said, just for the sound
of it. Returning to the house, I dialed her number and
waited. I'd have to be careful about what I said. I didn't
want to worry her.

"How are things in Heather Valley, Mom?"

"Idyllic, if your idea of romance is being strapped in
a straitjacket at the mercy of a psychiatrist. He can't
decide if he wants to give me shock treatments or make
love to me."

Five years ago, my mother, Vera Anders, had lucked
into a bit part in a daytime soap, which was either *To
Live Is To Love* or *To Love Is To Live*, I could never
remember which. Lucky for me, the title was usually
shortened to TLTL. Her short-term role had been de-
scribed as a middle-aged sexy psychotic. When the writers tried to kill her off, soap fans initiated a letter-writing

campaign that resulted in her becoming a contract member of the cast. She'd been in California ever since.

I'd missed most of what Mom had just said, something about the re-release of her one hit jazz record, "What a Difference a Day Makes." It was also her philosophy of life.

"I went to Tony's funeral," I blurted out.

"You'll get through it. Give it time. When your father died, I thought my life was over, but then I looked at you and Christine, and I knew I had to be strong." As she spoke, I found strength in her calm, mellow voice.

She had managed to pay off debts my father had kept hidden, put both her daughters through college, pay the rent on a Lake Shore Drive apartment, and never let us feel the pinch—all on a lounge singer's salary. The only problem was, she had rarely been around.

"Keep busy," she said. "That'll help. What are you working on?"

"Nothing much, you know . . . another mural." Why had I said it?

"A mural? Why in the world would you go back to that?"

"You went back to lounge singing after Dad died."

"That's different. It's all I knew. I didn't go to college." When times were good, she had sung and played piano at local lounges. In bad times, she had gone on the road.

I began to draw concentric circles on a scratchpad. "They made me an offer I couldn't refuse." The circles grew bigger.

"Don't get in the habit of doing things you hate just for the money."

The circles turned into jagged lines. "It's a lot of money, Mom. I mean a lot of money." With the portable phone, I began to pace the room.

"There are more important things than money. Your problem is you're lonely. You need to get out and make some new friends."

Here came the advice. I opened the front door and rang the bell urgently. "Gotta go, Mom, the gang's here."

"There's something you're not telling me, Carrie. I can hear it in your voice."

"There's nothing, Mom, really." I rang the bell again. "Hold on, guys. I'll be right there."

"This is your mother you're talking to."

I punched on the CD player. "I guess I just miss Buttons." Mistake.

"Oh, Carrie. That dog was old." She sighed. "Why do you do this to yourself? When your father died, you moped in that big old tree all summer."

"I wasn't moping." I had clung to the tree thinking if I didn't let go, my life wouldn't change. One day Mom came out to the tree and told me I had to give up not only the old oak, but the house we'd lived in as well.

"You have to learn that life is change. You can't be so inflexible."

"I'm tired of being told my faults! I'm too naive, I'm too loyal, I'm too trusting, I'm too untrusting, now I'm too inflexible."

"Listen to the music you're playing. Jerome Kern. My God, Carrie, he was even before my time." The Smashing Pumpkins were playing on her stereo.

" 'All the Things You Are' is possibly the greatest song ever written. You sang it."

"That was a lifetime ago, honey. And it was an old song even then. Why are you always looking backward when you should be looking ahead?" She hesitated, but I knew it was coming. "Are you seeing anyone new? You're not still brooding about David . . ."

Traditionally I avoided one topic with my mother, best summed up in two words: sex life. At fifty-six my mother had one, and I didn't.

"I gotta go, Mom." The comfort her voice had brought me had been snatched away.

"Take care of yourself, hon. And call Christine once in a while. She says you never go out there to see the baby. I love you, honey."

119

In spite of it all, I had never doubted that she did. I heard a door open and close on the other end of the line.

"I've gotta dash, too, hon. Roberto's here."

"Roberto?" Why did I ask?

"We're going windsurfing."

Mom never played favorites with my sister and me, I'll say that for her, but Christine was like my mother. I wasn't. I wasn't like my father either. I was like my Gram.

I pulled into the driveway of Gram's bungalow in Elmhurst. Her golden retriever, Brandy, bounded up to the car. The barking outside the house set off a chorus of yapping inside. Gram was in the backyard, on a ladder, hanging another bird feeder in the tree.

I hurried forward to steady the ladder. "Careful, Gram. You could fall."

"Oh, horsefeathers." She descended the ladder and hugged me.

I didn't let go right away.

"Something tells me you talked to your mother today," she said. "Come on inside. Let's have a drink."

When we moved to an apartment on Lake Shore Drive, Gram moved in across the street. Our building didn't allow animals, hers did. Gram baby-sat us at night, and when Mom toured, we lived with Gram. My best memories were of New Year's eves. Mom always had a gig. Munching on popcorn, we'd watch wrestling on TV—the women were our favorites. After Gram and Christine dozed off, I'd watch old movies and pretend I was Ginger Rogers. I'd dance around the living room until I broke a lamp or fell over a table. Finally, I'd fall asleep with Gram, Christine, and assorted pets in a pile on the sofa bed.

Gram's voice brought me back to the present. "Whiskers, get down from there." She removed a Siamese cat from the kitchen countertop and wagged a finger. "Or you just might lose your good home."

"Good home. Good home," a parrot mimicked from a perch in the corner.

I smiled and slid into the breakfast nook. At its end an aquarium glowed. "What's the population up to now, Gram?"

"Who can keep track?" Gram's backside was all I could see of her as she bent into the old Crosley refrigerator. "Wine okay?"

Like Mom, Gram had always had a steady man in her life, too. But his name was Johnny Walker, and he lived in a square bottle. Recently she had switched to wine.

"Wine's fine," I said. "How are you feeling?"

She tap-danced as she poured the wine. "And you can tell your mother I said that."

"What's she been bugging you about?"

"She wants me to move out there, says I shouldn't live alone anymore. How old do I have to be before she'll let me make my own decisions?" She began to sing.

Oh, Maresy Dotes and Doesy Dotes
  and Little Lamsey Divey
A Kiddely Divey too, wouldn't you?

Although Mom was the professional, it was Gram's singing voice I treasured. Christine and I always sang an octave lower than the other kids in the Christmas program, because that was the register in which we'd practiced with Gram. It was Grandma who wrote an angry letter back to my third-grade teacher, who urged counseling because I included a squirrel in every picture I drew. It was Grandma who first explained the birds and the bees to me. Men's parts and women's parts, she said, were like an electric plug and socket. And it was Grandma's fault that for a long time I was sure I'd be electrocuted the first time I had sex.

Gram gave me another hug. "What's wrong?"

I didn't want to worry her, so I gave her the barebones version. Why was it so easy to talk to her? Maybe because she listened without judging or giving advice. Maybe because she accepted me the way I was. But mostly because she made me laugh.

"I remember that Vince boy," she said. "He came over here one day with you, didn't he? You were on the back of his motorcycle. Remember how afraid he was of all the animals? Course, they did growl and hiss at him. Animals sense when someone doesn't like them."

"I'd forgotten about that."

"I think he was sweet on you."

"Well, he's not sweet on me anymore, Gram. In fact, Barb's probably the only old friend I have left."

"Barb." She ran the name through her memory bank. "Isn't she the one who took in those Manx kittens? The ones you brought home from college and your mama wouldn't let you keep?"

"Mom just never understood. You're the one who taught me to love animals."

"Horsefeathers. That's not something I taught you. That's just who you are." She kissed the top of my head. "I know what you need. A pet."

"I don't want any more pets, Gram. Sooner or later they die. Like Buttons." I felt the tears well up, the way they always did when I remembered her sweet face.

"That's the cycle of life, honey. I'm gonna leave you someday, too, but wouldn't it be worse if we never had each other? Or these times together?"

I tried to imagine Gram gone, but I couldn't. Maybe because I just didn't want to. "Promise me you won't die before I do," I said.

The breakfast bench creaked as she sat down next to me and put her arm around me. "That's not the natural course of things, honey. Think how many animals I've seen come and go in this house. I cry for every one of them when they leave me. But they just don't live as long as us, and I can't live as long as you. You've got a lot of love to give. Don't let someone's leaving make you afraid to get close to them, honey."

I put my arms around her and kissed her cheek. "I better go, Gram. I start my new job tomorrow."

She made me promise to be careful and then asked

me to fill a few bird feeders before I left. I had the feeling she was up to something, but I couldn't guess what.

It wasn't until I was halfway home that I noticed the box on the back seat of the car. The blanket inside it stirred. A silver Persian kitten poked its head out.

18

ALL ELSE PASSES . . . ART ALONE ENDURES.

The carved words in the marbled lobby of Tony's studio scrolled through my mind. Semiconscious, I bunched the pillow and twisted in the clammy sheets, wanting to turn over, but knowing it took too much effort.

A musty odor filled my stifling bedroom. It brought images of long ago: my Girl Scout troop roasting s'mores over a late-night campfire; my little sister Christine and I dancing around smoldering piles of leaves in the autumn chill, years before we were aware of the environmental dangers. Innocent times. With a sleepy smile, I rolled over onto my back.

All else passes . . . art alone endures.

The odor drew me closer to consciousness. The movie in my head changed to a Wisconsin cabin in late October and the woodsy smell of David's hair as we lay in front of the fireplace, when we were still happy and together.

My leg searched the sheets for someone, something. But the search ended emptily. *All else passes . . . art alone endures.*

My nostrils flared. The odor demanded my attention. The pleasant images didn't fit. I wrinkled my nose.

Smoke!

My eyes snapped open like window shades. Two more seconds and my feet hit the floor running. I flew down the stairs and ran toward the back of the house where the smoke drew me like a moth to the . . .

Flames!

From the huge back window in the chancel, I watched the hot yellow tongues, hungry for air, lick out from my studio's louvered side window, the one I always left open for ventilation. The walls of the chancel glowed cadmium orange, reflecting the light emanating from the one-room schoolhouse studio.

My brain commanded my legs to move, but my eyes refused to leave the scene. I pictured myself running to the kitchen and picking up the phone. In the next moment, systems kicked in, and I was doing just that.

I tore the receiver off its perch and punched in 9-1-1. I was almost ready to hang up and redial when the phone clicked.

"Emergency," a cool-headed voice intoned.

"I'm on fire!"

"What is your location?"

"It's my school . . . behind my church."

"Is it a school or a church?" the voice asked calmly.

"It's a church that was a house, no a house that— 1331 Willow. I have a steeple."

"Is that Willow Lane along the river, or Willow Street near city Hall?"

"Lane by the river!"

"Are you or anyone else in immediate danger?"

"No, just me and . . ." My mouth stopped working. I dropped the phone. The cat, where was the cat?

I vaguely remembered she had disappeared as soon as I'd set her down in the house. Had she followed me out to the studio earlier? My first impression had been that she didn't want to get any closer to me than I wanted to get to her. I called out frantically, knowing she probably wouldn't respond. I stumbled through the central part of the house and back up the stairs to the bedroom. "Kitty, where are you? Here, kitty."

I searched the closet, under the bed, on top of the VCR. But no kitty.

Down the stairs again, hysterical now, lights on everywhere. Oh, God! The studio! I ran back to the kitchen. Hopping on one foot as I fumbled to put shoes on, I reached for the studio key on a hook next to and above the refrigerator. Hot breath hissed across the top of my hand. A tiny white paw swiped out at me.

The kitten sat regally on top of the refrigerator. She watched my nervous breakdown with utter detachment, gazing condescendingly down at the maniac she was being asked to tolerate.

I reached up for her. The feline Queen of Mean trilled once, backed into the corner and hissed at me again. My prayer for her safety had been answered. I wouldn't ask the impossible—a sweeter disposition.

A blast of sirens filled the air, and a red light circled the four walls of the kitchen. Bursting out the back door, still in my knee-length night shirt, I collided with the fire department's lead hoseman. Another fireman helped me recover my balance. Taking me by the arm, he led me like a child toward the front of the house.

"It's best if you just keep back. You can help most by telling me what you have stored back there."

"Unly eye leich." My upper lip was stuck to my teeth.

"Say again?"

I used my tongue to separate lips from teeth. "Only my life."

He frowned. "Any flammable materials?"

"I'd say the whole thing is flammable. Wouldn't you? Or else what are we doing here in the middle of the night?"

"I meant anything explosive or chemically dangerous."

"Plenty. I'm an artist," I answered. "Paints, solvents,

thinners, take your choice." Why was he just standing there? Would he ever move?

"How 'bout compressed-air tanks? Anything that might blow?"

"Oh, no, I don't do airbrush art," I said as though he were interviewing me for a job.

The breeze shifted and the first waves of dense smoke slammed into my face. My eyes began to tear, and I coughed. The fireman pulled me backward, but my eyes stayed riveted on the fire. He relayed the information to one of his men.

An ax slashed through the studio's door. I cringed. Water from the fire hose crashed through the large fan-shaped window facing me. A fraction of a second later I heard the window opposite, facing the river, shatter into a million pieces. I couldn't bear to watch, yet I couldn't look away.

"Well, we'll get 'er now," the fire chief assured me. "With the wind shift, the flames could easily have spread to the church here. Lucky you caught 'er when you did."

"Yeah, lucky, that's me."

"Stay back now." Unbuckled galoshes slurping across the driveway, the chief headed toward his men.

I stood alone. *All else passes . . . art alone endures.* Right. Much of my artwork would not only not endure, but was passing before my very eyes. Including the drawings on the floor that I'd worked so hard to find. And there wasn't a thing I could do about it.

A creaking sound and shouts to stand back kept me transfixed. Slowly, almost reluctantly, the roof of the old schoolhouse shifted slightly to the left. It hesitated, then changed its mind and sashayed right. Like watching a horror movie, I squeezed my eyes shut and waited. And again, like watching a horror movie, I opened my eyes a moment too soon.

Just in time to see the roof cave in on my entire career.

19

ARTISTS DREAM OF SETTING THE ART WORLD ON FIRE. IN my case, only my studio had been ablaze.

By dawn little remained of the studio, except smoldering ruins. The roof had taken the north wall with it when it collapsed. The pile of wooden debris lay like a huge shingled beaver's dam next to the river. The other three walls around the studio survived, forming an open-air barbecue pit. My car stood on the gravel driveway wearing a wet, sooty coating.

I walked around to the open side of the old schoolhouse. Overnight my large oak drawing board had been transformed into a lifetime supply of stick charcoal. On top, the remnants of the safari park photos took wing in the breeze. My rep would have to pass the news on to the ad agency. A big chunk of the money I was about to inherit could easily go to paying off clients' claims for lost property if my insurance didn't cover it.

The vellum drawings taped to the floor were history. Just ashes remained. Gone to the big art gallery in the sky. Had someone wanted to destroy them so badly they burnt down my whole studio? If Tony had been killed over the mural, surely setting a fire was small potatoes. Who knew I had found the drawings? Who didn't? Vince had announced it to practically everyone during yesterday's conference call.

The fire marshall arrived early on the scene. I watched him search through the rubble surrounding my drawing board as he snapped pictures and made notes. He studied the louvered window next to the side door, extracted something with tweezers from between the glass panes and placed it into a baggie. Did he suspect arson? I wondered if I should mention that I did. Would it affect my insurance claim? Insurance was something I bought and promptly forgot about. Why hadn't I checked my policy? He bent to study the burn pattern on the south wall near the louvered window. His finger traced the path of the burn.

Before he left I asked him if he could determine the cause of the fire. He was a man of few words. "You'll get a copy of my report" was all he would say. He warned me to be careful if I chose to explore the wreckage.

As soon as he left, the claims adjuster showed up. I hadn't expected such prompt service from my insurance company. I approached the drenched ruins with the short, tired-looking, middle-aged man dressed entirely in black. A heavy stale odor rose from his clothes. Maybe he got a professional discount on his apparel at fire sales. He shook his head a lot and kept his shoulder at all times between me and his metal clipboard. When I asked how soon I could expect to be compensated, he pretended he didn't understand.

He made a whirling motion with his hand over a soggy pile of burned cloth near my charred drawing board. "Vaht deez pile uff rag iz?"

"Paint rags—to clean my brushes, wipe up spills, that kind of thing."

"Do you zmoke?"

"No way. It's a filthy habit." I noticed the nicotine stains on his fingers. "Not that I don't have my share of filthy habits," I added quickly.

He lifted one of the rags with his fingertips and sniffed it. Was that really his job?

"Aren't you here to assess the extent of the damage so I can be compensated fully?"

"I am here to make sure my employer does not pay out on a falzified claim."

"Right. Are you thinking spontaneous combustion?"

"Spontooneous comboostchun?" He dropped the paint rag like a dirty sock. "I dink naught."

"Well, it was awfully hot last night and I've read that linseed oil can—"

He glared at me. "Are you trying to influence my chudgment?"

"No, I just . . ."

He floated around the debris, making notes and glancing at me frequently as though sizing me up. I peered over his shoulder, but his scribblings were as abstract as a Franz Kline painting. Too bad I had let my Transylvanian language skills slide.

"You make lizt uff vaht's deeztroy-ed," he said. "Then we pro-zezz your claim."

"I have receipts," I assured him.

"Goot." He ruffled through the papers on his metal clipboard, like a doctor with medical records. "You hoff re-plaze-ment value?"

"I believe zo," I answered. His accent was catching.

He nodded. "I check." Did that mean he'd check or that he was Czech?

He snapped his clipboard shut. *Caze clozed.*

20

By noon I had put food out for the cat—wherever she was hiding—had wiped the soot from the Camaro's windshield and was heading for the zoo. I'd made the commitment to the project, if not the cat. I knew Gram meant well, but I'd have to find it another home. I decided not to mention the fire to anyone. Maybe someone would slip and mention it to me first.

The first thing I did was head for Tiger Forest. With the tissue drawings now destroyed, I wanted to see if I could detect any differences in the mural, while the drawings were still fresh in my head. I scanned the wall. My eyes kept coming back to the smeared section. The area above showed the banyan tree's trunk with the snake wrapped around it, just as in the drawings. I found nothing new.

The time had come to acclimate myself to the scaffolds. I inspected the wheels of the metal tower, making sure they were fully locked. With Tony's paint-spattered wooden ladders connecting the open mesh platforms, I took a deep breath and started the climb.

I reached the first level with little anxiety, so I continued the ascent. On each level I stopped to inspect the hardware connections, even though Miles had assured me a complete inspection of the tower had followed Tony's accident. By the time I reached the fourth level, I was feeling much less secure. Standing as high as the suspended public walkway from the floor, but twenty feet away from it, and with no railing, my legs trembled.

I began a slower climb to the highest two levels. Three years had passed since my near-fatal fall—the last time I'd made this climb. Death had been the cruel reward for the two mural painters who had preceded me up these ladders. The ease with which I knew I could fall at any moment made me extremely cautious. Several times I stopped to grasp the handrails to steady myself. Stay focused on the wall and don't look down.

Naturally I looked down. Below me the skeletal forms of banyan trees rose from the floor. My eyes followed past the largest tree's elongated aerial root system, up its trunk and limbs, now covered with gunite, to the spindly fingered branches reaching for the glass-paneled ceiling.

Gripping a crossbar of the metal structure for security, I returned my attention to the mural. Painted cumulus clouds interrupted by an occasional soaring bird spanned the wall above me. Gino's work. Grateful at least that the highest part of the wall was complete, I leaned back on the fifth platform to get a better look at the painted tiger, or liger, whichever it was. If I wanted a nose-to-nose view of it, I'd have to climb up one more level.

I gripped the ladder and started up. When I reached the sixth platform, I let go of the ladder and edged my way across the landing, getting the feel and spring of the open mesh platform beneath my feet.

"About time you showed up." The deep voice boomed and bounced off the concrete.

I lurched forward. The tower of pipes shuddered. "Jeez!" I dropped to my knees and clutched the platform beneath me. On all fours, I took a deep breath before turning my anger on Miles standing on the walkway. "While I'm at work here, I expect—I demand—complete privacy," I shouted.

"Privacy?" He cocked an eyebrow. "Something to hide, Canfield?"

While considering how best to discourage future drop-in visits, I slowly pulled myself upright. "Interruptions will only delay me. Do I make myself clear?"

Sweat stained the underarms of his safari suit. My underarms were none too dry, either. I made a mental note to order a safety harness.

Miles crossed his beefy arms. "Just remember, the meter's running. Our opening is only two months away. Make sure the mural's finished by then, or you'll face a lawsuit for breach of contract. Do I make *my*self clear?" He pivoted on his heel.

Ellen Riggs stood in the rear holding area with another keeper. She was discussing the plans for moving Kiara to her new quarters in Asia World. I waved hello and opened the door to Tony's supply closet. Ellen finished her conversation, then walked over.

"Still looking for Tony's drawings?" she asked. "I thought you searched there."

So she didn't know I'd found them, or was pretending not to. No, Ellen didn't seem the type. But had I met a murderer before? "I came back to check supplies, order what I need." I flipped a switch and light flooded the walk-in closet. The shelves of a utility rack were piled high with small jars of powdered pigments and larger jars of mixed paint. On the floor, along with brushes, rags, and various tools, sat a large drum of acrylic medium. "Acrylics? That's odd," I said. "We usually worked in oils for interior murals."

Ellen shrugged. "Tony said that acrylics would be better, since the walls would be subjected to a lot of water and humidity."

"That's true," I said. "With the monsoon and the waterfall, the conditions are more like that of an exterior wall. Acrylics are a better choice."

Ellen's beeper went off.

"Go ahead. I'll just have a look around," I said.

Inside the closet, I sifted through the baby-food-size jars of ground raw pigments. Once ground, they are suspended, or mixed with some medium, like linseed oil, egg tempera or, in this case, acrylic. Unlike Tony, I had no problem using manufacturers' paints. Referring both to the pigments in the closet and the color notes in the black sketchbook I'd found in his trunk, I started a list of the colors and the quantities I'd need.

Determined to be faithful to Tony's palette down to his favorite white, I added flake white to the list. Then I scratched it out. Surely Tony wouldn't have used flake white, which contains lead, in a zoo mural. If the paint chipped off, an animal might ingest it. I went back to the closet and shuffled jars around until I found the white powdered pigment. The handwritten label on the larger size jar read "titanium white." Of course. Titanium was the only possible choice of white in acrylic paint. Lead was incompatible with the medium, so flake white wasn't an option in acrylics. But if there was no acrylic flake white, then why had lead been found in the white acrylic paint on Tony's lips?

I studied the jar. It was larger than the others, but that was only natural. An artist uses white more than any other pigment. The handwritten label on the jar of white pigment didn't match the others. It wasn't Tony's writing. Could it be Gino's? I picked at the corner of the label and discovered another label underneath. Carefully I peeled it back, but I ripped part of it.

In one of the holding cages, I heard Ellen instructing a workman where to install the elevated wood planks that the big cats would sleep on in each of the cages. Their voices echoed around me.

"Ellen," I called out, "you mentioned you have a degree in chemistry. What's lead, uh . . . ?" I tried to make out the part of the underlying label I'd ripped, but with no success. "What lead compound is used in paint?"

"Lead carbonate?" she said, walking toward me. "Lead chromate?"

I shook my head. "Looks like it starts with an 'a.' "

Her eyes grew round and big when she saw the jar in my hands. "Lead arsenate?" Her grip visibly tightened on the clipboard she held.

I looked back at the label. "Could be."

Slamming the clipboard to the floor, she stormed toward me and ripped the bottle from my hand. The gentle, doe-eyed woman had been transformed into a snarling beast. "Damn him! Didn't he realize there are better ways to get rid of rats?"

I wasn't sure if she was referring to the ones with tails or without.

The intensity of Ellen's anger had shocked me. When I caught up with her outside Asia World, she gently pushed a few stray hairs back into her French braid.

"Sorry I lost it in there. Maybe I can explain," she said, collapsing onto a park bench. "You see, before the new building was secured, we had a rat problem. Vince said it was common at construction sites." She gripped the jar tightly in her fist. "Around the same time our liger died. Rob said it was poisoned, that he found lead in its system."

"And you blame Tony?"

"I knew lead had been banned in house paint, but I knew it was still used in artists' materials. I assumed it was Tony's paint that killed the liger. He denied it when I confronted him. But now I see what really happened. He spread this rat poison."

"Rat poison?" I shook my head. "Tony wouldn't have been foolish enough to sprinkle poison so close to animals." I didn't tell her it had been labeled titanium white.

"Close or not, it doesn't make any difference. A rodent can nibble at the poison, but it doesn't die in its tracks. No, it runs off into other areas of the zoo. If that rat or even a mouse, let's say, enters another cage containing an animal who catches it and eats it, that animal ingests all the poison in the rodent's system."

"Anyone could have put that in the closet," I said.

"Why would anyone do that? This damn lead arsenate has been right there all along. That's what killed our liger."

"Lead poisoning?" I asked.

"Not lead," she said impatiently. "Arsenic."

"A" as in "arsenate." I had been slow to make the connection. "D" was the highest grade I'd ever gotten in science. "D" as in "dead."

Gino said Tony had complained about the gritty texture of his paint just before he fell. The grit must have been caused by lead arsenate mixed in with his paint. But Gino couldn't have been the murderer, or he wouldn't have disclosed that fact. Anyone could easily have mixed this powder with the white ground pigment.

Tony's murderer had to know his painting habits, to know that he'd ingest it when he pointed his brush by running it between his lips whenever he was about to paint fine lines. Fine lines, like the tiger's whiskers.

Ellen stood up. "I have to get rid of this before it does any more damage," she said.

"I need to hang on to that."

"No way! It's poison!"

"Exactly." I tried to take it from her hand. "It's evidence."

"Evidence! What are you talking about? This has to be disposed of properly once and for all. I won't risk more animals' lives." Ellen hurried away down the path.

I ran after her. "Ellen, you don't understand. I need that. It could have something to do with Tony's death."

When she didn't respond I tried to grab the jar out of her hand again. It bobbled between our grasps for a moment, before she grabbed it tightly and shoved me away. I lost my balance and fell down.

"Are you crazy?" she said. "What if this had broken? The birds, the squirrels could . . ."

I sat on the ground stunned, watching her recede down the path. The sweetness of the birds' songs in the trees seemed to refute the evil I felt growing all around me.

21

DAYLIGHT FADED IN THE GLOOMY RECESSES OF THE ZOO library, located in the rear of the administration building. The room looked more like an overstocked storage closet than a library. I flicked on the green-shaded desk lamp and sat down at a lone, battered walnut table.

I pulled a stack of large veterinary textbooks in front of me. On the cover was the symbol for a veterinarian, similar to the caduceus for a physician—two snakes wrapped around a wooden stick—except for the initial "V" carved into the stick. I recalled the snake wrapped around the banyan tree in the mural and how two of the aerial roots were crossed in such a way as to create the letter "v." Was Tony implicating Rob Bennett, the veterinarian?

I had to scan the indexes of several volumes before I found an entry for lead arsenate. All the medical book said was that it was sometimes used to treat tapeworm in animals. I pored over several more tomes, searching for a reference for lead poisoning. One book indicated the symptoms would be cerebral edema, nerve and muscle cell damage. I wasn't sure what all that meant, but it sounded like it could account for a fall, at the very least.

As to arsenic, the index had multiple listings. I looked up the first reference. Though I knew lead could be found in paint, the fact that arsenic could also be present surprised me. I read on, scanning the text for symptoms of chronic arsenic poisoning. The side effects included jaundice and exfoliative dermatitis.

I remembered the two Toulouse-Lautrec women at Tony's funeral. They had brought his yellowish skin color to my attention. The woman with the beehive had additionally mentioned his dry skin.

What other symptoms could I recall? Gino had mentioned Tony's red, puffy eyes the day of the accident. Ben Rudolph had confirmed that, attributing Tony's fall to it. What was the condition called?

Scouring countless pages of text, I created a mountain of books on the table before I found the one I needed. I bent over the page. "In cases of chronic poisoning, arsenic may cause conjunctivitis, an inflammation of the membrane surrounding the eye."

The sentence was underlined in dark black ink. By the murderer? I knew the how of Tony's murder, but I still didn't know the who or the why.

I flicked off the desk lamp. Darkness surrounded me. I hadn't realized how long I had been sitting in the library. Jake Statler had told me things happened at night at the zoo. Now was as good a time as any to take a quick, unobserved look around.

A crescent moon greeted me as I exited the main doors of the administration building, empty except for a janitor sweeping up. Before leaving, I had tried several office doors, but they were locked.

Moonlight glistened off the zoo's wet sidewalks. It must have rained while I was inside. I breathed deeply, taking in the cooler, but still humid, August night air. The invigorating scent of fir trees filled my lungs. As I crossed through the darkness of the zoo grounds, the glow of light from a window in the veterinary building drew me.

Pushing through the shrubbery, I settled in the bushes and peeked over the windowsill. A female veterinary assistant read a computer printout, while her male associate prepared some injections. Their conversation drifted through the screened window.

"The initial results from this blood sample don't look good," the woman said.

"Yeah, well, I don't want to be the one to tell Ice Queen Barbie." The man drew a clear liquid from a vial into a syringe. "If the results are that bad, it's blue juice time for Kiara."

"It's the only humane thing to do," the woman replied.

"At least we can help this little girl," the man said, holding the syringe up to the light.

The tips of my feet sunk into the loamy, cultivated soil of the evergreen bed, as I stood on tiptoe to watch. A snow monkey, out cold, lay strapped to a table. The man injected the fluid into the animal. The woman came over and hooked the monkey up to an intravenous solution hanging from a pole attached to the table.

"Poor Ellen," she said. "That white tiger is special to her. I think she'd kill to save it. Remember when the liger died? She really freaked."

"Ellen should get a life," the man said.

The woman laughed. "So ask her out. I see you always looking at her."

Wearing a chartreuse and orange shirt, Rob Bennett hustled into the room. "If you two spent as much time on procedure as you do on your love lives, we wouldn't have any problems. Are we set?"

"I just gave her the anesthetic. It'll be a few minutes before she's ready," the man said.

"Get that crash cart over here," Rob said impatiently. "How many times do I have to remind you? What happens if she should suddenly go into cardiac arrest? We could lose her while you're taking your sweet time wheeling it over. What do they teach you people?"

Mosquitoes were eating me alive in the wet shrubbery. I struggled to scratch the latest welts rising on my arms and legs. Rob Bennett glanced at the open window. I ducked down.

"And close that goddamn window. Finish prepping her while I scrub up," he said.

"Do you want me to assist?" the man asked.

"I'll need you both," Rob answered. "Let's see, that's four extra hands and a half a brain between you."

"I just thought—"

"You don't have to think. That's why we color-code lethal injections for you morons."

So that's what blue juice was. A lethal injection. I stayed hunkered down in the bushes until I was sure Rob had left the room.

"He must have really lost his shirt at the track today," said the man. "I can always tell."

"He'd be lucky to lose some of those shirts he wears," the woman said.

The man approached the window. I moved to the right of it, my face pressed to the bricks. The window slammed shut. I heard a rustling in the bushes behind me.

A voice filtered through the needly branches. "I've heard of peeping Toms, but never a peeping Caroline."

I swung around. Light spilled out the window, illuminating Rob Bennett's smile. I recognized an unfriendly grin when I saw one.

The fluorescent colors of his shirt practically glowed in the dark.

"What are you up to?" he said.

I stood my ground as best I could, considering I was standing in zoo fertilizer. "I was taking a stroll, heard some voices and was curious, that's all."

"Curiosity can kill more than a cat," he said. "If you wanted a tour all you had to do was ask. But nobody likes to be spied on."

"You make it sound so sinister. Of course, if you have something to hide . . ." I pushed my way through the shrubbery. When I emerged from the evergreens, he was waiting.

"The lot's dark at night. I'll see you to your car," he said.

"That's not necessary."

He walked at my side. "You'll need a key to get out."

I walked in silence, but my hands were busy searching for the car keys in my purse.

"Look, maybe I overreacted," he said. "Miles has cut back on security. Says there are better uses for the money. So we're doing our own policing. Can't be too careful. Sometimes kids decide to climb over the fence at night. They don't realize how dangerous some of these animals can be." When we reached the staff exit, he said, "Too bad about that fire at your house."

"How do you know about that?"

"We have a switchboard operator with a real green thumb when it comes to grapevines. Didn't you pick up your messages at the zoo office? Your insurance company called. They can't process your claim till they get the fire department's report."

"Thanks for minding my business." I pointed to the gate. "You wanna open that?"

He didn't move. "Did the fire do much damage?"

I turned to study his face. I found its clues as puzzling as the mural's. "Yeah, practically gutted my new ranch house," I said.

There was no flicker of surprise in his face. "Wow, good thing you're okay."

He unlocked the gate to the parking lot. As I started to pass, his arms closed around the bars, trapping me between him and the gate. He leaned against me, his face inches from mine.

"I know what would make you feel better," he said.

The biting smell of antiseptic filled my lungs as he reached over and fingered the lapels of my blouse. The side of his hand rested on my breast. I shoved his hand away.

His voice was a harsh whisper in my ear. "Now that's not nice."

"I don't like your style, Dr. Bennett, charming as it is. I suggest you remove your body block and let me past, or . . ."

"Or what?" He seemed amused. "I'm just trying to

be friendly. You came on to me the other day. Now you start playing games?"

"You've got a patient waiting for you, remember?" I ducked under his arm and tugged on the gate.

"She's not going anywhere. She's anesthetized."

"I imagine you have to drug every female you're with."

He laughed and leaned into me against the fence. "Pretty smart mouth on you." He ran his thumb over my lower lip. "Maybe that mouth is good for other things."

I shoved him away. He lost his balance. I yanked open the gate and ran. My hands fumbled for the car door key.

He caught up with me before I could slide the key into the lock. Pulling me around to face him, he slammed my back into the sooty side of the Camaro. "You think that's funny?" Towering above me, he pushed against me. "Well, joke this."

I pictured "Evvie" and delivered the uppercut directly to his gut, just below the "E" in Everlast. Yanking open the car door, I jumped in, slammed the door closed and locked it. From the safety of the Camaro I gazed out the window to see him bent over, clutching his abdomen. I turned the key. The engine turned over instantly. I circled his crumpled form once, honked, then sped for the exit.

"Now that's funny," I said out loud.

22

HUMOR HAD ALWAYS BEEN MY FIRST LINE OF DEFENSE, but I'd never been tested in such a physically threatening situation. I was lucky to have taken Rob Bennett by surprise.

Not bad for my first bout. All through school I had been the last kid picked for relay races. The only way I ever crossed a finish line was to trip across it. But when I brought Rob Bennett to his knees, I felt a sense of confidence I'd never known before. The potential victim had turned into a capable defender. Had it been a simple case of sexual harassment, or were there deeper motives behind his actions?

When I walked in the kitchen door, the phone was ringing. I set down the mail in my hand—mostly bills— and picked up the receiver.

"You handled yourself pretty well in that parking lot."

At first I couldn't identify the voice.

"I was just about to come to your rescue, when you proved you didn't need my help."

"That's right, Jake. I don't need you."

"Ouch," he said.

"So if you'll excuse me, I'm tired and—"

"Dealing with a lech will usually do that," he said. "Not to mention finding a corpse. Want to talk about it?"

"I don't need any more problems tonight." I hung up and poured myself a glass of champagne. No celebration. It was just that champagne worked its magic quickly.

I stared out the back window at the pile of rubble that was once my studio. It could be months before I saw any actual cash from either the inheritance or the mural commission. I needed to rebuild my studio as soon as possible.

I felt eyes on me and glanced around. On the kitchen counter sat the kitten. Her large green eyes, punctuated with black slits, glowed with resentment. I had basically ignored her since her arrival. In a lame effort to interact, I tossed a drawing pencil on the floor.

The white ball of fur jumped down and sniffed at the pencil. Like a switch-hitter, she batted at it with one paw, then the other, sending it rolling across the floor. She began to stalk it. Rump up in the air, head and shoulders low to the ground, she did a little drumbeat dance, then tore across the floor. She cut back to the left and shot back across the floor once again. It felt good to laugh. Sensing a treat was on tap for the entertainment, she pranced toward me with her tail high.

While visions of fish heads surely danced in her head, she sprang to the kitchen counter again, next to a sample box of Katey's Kitty Kandies. I had provided the illustration for the cat on the box front and had been sent a carton of it in lieu of a check. The company went bankrupt after being listed on the stock exchange as KKK. So I couldn't even take Katey and her Kitty to Kourt. My hands fumbled with the cardboard flaps. Only cats could like food that smelled like it came from the bottom of a septic tank. I held my breath, extracted several odoriferous morsels, fed them to the kitten, and quickly rewrapped the remainder.

I looked at my mounting pile of bills, then checked my watch. It was nine-thirty, but it was worth a try. I picked up the phone.

"How soon can you get a report to my insurance company?" I asked the River Ridge fire marshall as soon as I was connected.

"In a hurry, are we?" A loud thud sounded like he'd just dumped a stack of file folders onto the floor.

"The insurance company told me they can't process my claim until they hear from you."

"That is such a bother," he said, "to have to wait for them to cut a simple check."

"Well, you know, that's why people buy insurance, and it is my business location."

"Hmmm. Well, I haven't had time to write up the report yet, but I can give you a one-word preview of what it will say."

I was afraid I already knew the one word, but I waited for him to speak.

"Arson," he said.

I said nothing.

"You don't seem surprised that it was arson."

"Well, I, uh, I mean . . . how?" I should have prepared before I called.

"Burn pattern indicated it originated outside, then traveled through the louvered window to the pile of rags under your drawing board."

"How'd it get from the window to the rags?"

"Take your best guess." He chewed something and swallowed. "No? Wax paper. Found some stuck in the window. The arsonist unrolled just enough through the window of your studio to reach the rags, then lit a match. Strictly amateur. Didn't even make sure all the evidence burned." He slurped through a straw. "Business been good, Ms. Canfield?"

"Fairly good."

"But not so good you couldn't use a little extra cash?"

"Who couldn't?"

"Your insurance agency says you added a separate office policy recently."

"I just had the place remodeled. My house insurance didn't cover the studio."

"Remodeling took place . . ." Sound of pages flipping. ". . . two years ago July. Insurance coverage increased only six months ago."

"Well, I should have done it right away, but you know how it is."

"Boy, do I know how it is."

"What do you mean?"

"Look, lady, if you wanna set fire to your own property, that's your business. But filing a claim is a different story. That's fraud, and that'll buy you a room at Dwight."

"Fraud?" Surely this was some sick joke.

"Still want me to rush a report to your insurance company?"

The handles of the kitchen cabinets dug into my back as I sank slowly to the floor.

The clock read 3 A.M. After two sleepless nights, it was no wonder I had fallen asleep as soon as my head hit the pillow. The old bell in the steeple overhead must have awakened me. Whenever the wind was high, it swayed slightly, like a gigantic wind chime. Lightning flickered outside. A moment later thunder crashed. I flicked on the bedside lamp.

The cat lay on her back, spread-eagled at the end of the bed. I propped up my pillows and stared up at the plaster ceiling, wondering if the hairlines in it were plaster cracks or spider webs? *"What a wicked web we weave . . ."* Except I was the one being deceived.

Somewhere out in the stormy night was a murderer who was getting away with, well, murder. First I'm suspected of killing Gino. Then the local authorities accuse me of being a pyromaniac. If my bad luck held, I'd end up convicting myself of my own murder. I shivered and got up to close the choir loft window.

Rob Bennett had to be the arsonist. Except why then had he bothered to ask me what artwork I'd lost in the fire? A crack of thunder shook the room. The cat jerked awake. I bent forward to take her in my arms, but she jumped from the bed and ran off.

I plopped into the bedroom chair, throwing my arms over its sides. My hand grazed a plastic bag sitting on the table beside me. The bag containing Tony's final effects had been too hard to look at before. Maybe now was the time.

I opened it and carefully laid the articles on the bed. They hardly defined the man I had known.

One gold money clip—empty. Vince had probably kept the cash.

One black comb. I'd never seen a hair on Tony's head out of place. I always suspected it was airbrushed on.

One Rolex watch. I turned it over. The inscription on the back read, "To Anthony—with eternal love. Claudia." No wonder he dumped her. Tony couldn't commit to a lunch date, let alone eternity.

One cash register receipt for $1.35. He took every deduction possible.

Something was missing from the items. I thought of all the things I carried with me every day. Keys. There were no keys. Surely Tony would have carried keys to his car and his studio. Had someone taken them to search the studio—and his trunk—before I got there?

Remembering the drawing I'd found that day taped to the sliding door, I opened my shoulder bag and slid the drawing from my sketchbook. Just as in the mural, the proportions of the tiger were wrong. Admittedly, the differences were subtle, but the head was clearly too big for the body. The hind legs appeared longer than the forelegs and the back arched. In fact, except for the head, this creature looked more like a rabbit than either a tiger or a liger. What was it, a mythical creature?

The lights in the room flickered. I turned back to study the items laid out on the bed.

One drawing pencil. It must be the one Tony had jabbed into Gino's arm as he lay dying. What was he trying to communicate? I studied the lettering on the shaft of the pencil.

GERMANY—STAEDTLER—MARS LUMOGRAPH—100—2B.

STAEDTLER was the manufacturer's name, but it bore an eerie resemblance to Statler, as in Jake Statler. Coincidence?

The bell in the steeple began to peal as the wind whipped around the walls outside.

GERMANY seemed irrelevant in lieu of all the Italians involved, although I'd heard the Italian word for "Germans" muttered often enough—*Tedeschi*. I heard it every time Tony had trouble with his Porsche. Gino's last name was Tedesco. A connection? Ben Rudolph was possibly of German extraction. But Ben was a friend.

MARS was the Roman God of War. Perhaps a reference to Miles's military background. Mars, Martian, Marcia Wilhelm, the animal rights woman. Wasn't the name Marcia derived from Mars? Wilhelm was a German name. Mars. A reference to the color mars black?

LUMOGRAPH was a pure mystery. Light? Drawings?

If the number 100 was a clue, I didn't see how.

2B indicated the hardness of the graphite in the pencil, but what if 2B was converted to initials? Robert Bennett? Bob Bennett? A real possibility given my encounter with him. *2B or not 2B? That was the question.*

My eyes kept returning to the word STAEDTLER. Could Jake be leading me down some garden path? Why was he being secretive? The rain outside beat against the windows.

I came back to the number 100 on the pencil shaft. In Italian, wasn't one hundred *centa*? Senta was an Italian woman's name. Could it be the name of the young Italian girl with Tony in the photo I'd found? Senta was close to the word Santa. Great! Was I actually sitting here thinking Tony might have been fingering Santa Claus for his murder? I shook my head and set the pencil down.

In frustration I tossed my bag across the bed. Several items fell out of it to the floor. I bent to pick them up. One was a business card I'd been handed the day of Tony's funeral.

Claudia B. Water Tower Place. 845 N. Michigan Ave. The suite number jumped off the card.

2B.

23

DRAWING IS THE BEST WAY TO SEE. AT LEAST THAT'S always been true for me.

The summer my dad died, I sat in the old oak tree and sketched from dawn to dusk. But I wasn't moping, as my mother thought. I was finding my way. With each successive leaf and acorn I drew, I realized how individual they were. It became my goal to capture the essence of each one. When I tired of leaves and acorns, I discovered the spiders, the beetles, the birds, the squirrels, all the life forms that thrived in that old oak tree. That was the summer I found myself. I knew I'd become a wildlife artist.

Knowing I had a full day at least before my painting supplies were delivered to the zoo, I booked an afternoon appointment at Claudia B. I decided to check her out first for one overpowering reason. Of all my suspects, I liked her the least. I could live with it being her. I made the hair appointment, then spent the rest of the morning drawing Kiara.

Captivated by her every movement, I sketched Kiara on page after page of my sketchbook. I envied the grace she displayed in merely pacing her cage, the way she turned rhythmically, never missing a beat or falling out of sync. My breathing became more regular as I sketched. Just watching the magnificent cat walk and turn had a calming effect on me. Why had my consciousness been forced to reside in this clumsy human body, instead of a graceful feline?

I wondered what Kiara observed through her line of vision that converged in the center of those ice-blue eyes. What thoughts went through her head as she stared back at me through the filter of iron bars? Were bars a permanent part of her vision, burned onto her irises the way a computer image could be burned onto a monitor? The way the image of a murderer is supposed to be burned onto the irises of a victim?

For an hour I lost myself in drawing Kiara, and then like the approach of a bad storm, the winds began to whip around me until I couldn't ignore them any longer, until they dragged me down in a whirlpool of emotions.

If Tony had died from arsenic, wouldn't the pathologist have noted it in the autopsy, just as he had the lead? Maybe it had been listed in the report. I couldn't recall. With all the chemicals in Tony's body, how suspicious would a little arsenic be? After all, how much could he have ingested by just running the tip of a brush through his lips? Had there been a cover-up? An official crime scene would have delayed the completion of Asia World and risked the endowment. Miles wouldn't have stood for that.

I thought about the mural. If the misshapen tiger was the main clue, then why wasn't that panel missing? And how could I find out what was in the missing panel? My thoughts kept me a prisoner as much as bars kept Kiara. Yet I had the option to run. So why didn't I? The invisible bars that held me were just as real as Kiara's.

When I closed my sketchbook that morning, my vision hadn't improved. For the first time, drawing hadn't helped me see anything beyond the tip of my nose.

24

CLAUDIA B, NO PERIOD, SNUGGLED BESIDE MARSHALL Field's on the second level of Water Tower Place. I pushed open the gold enameled door marked 2B and entered the salon.

My options had been half-day, full-day, or something called "spa," which suggested luggage and travel. I took the half day. Once inside the salon, I'd get lost in the crowd of customers, track down Claudia's office and find out what I could about her.

The receptionist sat in the center of a circular white desk in the middle of the room. I noted his nameplate on the desk as I approached. Enrique wore a colorful dashiki that I personally felt clashed with the salon's botanical display, but I was far too diplomatic to mention it. I told him I had an appointment and gave him the name. He handed me several forms. One requested my full medical history, the other covered my credit references.

"I just want my hair styled, not brain surgery."

"Then you must sign this disclaimer that we can't be held liable in the event of an allergic reaction, heart attack, stroke, migraines, or anything else hah-penning as a result."

I looked at the hairstyles displayed in photos on the wall. "What about loss of sex appeal?"

"We can't be sued for anything that hah-pens."

Was this guy a receptionist or a barrister?

I shrugged and signed the form in the phony name I'd used to make the appointment. He pulled out a card and checked off a half-dozen boxes. Like reading a French menu, I wasn't sure what he was ordering for me. "Like I said, Ricq, I just came in for a shampoo and set."

He stopped writing, sighed, and stared away out of the corners of his eyes to let me know he was plenty perturbed. "With that attitude, I'd seriously consider aroma therapy and an herbal wrap if I were in your . . ." He glared down at my tennis shoes, shook his head and resumed checking off boxes on the card. "First you'll need to be detoxified, you'll need to be vitalized, you'll need to be hydrogenated, fused, chromatized, detoxified again, oxygenized, energized, transformed and—finished." It sounded like I'd be leaving in an aerosol can.

Ricq toted up the score. Everything was à la carte. This detective business was more expensive than I had planned. I handed him cash. He picked up the filthy lucre, slipped it into a drawer and picked up a microphone. Maybe he was going to do show tunes.

"Raphael, your afternoon is here. Raphael, your afternoon is here."

A man in tuxedo pants and tie with no shirt opened the inner door. He stepped forward and handed me a white rose, as he pushed the long dark hair back from his face. "Hello, I am Raphael, your coiffure artiste. My only goal is your satisfaction." He extended his bronzed arm and ushered me in. I had my first clue as to why Claudia's salon was so popular.

My muscle-bound escort led me to the first stop, the Aqua Pool. It looked like a shampoo bowl to me. After I was detoxified and vitalized with something called Rain Forest Essence, which looked and smelled like crushed bananas, Raffy took me and my towel-wrapped head down a long sterile corridor of white doors to a private room. Where were the other customers? My plan to get lost in the crowd needed to be rethought.

New Age sounds played across the speaker system as

Raffy seated me in a leather bucket seat and wrapped a gold cape around my neck. He handed me a glass of champagne. The lights dimmed.

"First, I need to feel your aura, so that we are in tune." He leaned forward and whispered, "We must be at one in this." Pressing his palms together, fingers up, as though in prayer, he announced, "I am ready to begin." The lights came up. He brandished a scissors.

"Aren't we going to discuss this first?" I asked.

He took my hand in his. "You must clear your mind of all stress and strain. Rest your eyes and visualize your personal safe haven. May I suggest a blindfold?"

"Are you going to cut my hair or shoot me?" I asked. "And where's the mirror?" Unlike other salons I'd been in, this one didn't have one on the wall. I squirmed.

"Mirrors encourage distrust between an artiste and his creation," Raphael said. "There must be a complete bonding between us if our relationship is to work."

"I don't want a relationship, Raphael, I just want a new style. But, you know, maybe I didn't think this through. I'll just be going." I struggled out of the bucket seat.

His downcast eyes told me what was coming. "If I haven't pleased you, I will have failed." He looked up at me with pleading eyes. "You need to relax. Perhaps a massage first?"

"I'm outa here." I headed for the door.

"Okay, I'll level with you." Raphael's voice had dropped an octave. He tugged on the long strands of his hair. "Hair extensions. My name's Ralph. And I really need this job."

I had already given up my cash. I might as well get something for it. "Okay, Ralph. How about if you just take off my split ends?"

His eyes lit up. "No problem." In half a dozen snips, he whisked the cape away from my neck.

I looked at the mass of hair on the floor with horror. "I . . . I . . ." I couldn't talk.

"You'll love it. It's retro. Ready for highlights?"

Before I could say "mutilation," Ralph had coated strands of my hair with some foamy liquid he called Essence of Blanche and wrapped them in tin foil. I was more determined than ever to get what I came for. I wondered if Ralph liked to gossip as much as some of his clients probably did. I asked him how he liked working with Claudia.

"She's great." He seemed to have relaxed knowing I didn't mind that he was Ralph and not Raphael. "And she has a knack for making the right choices. Take the name of the salon, for instance. When she opened this place her name was, uh, Benson, Bertram, whatever. But she was lucky enough to marry a man with the same last initial—Baxter. I mean, what if she had married someone named Fliegel? Claudia F. The name just wouldn't have had the same ring to it." He reached over to set the timer.

Time to look around. "You know what, Ralph? I really have to go to the bathroom."

"Well, you should sit under the dryer, I mean the oxygenizer," he said with a grin, "but I'll take you to the john first." He helped me from the chair like I was ninety years old.

"Can't you just tell me where it is?"

"I'm supposed to escort you. I'll get in trouble if I don't."

With aluminum foil spikes shooting from my skull like the Statue of Liberty, Ralph led me down another white corridor. At its end were gold double doors. They could only be the portals to Claudia's office.

"Where's Claudia B today?" I asked.

"She's having lunch with her fiancé. You should see the rock he gave her." It appeared Claudia had moved on. Ralph held open the bathroom door and started to enter with me.

I put a hand on his chest. "Thanks. From this point I know where everything is."

Once inside I noticed there was no mirror on the wall here either. Probably just as well. Still, the glaring ab sence of mirrors made me wonder. I pictured Claudia as a blond vampire, like Catherine Deneuve in *The Hunger*. I waited a moment, then cracked the door.

"Need more toilet paper?" Ralph asked.

"I'm just a little . . . claustrophobic. I'll be out in a minute." I closed the door and sat down on the toilet lid. How was I going to shake him? Beside me a cord dangled. I glanced up at a wall phone. The titles on each of the push buttons indicated three were outside phone lines. The fourth read, "Intercom."

I picked up the receiver, pushed the intercom button, and put my mouth to the speaker. I could do a bad English accent as well as Enrique any day. "Raphael to reception. Raphael to reception." I wasn't Vera Anders's daughter for nothing.

A timid knock rapped on the door. "I'll be right back."

I waited, then opened the door. I looked both ways, then hurried down the hallway to the gold doors and slipped inside.

My first impression of Claudia had been correct. The huge desk was indeed a slab of glass on a chrome pedestal. No drawers.

I ripped open the drawers of the filing cabinet. The middle drawer was full of boxes of junk food amid discarded Snickers wrappers and empty Fritos bags. An eating disorder? I cringed at the thought of someone invading my privacy this way. After shuffling through eight years of canceled checks in the bottom drawer, I felt I knew Claudia better than I had any right to. She had donated a fortune to various charities. I had really misjudged the book by the cover. In checks dated nine years ago, she had signed them Claudia Bentley-Baxter. The name rang a bell. The Worthington-Bentley trust.

I noticed the desk calendar sitting on the glass desktop. I flipped through it to the date of Tony's death. The notation read, "Pick up animal protein. Deliver portrait of Aunt Regina." Of course, the zoo philanthropist. Claudia had ended up with Aunt Regina's emerald ring.

And Aunt Regina had ended up in the cornerstone of Asia World.

I heard voices down the hall. I couldn't hide under the desk with its see-through top, so I pulled the file cabinet away from the wall and slipped behind it. I bent my knees and hoped my head's aluminum spikes didn't extend beyond the top. The door opened.

"Thank you, my love, for a marvelous lunch," Claudia said. She walked over to her desk. "Here are those papers you wanted signed."

"We really should discuss the trust before I leave, dear."

Where did I know that male voice from?

"Let's discuss it over dinner, darling," Claudia said. "Come on, I'll walk you to the elevator."

"All right, but as administrator, I do hope you have some plans for all your aunt's money if the zoo can't meet the d-d-d-deadline."

25

I HID IN A SUPPLY CLOSET DOWN THE HALL AND WAITED until I heard Claudia return to her office. With my head wrapped in a hair towel, I headed for the waiting room. I passed Ralph in the hallway. "Emergency. Have to go," I said. Enrique was on the phone, so I merely dashed out the door. Since I'd already paid cash, he wasn't about to detain me.

The revelation that Ben Rudolph was the attorney for the Worthington-Bentley trust, as well as Claudia's fiancé, sent me reeling. I didn't want to think that he could be involved. I wondered about the terms of Aunt Regina's trust. Had Aunt Regina named her niece her secondary beneficiary, as Tony had named me? If so, Claudia stood to gain a fortune if the mural wasn't finished on time. Was Ben pulling the strings to make it happen?

Could I be sure of anyone? Tony's family hated him. His girlfriend welcomed his death. Had even his lawyer in the end betrayed him? Tony referred to lawyers as snakes in the trees. Did the snake in the mural represent Ben, not Rob? Had Tony been killed by someone we both trusted? With all the doubts came the dawning realization. Tony's murderer was someone I knew.

For the next two days I pulled back from the investigation. My supplies arrived, and as much as I dreaded the scaffolds, I welcomed the chance to immerse myself in work. With Tony's color notes at hand and the drawing grids to guide me, I moved ahead with the mural.

I loaded brushes, paints and palette into the basket on the side of the scaffold. In hand-over-hand fashion with the help of a pulley, I raised the basket of supplies to the scaffold's top level and tied off the rope. I walked over to the ladder and placed my foot on the bottom rung.

Gripping the sides of the ladder, I let my eyes travel up the six staggered levels of scaffolding. I checked the leather safety harness strapped around my waist. Slowly my paint-spattered tennies began the ascent. The drop cloths beneath me, like the colorful dripped canvases of Jackson Pollock, receded with each step. Tony had often threatened to sign the tarps and sell them as expressionist paintings. Colorful droplets. Red drops. Blood. White-knuckling the ladder to the fourth level, I stopped to take a deep breath.

Finally, thirty feet above the cement floor, I eased to the center of the fifth platform with paint, brushes and water. I secured the lines of my harness to either end of the scaffold, tugging on the ropes to test them. Picking up the largest of my brushes, a two-inch flat, I resumed painting where Tony had left off. I began by blocking in large shapes with a middle tone of raw umber. Using an earth color for the ground would help to unify the final hues.

It surprised me how quickly I slipped back into the rhythm of mural painting. In my head Tony's voice coaxed me, corrected me, reminded me. Shape. Tone. Color. They all came together. The colors flowed from my brush almost effortlessly. A touch of warm yellow light against the cool purple shadow. I worked as long as possible, taking breaks by sitting on the platform, rather than descending to the floor. To avoid making too many trips up and down the ladders, I had even cut back on my liquid intake.

When I did visit the ladies' room, I consciously avoided the mirror. The highlights that Ralph had intended for my hair had turned into white streaks by the time I fled the salon and drove home. A home rinse I'd used on the medium-length strands hadn't covered and had merely turned the streaks to straw, both in color and texture. I didn't have time for another appointment. Instead I tucked my two-toned hair under a Sox baseball cap.

What I couldn't ignore was what I'd overheard the night outside the zoo hospital. Each morning before I started painting, I dropped by the old lion house to check on Kiara's health. But whenever I broached the subject to Ellen, she avoided talking about it and would only say they were continuing to medicate the white tiger.

One morning I found Kiara's cage vacant. When Ellen came through the side door, I rushed up to her. She looked exhausted, her eyes swollen.

"Kiara's been moved to the hospital. I was up all night with her," Ellen said. "Rob says the latest blood tests indicate she's going into acute liver failure. It's common in white tigers. We'd hoped that because Kiara had mixed bloodlines, she'd avoid it." Ellen looked like her own bloodline had been drained.

I struggled to find some words of encouragement. "Kiara hasn't looked sick or seemed to be in pain."

"Wild animals hide sickness. Weakness signals vulnerability. It's an instinct they display even in captivity. That's why we keepers have trouble monitoring their health." Ellen's voice cracked. "Sometimes I think I'm not cut out for this work. I don't seem able to spot symptoms early enough."

She lowered her head and ran her left hand over the top of it. I noticed again the space where her two fingers were missing. She looked up in time to see me observing her hand. Of all times for her to smile, I didn't expect this moment to be one. "I use this as a scare tactic," she said, "to warn kids to keep their hands out of the cages."

"Is that how it happened?"

She shook her head. "I was born this way. You might say Kiara and I both have birth defects. But mine's just an inconvenience. Hers is fatal."

26

THE NEWS THAT KIARA MIGHT BE TERMINALLY ILL PULLED a black curtain over my day. Like Ellen, I too allowed myself to get emotionally involved with my animals, and I resolved never to feel that particular pain again. I remembered the kitten waiting for me at home. No way was I going to go through losing another pet someday.

I made a mental note to ask Ellen if she would like the kitten.

There wasn't much I could do to help Kiara but hold onto hope. Her fate rested in the hands of the people who knew and cared the most about her—Ellen and Barb, certainly. Even Miles, with all his financial and public relations concerns, wouldn't be eager to put down the tiger if it could be avoided. I wasn't so sure about Rob, but the seed of whatever had made him choose veterinary medicine in the first place couldn't be completely dead.

After leaving Ellen, I headed for Tiger Forest. But I had no enthusiasm for my work or the scaffolds today. By mid-morning I still stood uncertainly at the base of the ladder.

"I hoped I'd find you here."

I whipped around.

Jake Statler stood behind me. He picked up my sketchbook from the floor and slowly turned the pages.

I walked over, reached across and closed the spiral-bound book.

His eyes scanned the mural, then dropped to my hat. "You a Sox fan?" He peered under the cap's brim. "What happened to your hair?"

I gave him the warning look I'd perfected over the last few days that made the receiver think twice before pursuing the subject.

He hooked his thumbs into the back pockets of his jeans. "How 'bout giving me a second chance? Coffee?"

I turned my back, again placing a foot on the ladder. "I've got work to do."

"Come on. I'm ready to trust you."

"You're ready—" I gripped the ladder to get hold of my anger. "I'm delighted to know I've earned your trust." I put my foot up again. The damn thing wouldn't go any higher today than that first rung. "Go away. I don't need distractions."

"Well, if you consider saving Kiara's life a distraction . . ."

I spun around. "What do you mean?"

"You can help her."

He bought coffee and doughnuts at a kiosk, and we strolled beyond the zoo gates to the banks of the Fox River. It had rained the night before, and the grass was damp. As I bent to sit down, my heel slipped out from under me. I tried to pretend the quick glide to the ground had been planned.

The sides of his mouth turned up. "You, uh, land on that part of your body a lot."

"I'm glad it amuses you."

Jake handed me a paper cup and a doughnut. "I'm sorry. It's just that . . . you have no idea how refreshing it is to find a beautiful woman who's—"

"Who's such a klutz?" I tugged on the bill of the baseball cap.

He sat down next to me. "Why do you put yourself down?"

"I'm just a realist."

"That's the last thing you are." He stretched out his long limbs. "You're an idealist. You want everything to be perfect. I'm the realist. I know things'll never be perfect."

"Then you'll be pleased to know you're living up to your own expectations." I turned toward him. "Get to the point. You said I can help Kiara. How?"

"Okay." He put down his food and dusted his hands. "My name's Jake Gavin. I'm an agent for the U.S. Fish and Wildlife Service—Law Enforcement."

"Why not tell me that in the first place?"

"Flash a badge and people clam up."

"Try me."

He reached into his jacket and displayed his ID.

"Is Statler your undercover name?"

He laughed. "No, not really."

"Not really?" I unwrapped my doughnut, tore off a chunk and tossed it to the purple grackles flitting around us.

Jake looked deep in thought, then his head jerked up. "You dropped a drawing pencil in the restaurant, and I picked it up. The name was on the label. I don't do a lot of undercover work in my business."

I remembered the incident. "Why's the Fish and Wildlife Service investigating Tony's death?"

"We're not—directly. We got a lead a few months back from Agriculture. Shipments of rare and exotic animals leaving the Midwest heading south. We figure they're coming from a zoo. I suspect Fox Valley."

"It's not illegal to relocate animals, is it?" I asked.

"Not as long as the proper permits are completed. But I'm betting these animals are being sold under the table, leaving no paper trail."

"Sold to whom?"

"Trust me, you don't want to know. Let's just say they haven't gone to a better place."

"You're way off base then," I said. "I know the curator of mammals here, and I can tell you there's no way she would let that happen."

"Who says she knows about it?" he said. "It could be going on behind her back."

"You think it's related to Tony's murder?"

"I don't know how he found out, but he must have known who was involved. And that person had enough at stake to kill him rather than be exposed."

"I think it could be Rob Bennett." I told him about the veterinary symbol I'd found in the mural. "You told me I could help Kiara. How?"

"How sick is she?"

"They may euthanize her."

A smile crossed Jake's lips. "This just might be the break we've been waiting for."

27

THOUGH SHE WAS ON THE PHONE, BARB WAVED ME INTO her office. Her red hair provided the brightest splash of color in the decor of earth tones. "No, ma'am, I can assure you no bears, white or otherwise, have escaped from our zoo."

I sat down on the beige love seat. A grouping of photos and drawings on the wall occupied my attention as I waited. The Dodo Bird—Extinct 1681. The Bali Tiger—Extinct 1982. The Caspian Tiger—Extinct 1987. The Javan Tiger—Extinct 1987. The Polynesian Tree Snail—Extinct 1996. The Javan rhino, the Carolina parakeet, the New Zealand moa. All extinct.

"Our polar bears don't wear red collars, ma'am," Barb said into the phone as she rolled her eyes at me. "What you probably saw in your backyard was a large dog. But we appreciate your concern." She hung up the phone. "I hope the zoo restaurant is okay with you for lunch. I'm leaving in a couple of days for the AAZPA convention in New Orleans, and I have a lot to do before I go."

"Maybe we should skip lunch," I said. "I've got a lot of work to do myself."

"Don't be silly." She pulled her purse out of her desk, and we walked to the door. "Hang on a sec. I better take this with me." She returned to her desk and picked up her portable phone before rejoining me at the door.

"Can't go anywhere without it." Her eyes studied my baseball cap. "What's happening under there?"

"Never mind."

We left the administration building and turned up the path to the restaurant. A carved and painted wooden hamburger with arms and legs pointed the way. Barb walked slower than her usual confident pace, as though bearing a huge burden.

I guessed the source of the weight. "Ellen told me about Kiara," I said.

"We're meeting tomorrow morning to decide what to do."

"It's not easy, is it? Having to make that decision."

"No, it never is. Especially when you're dealing with endangered animals. It goes beyond the loss of an individual animal. The species itself is one step closer to extinction."

"I noticed all the pictures on your wall," I said.

"Sometimes, when I get discouraged, I look at that wall to remind myself of the importance of the work I'm doing."

"This may be bad timing," I said, "but would you be interested in a kitten? My Gram gave me one, and I just don't think I'll have time—"

"What's wrong with it?"

"Nothing. She's a little aloof, but . . . ."

She smiled. "The last time I accepted one of your kittens in college, I ended up with all four. Remember how we kept them hidden from our house mother?"

"How we stuffed them down our blouses when she inspected our room?"

"Remember her staring at your chest when your boobs starting moving?" We laughed so hard our eyes began to tear.

"You still have them?"

Her smile faded. "Unfortunately Manx kittens are bred to be tailless, so they're often born with defective spines. Eventually I had to put them to sleep."

The simple reason I didn't want another pet. We

passed Ellen and Rob outside the zoo hospital. Ellen seemed to be plea-bargaining with the vet. He sported another of his garish shirts.

"How much do you know about Rob?" I asked. "Do you trust him?"

"He hit on you, right?" Barb stopped walking. "I should have warned you. The only females here he hasn't hit on are the four-legged ones, and I'm not so sure about that anymore. But I'll say one thing for him. He has a great tan." She turned to me. "You're not interested in him, are you?"

"Only in whether he's a good vet. I mean, are you sure he's being straight with you about Kiara's condition? Would it be possible for him to fool you, fake test results?"

"Now you sound like Ellen." She stopped and caught my arm. "If I could change Kiara's genetic makeup, I would, but I won't let her suffer if we can't help her."

Children darted around us in every direction. Life went on. One generation replacing another. Barb intercepted a five-year-old girl who was walking backwards and stumbled into us. Sending her on her way, Barb said, "Careful, kid, or you'll grow up to be her." She pointed at me and laughed, but I didn't feel like joining in this time.

Barb put her arm around my shoulder. "Cheer up. Euthanization is always a last resort. Ultimately, we'll do whatever's best for Kiara. You know that, don't you?"

For the balance of our walk, Barb talked nonstop about attending the upcoming AAZPA convention, about her desire for Fox Valley to gain accreditation and the exciting research being done by zoos in genetics and in vitro fertilization. I recognized the signs. She was immersing herself in work just as I was.

When we reached the restaurant, she led me through the self-service line.

"Let me treat," I said, struggling with my purse and the tray.

Barb headed for a table as I shuffled through the contents of my purse, pulling out the items blanketing my wallet at the bottom. I rested a handful of purse contents on my tray as I paid the cashier and joined Barb.

She nodded at the envelope that sat on top of the pile. "Are you two corresponding these days?"

I glanced down at the heavy black felt-tip lettering on the envelope addressed to Tony. It had contained the threatening note the police had confiscated. "What do you mean by that?"

"I'd know that handwriting anywhere. I've seen it every morning for the last two years in written reports to me. It's Ellen's."

I don't think Barb noticed my body tremble. Though it was now in police custody, the words of Ellen's note came back to me, burned into my mind like a hot brand.

Our Baby died this afternoon thanks to you. But losing a baby or its mother has never particularly bothered you, has it? I hope you ROT IN HELL!

Was Ellen a split personality, capable of killing Tony yet caring enough to cry for Kiara and the liger?

I tried to keep my voice steady. "Barb, what was the liger's name? The one that died."

Barb stopped munching on her salad long enough to answer. "We just called her Baby."

A searing pain stabbed through my brain—an instant headache. I pinched the bridge of my nose. Was the liger's death enough motive for Ellen to have killed Tony? Or did she have an even bigger reason?

28

MY CAR TIRES SQUEALED AS I PULLED INTO THE DRIVE-way. Hurrying up the front stairs, I struggled to get the key into the front door. On the dining room table, I emptied the bag of art materials I'd purchased on the way home: cotton swabs, turpentine and blotter paper. From the closet, I removed the rolled canvas—the Chirico family portrait.

As I stretched it across the table, its slick surface glistened under the light fixture, just as I had hoped. Tony had given it his usual two coats of gloss damar varnish. However, the bouquet of roses Vince had painted had a comparatively matte finish to it. He had probably not varnished it or had merely used a nonpermanent retouch varnish. If so, I should be able to remove the top layer Vince had painted without destroying Tony's painting underneath.

I dipped a cotton swab in the turp and with a small circular motion began delicately removing the top layer of paint. Gently massaging one of the roses, the swab turned pink as the top layer of paint began to lift away. Working just to the right of the slash in the canvas, I glanced up at the faces in the portrait. Antoinetta's reproving eyes dared me to continue.

I took a fresh swab and began to remove more of the red pigment. Methodically and with as much patience as I could muster, I kept at it. One by one the rose petals disappeared, exposing a more delicate pink tint underneath. I had to be careful to stop at the exact moment the red faded. The layer of damar varnish between the two painted surfaces was working in my favor, preventing me from removing the underlying original painting.

One hour and at least fifty cotton swabs later I had uncovered about two square inches of the portrait. At three in the morning I found what I had suspected: a tiny baby painted masterfully down to the last detail. Its left hand was missing its fourth and fifth fingers.

29

NOW I KNEW WHAT TONY MEANT WHEN HE SAID HE HAD taken the zoo commission to reunite his family. Ellen was Tony's daughter, the child born in Italy that Tony had brought back to America. Then, for some reason, she had disappeared from his life, until recently.

As long as Tony lived in the house, the portrait must have hung as he had painted it. But after the divorce, Vince had painted over Ellen's portrait to placate his mother. Anyone else would have simply removed the portrait. But not Antoinetta. That would have been admitting that Tony no longer belonged to her, that he would never be back. But the slash in the canvas told me she had never forgotten what lay beneath the roses.

The next morning I couldn't wait to find Ellen. I squeezed out of the driver's side of my Camaro in the staff parking lot. I'd parked too close to the silver van next to me. With my face practically kissing the side of the van, I hesitated just long enough to hear the voices escaping from the side panel door.

"I won't tolerate having a sick tiger for the opening." Miles's booming voice was unmistakable. "Whatever has to be done must be decided now. We have just seven weeks."

What was Miles doing inside a van in the zoo parking lot?

I leaned closer to the van's door and put my ear to the crack.

"Maybe Kiara will improve." It was Ellen's voice.

Ellen, too? I stepped back from the van.

"Barb, you've seen the test results. What's your opinion?"

How many people were in this van? And why were they meeting in the parking lot?

My questions were answered when the door rolled open and a hand yanked me inside.

30

IT TOOK A MOMENT FOR MY EYES TO ADJUST TO THE darkness of the van's interior. One meager beam of sunlight streamed through a curtain drawn behind the front seat of the truck. I lay on my back on the van's floor.

Kneeling next to me loomed a small but wiry guy with a shaved head and a tattooed arm—the arm that had pulled me in. "What'cha doing snoopin' round our van?"

"What're you doing parking in the staff lot?" It was

the best I could come up with on such short notice. I pulled myself up into a sitting position on the floor.

"Be quiet, both of you!" In the center of the van, Marcia Wilhelm sat at a card table with a black box in front of her.

From the box came Rob Bennett's voice. ". . . condition will continue to deteriorate."

"Recommendation?" Miles barked.

"Euthanize."

In the background someone gasped.

"That's just great!" A heavy thud made me jump. "No tiger for our opening. Intolerable," Miles said.

"What about finding a replacement?" a Hispanic voice said. It was Yolanda.

"As a matter of fact," Barb said, "several tigers are listed as available in—"

"Are they white?" Miles demanded.

"No," Barb said, "but they're purebred Siberians—"

"Siberians, Mongolians. Goddamn it, if they're not white, I don't want them. Without a white tiger, we're just another zoo."

"Siberians have a lot of white on their chests," Yolanda said.

"What's the matter with all of you?" Ellen said. "You act like you're ordering new furniture. This is Kiara's life."

"That's uncalled for, Riggs. Thanks to you, we're in this predicament." Miles's voice caused the card table in the van to shimmy. "You're supposed to keep these animals healthy."

"That's unfair, Miles." I was surprised to hear Barb defend Ellen. "Kiara's problems are genetic. When will you understand that inbreeding creates serious consequences?"

"Don't change the subject, DiGenova. Find another white tiger. Cincinnati has more than their share."

"They won't deal with us. Our reputation still isn't very good, remember?" Barb said.

"What about those fancy boy magicians in Vegas? They must have thirty or forty."

"But—"

"I don't want excuses, I want results. I don't care how you get one, DiGenova. Pull some strings. Throw your weight around. Beg, borrow or steal one, woman, but on October thirty-first when we open, I want to see a white tiger!"

"None of you cares about the animals!" The volume of Ellen's voice rivaled Miles's.

There was silence, then Barb spoke. "Let's not be hasty, Miles. Let's give Kiara a chance to respond to treatment."

A chair scraped back. "I'm surprised at you." Rob Bennett's voice. "You saw the test results. How can you even suggest waiting? The sooner we put that cat out of her misery, the better. The latest tests indicated—"

"I want new blood samples and new tests run!" Barb's voice was firm.

"There isn't time for that. The animal's suffering, for God's sake!" Rob shouted.

"Ellen's right. We're dealing with a life here," Barb said. "Kiara may well rally."

"I'll watch her night and day," Ellen said.

"As director and the voice of reason . . ." I pictured Miles's red face and bulging neck veins. ". . . I've decided we'll wait until we secure a replacement."

Rob broke in. "And what if her condition worsens? My vacation starts tomorrow, and Barb is leaving for the convention. You know the board of directors demands all three of our signatures on euthanization papers."

"I'm in charge!" The sound of Miles's fist hitting the conference table made all of us in the van jump. "Now get on the horn, DiGenova, and track down another white tiger. Move!"

Chairs scraped and the voices drifted away.

Marcia Wilhelm's eyes were riveted on mine as she clicked off the tape recorder.

I pointed at the black box. "How did you . . ."

"We bugged the smoke alarm. Now you've heard for yourself in what low esteem they hold these animals' lives. Once we release this tape, the public outcry alone will close them down."

The tattooed arm pulled back in a violent jerk. "Yesss!" His tattoo consisted of the words "Mother Earth" on a banner encircling an anthropomorphic globe with collagen lips and D-cup breasts.

"I don't think you and I heard the same conversation," I said. "That tape won't make great PR, but I didn't hear anything particularly incriminating. What do you have on them?"

Marcia Wilhelm's eyes glowed in the dim light. "We'll bring down the whole corrupt system." Like a true zealot, she was long on rhetoric, short on facts. "No longer will our friends in the animal kingdom be humiliated in live displays."

"People will always want to see live wild animals—"

"Some people want to see live sex, too. Does that mean society should cater to them?"

"What do you propose in place of zoos? Home videos?"

"Virtual reality," she replied. "The next generation of zoos won't need live animals. The prototype is being built right now in Leicester, England. By putting on a pair of goggles, you'll soar with the birds, hunt with the tigers, frolic with the dolphins."

Mr. Tattoo grabbed my arm. "And if you blow our cover, babe, you're gonna swim with the fishies," he snarled.

"You plan to substitute pictures of animals for the real thing?"

"Isn't that what you do?" Marcia's silvery hair glimmered in the light. "Are these animals to give up their rights so that selfish people like you can stand back and ogle them?"

"But to never be able to see a real tiger—"

"Real? What you're viewing is living taxidermy, not real animals. Seeing animals in zoos only deceives people into believing that they're alive and well in the wild. Stop the deception. Help us. Miss the deadline."

So they were aware that I stood, or fell, along with the zoo's funding.

"You're very articulate," I said. "Far more articulate than I am. But have you really seen this zoo, or do you just march around the gates? Have you looked into these animals' eyes the way I have? Maybe if you saw them as individual creatures, not abstract symbols, you'd see them looking to us for survival. Whether or not you believe it's right to keep them in captivity, these specific animals here and now are already in captivity, and they need our help. Where do you propose these animals go if you shut down Fox Valley Zoo?"

She was silent for the first time.

"You don't want to think about that, do you?"

"So, you're not with us, then?"

"I'm with the animals," I said. "I want what's best for them, even if I'm not sure what that is at this point. But people who care are trying to find solutions, not create chaos."

Mr. Tattoo's sleek skinhead and ratlike nose were in my face. He pointed at the tape recorder, then jabbed his finger into my chest. "Yeah, well, nobody better find out about our bug. Unless you want to get squashed like one."

31

THE KEEPER'S DOOR IN THE WALL BELOW ME SOFTLY opened and closed. The scaffolds blocked my view. "Who's there?" I called, but there was no answer. I was used to various people poking their noses in to check on my progress, but they usually announced their presence.

My stomach growled in displeasure that I'd skipped lunch. I checked my watch. Four o'clock already. I'd grab a bite to eat, then work until the daylight faded. I had to quit a few minutes earlier each evening as the days shortened, and I still had a lot of mural to paint. I rinsed my brushes in a bucket. The water turned a muddy gray, the color of Gino's dead face.

I unhooked the safety harness from the scaffolds. Descending the tower of metal pipes was worse than climbing up. I eased myself lower on the ladder. My left foot felt for the next lower rung. Before the right one could catch up, the left one slipped out from under me.

My heart dropped to my shoes. The wooden ladder tumbled away to the concrete floor. I grabbed the side of the scaffold with one hand. Struggling to gain a hold with the other, I swung back and forth by one arm like a monkey, but with far less glee and agility. I lunged for the bars again without success. My arm stretched to its limit. My flailing feet struggled for a foothold, but it eluded me. Each time my foot landed on a bar it skidded across.

I kicked off my left shoe, swung the opposite arm around and planted my right hand on a crossbar. At last my stockinged foot found a hold. I lowered myself slowly arm by arm until my feet touched ground. Collapsing onto the floor, I gasped for breath. My arms tingled as blood began to rush back into them. I lay back and stretched out on the drop cloths.

The runaway ladder lay several feet away. I crawled over to it. My fingers were numb as I ran them across the rungs, but not so numb that I didn't know what I felt. Grease.

Heading for the hot dog stand, I saw a wheelchair rolling slowly ahead of me.

"Yolanda!" I hurried forward. "Have you seen Ellen?" I had a lot to talk to her about—not only about Kiara, but about Tony, Baby and the letter I'd found.

Yolanda turned to look up at me. Her eyes were red.

"What's wrong?"

"We're going to put Kiara down," she said. "Miles just signed the papers."

"Where's Barb?"

"On her way to the convention in New Orleans. After she left, Rob Bennett marched into Miles's office. He said Kiara took a turn for the worse, that we can't wait. Miles agreed."

"When will . . ." I didn't have to complete the sentence.

"Tonight."

My fingers trembled as I jabbed the numbers on the phone. Pick up, pick up.

"This is Jake Gavin. I'm away from the phone . . ."

I waited for the insipid message to run out. Beep.

"Jake, where are you? This is Caroline. It's happening."

I tried to call Barb. All I got was her voice mail. I wondered if she had taken her cellular phone with her to New Orleans. I left a message about Kiara and asked her to call. I got Ellen's home phone number, but there was no answer. Where was everyone?

32

WHEN THE ZOO CLOSED THAT NIGHT, I FOUND A THICK clump of mulberry bushes near the hospital and hid there until it got dark. Somewhere inside the infirmary lay Kiara. I hoped Jake's instincts were right about this.

Armed with a camera stuffed into my shoulder bag, I planned to document Rob Bennett's activities. I'd come to know his schedule: mornings for his rounds at the zoo, afternoons at the racetrack. Evening was when he did most of his procedures.

A lone guard came past the hospital after sunset. He swept the ground with his flashlight. I stopped munching on the granola bar I'd brought for dinner and withdrew deeper into the foliage. The guard pulled out a flask, took a swig and moved on into the night.

At nine-thirty Rob hurried up the path. Passing under the arc of an overhead light, he had the look of a man on a mission, clenched jaw and eyes fixed straight ahead. When he entered the building, I stuck the granola bar into my pocket and scurried to the shrubs beneath the darkened surgical room window. The fir trees scratched the nape of my neck as I waited.

It didn't take long. A light flicked on. Rob entered the surgical room, opened a cabinet and took out a vial. He turned out the light and left the room. The action must be elsewhere. I'd have to get inside.

Abandoning the shelter of the shrubs, I crept up the front steps of the hospital. The front doors were locked tight. I slipped around to the back. The trees blocked out the light of the moon. Everything lay in darkness. A beat-up unmarked midsize panel truck had been pulled up to the back double screen doors. I ducked down, then realized the truck was empty. Rob appeared to be alone. But where was Ellen? She'd been absent all day. Why would she abandon Kiara at this most critical time?

One of the hospital's warped screen doors gaped open. I slipped through it. Approaching footsteps sent me scurrying to a supply room, where I ducked inside. Through a crack in the door I spied on the room across the hall. In the center of the well-lit room sat a squeeze cage. I couldn't tell if the motionless white form behind its bars meant Kiara was sleeping, tranquilized, or just unable to move within the confined space. I pulled out my 35-millimeter Minolta and snapped a picture.

The sight of the crash cart next to the cage gave me a sense of relief. If Rob was intent on euthanizing Kiara, why take precautions to resuscitate her? The phone on the wall rang. The vet entered the room.

"We had a deal," he said into the phone. "I'm just keeping my end. I said I'd deliver by the fifteenth." He listened. "No one's gonna know about it, if you keep your mouth shut. You get what you want; I get what I want." He glanced around the room. "I thought you didn't want to know the details. What's your sudden interest?" He smiled. "More business? I can handle that. Okay, yeah, I think I know the place. I'd call you when I'm about an hour away. Of course I have it." He hung up and left the room.

Was he meeting someone later? In a moment he returned. He held up a vial and stuck the needle of a syringe into its top. He drew a colorless liquid—not blue juice—into the tube of the syringe. I opened the door just enough to accommodate the camera lens and snapped the shutter. I might as well have announced myself.

He wheeled around. I backed quickly into the shadows of the supply room, until a door handle jolted my spine. Pivoting around, I unbolted the lock and opened the heavy metal door. I retreated into the pitch-dark enclosure and closed the door behind me.

From the darkness of my cell, I heard Rob yank the outer hall door open. A sliver of light appeared under my cell door. I heard him shuffling around in the outer room. The scent of hay drifted up to my nostrils. I dropped to my knees and pulled clumps of straw on top of me. Fighting the urge to sneeze, I jammed a finger under my nose.

The door of my cell opened. A light beam circled the interior. A frightened whimper broke the silence. For a moment I feared it came from me, but when the crying changed to shrieks, I realized I wasn't the only one in the room who was scared.

"Damn it, who left this door unlocked?" Rob shouted. The shrieks became deafening as he approached. "Shut up. What have you got now? Give me back my cigarettes. Damn pickpocket." Mumbled swear words and the scraping of the metal door told me Rob was leaving. A lock clicked into place.

The hay stirred a few feet away from me. I remained motionless in my miniature haystack. When the rustling stopped, I rose up on all fours and pushed the straw from my face.

Wet flesh mopped my face. A tongue? I reeled back and slapped a hand over my mouth to prevent crying out. I peered into the darkness.

Through the barred window behind me, moonbeams fell across a shock of red hair. Below a sloping high forehead, a pair of close-set brown eyes sparkled. Wide round lips set into an animated fleshy face pulled back and displayed a set of choppers that needed the attention of a skilled orthodontist. Was it a smile, a grimace of fear or a threat?

33

On my knees I zigzagged backward across the floor until I was far enough away to rise to my feet. My roommate and I took a moment to size each other up.

The orangutan was short and stocky, its knuckles scraping the floor. Although I was confident I outweighed it, I would be no match if it became aggressive.

The moon went behind a cloud, taking with it the room's only light. From what I had observed of its compact face, the orang appeared to be a female. However, I knew the Sumatran male lacked the large facial flanges of the Bornean, as did immature males of either type. The moon came out again. If I hadn't been sure of the features, I easily recognized the fixtures of a female. She rushed toward me, her teeth flashing, her long arms pounding out at me. Was she threatening me or begging me to do something?

Like Sigourney Weaver in *Gorillas in the Mist*, I dropped to my knees, bent forward, and put my hands over my head. As I crouched there, I remembered what Ellen had told me about the zoo's new orang—the magician's assistant that couldn't adjust to being an animal after living her whole life as a human.

I raised an eyebrow and studied Houdina from the corner of my eye. She sat down next to me and lay a heavy hand on my back. I raised up slowly on all fours. My friend slammed my shoulders back to the floor. Like

Miles's tendency to pound the table, this was probably just a casual reminder of who was in charge.

I remembered the granola bar in my pocket. The wrapper rustled as I slowly extracted it. Houdina tipped her head. I offered it to her. She snatched it from my hand and lumbered over to a corner.

I heard activity outside, as though metal furniture were being rearranged. I glanced over my shoulder like a pitcher checking the runner at third. My dinner date was munching contentedly on the wrapped treat, paper and all. The noise outside sounded like a garbage truck in action. Houdina dropped her treat and charged to the window. She extended one long arm through the bars and appeared to be fishing for something below. She pulled a small paper bag through the bars and ran to a corner. I crawled to the window and rose, but the sound outside had stopped. Below the window was an open garbage Dumpster.

The sound of the hydraulic lift started again, but this time it sounded like it was straining less. The close-set bars on the window prevented me from seeing what was happening, but I had a good idea. Kiara was being loaded onto the truck I'd seen waiting outside.

Doors banged shut. The truck's engine turned over. I hurried to the metal door and tugged on it, but it didn't budge. There had to be some way out. But every possibility of escape was either nailed down, bolted to the floor or had bars across it. Even the ceiling had chain link fencing across it. Houdina must have been quite an escape artist. I was trapped. The truck pulled off. I slumped to the floor. Houdina sat in the opposite corner sorting through the lunch sack she'd pulled from the garbage.

Kiara was on her way to God knew where, and all I could do was wait to be rescued. I dragged my shoulder bag toward me and wrapped my arms around it.

Houdina glanced up at me watching her. We stared in each other's eyes for the longest time, like we couldn't believe that with all the gin joints in this world, we'd ended up in this place with each other. Legend has it that orangs can talk, but don't because they know humans will only put them to work. Houdina was living proof.

Apparently bored by the orange rinds and empty food wrappers she'd rescued from the garbage, Houdina rediscovered the granola bar. I pulled out my sketchbook. For the next ten minutes I sketched her by moonlight. After dragging the remaining granola crumbs to her mouth, she waddled over and peered over my shoulder. Reaching down to my lap, she dragged a long finger across the sketch, smearing the carbon pencil. I couldn't blame her for objecting to the drawing. No woman likes to be seen feeding her face.

She bent, pulled off one of my tennis shoes, and jammed her foot into it. She took several steps away from me, as though trying it out in a shoe store, then returned for the mate. She spent the next twenty minutes tying and untying the tennies on her feet.

I hadn't planned to sleep at all that night, but I must have dropped off when the moon vanished from view. I awoke just before dawn with a start, the way you do in unfamiliar surroundings. I lay on my side, strangely aware of two strong arms wrapped around my waist from behind. Red furry arms. Like any woman awakening in a strange bed, I hurried to piece together the events of the night before.

I glanced around. The contents of my shoulder bag lay scattered across the floor. Houdina had had a busy night while I slept. The film had been pulled from my camera, and she had drastically revised her portrait with a magic marker she must have found in my bag.

The gamy smell of urine in the straw reminded me. I had to go to the bathroom. My feet were ice-cold. The orangutan's grip loosened. Slowly I rolled over to face her. She bared her teeth, but this time it didn't scare me.

I rose up on my knees and surveyed the room. I pointed at my feet. "All right, where are my shoes?" She shook her head.

I stood up and roamed the enclosure. In the back corner one of the floorboards was raised. My tennies stuck up vertically from the gap like two white horns. I headed for the corner. Houdina got there before me. She started shrieking and jumping up and down when I bent to retrieve my shoes. I had to laugh. She reminded me of Tony's ex-wife, Antoinetta.

She clapped her hands, acknowledging my laughter, and let me pick up my shoes. Their removal revealed a treasure store underneath the floor boards. There were keys, a fountain pen, a screwdriver, various pieces of jewelry, even a condom in its original wrapper. Had this been part of her Las Vegas act? Relieving people of their possessions? Houdina tried to pull me away, but I was as captivated as she was by the items. I picked up one item, a gold pin in the shape of a cat. I remembered seeing it on Ellen's shirt the first day I met her. I turned it over in my hand and read the engraving. *To my little lost kitten. Love, Papa.*

I reached beneath the floorboards again and came up with a two-ounce tube of acrylic paint. Mars black. It couldn't be Tony's. He never used tube paints. And he seldom used black, even for shades of gray. He'd taught me to create grays by mixing complementary colors instead. On the rare occasions when he had included it in his palette, I know he preferred ivory black. Had someone tampered with the mural? If so, the tampering couldn't amount to much. Very little paint had been squeezed from the tube.

I reached down for the ring of keys, wondering whose they were. Had Houdina pulled them from the garbage or lifted them off a staff member? What did it matter? If I was lucky, one of them would work.

I hurried to the door. I had to try a dozen keys in the lock before I found the means to my escape. Houdina had lived up to her name.

34

I DROPPED A QUARTER INTO THE FIRST PAY PHONE I FOUND and punched in Jake's number. I left another message on his machine. I called my own number, but there were no messages.

I hurried on to the administration building. Only one office had lights on.

Out of breath, I barged into Yolanda Ramirez's office. "Where is everybody?" I scanned the room, feeling disoriented at first, then realizing the reason. Yolanda's office had a low center of gravity. Everything had been designed for wheelchair access, including the height of file drawers and bookshelves. It seemed odd that she would opt for hanging plants.

"I'm the only one here," she said. "It was all I could do to drag myself in today. I just can't stop thinking about poor Kiara."

"Where's Miles? And how can I get hold of Barb?" I knew she thought me unfeeling for not commiserating.

Her voice turned cold. "Miles was called out of town suddenly. Death in the family. He won't be back until Tuesday. As for Barb, she just phoned in. When I told her what happened last night, she was furious. She said as soon as she delivers her speech at the conference, she'll be on the first flight back."

"Where the hell is Ellen?" I demanded.

Yolanda gave me an icy glare as she pulled some papers from a two-drawer file cabinet. "I wasn't aware that

Miles left you in charge. In fact, when no one else is available, the chain of command falls to me." Spoken like a true Miles-wannabe.

"Just tell me where Ellen Riggs is."

"I can't remember."

"Try." When I didn't budge, Yolanda must have realized the only way to get rid of me was to answer me.

"Ellen left yesterday with blood samples. To consult on the test results with medical experts from another zoo."

"Which zoo?"

"I don't know."

I didn't like myself for doing it, but I walked over and glared down at her in her chair.

"It might have been the National Zoo." She turned on the paper shredder and ran a few sheets through its teeth.

"She left town, knowing Kiara was to be euthanized last night?"

"Rob and Miles made that decision after she was gone."

"So Ellen doesn't even know what's happened to Kiara?"

"She does now. When she called this morning to find out how Kiara was doing, I had the unpleasant task of telling her. She's on her way back, probably already at the airport."

I wasn't sure I could trust Yolanda, but she was all I had. "What if I told you I had evidence that Kiara is still alive?"

She spun her chair around. "What kind of evidence?"

"I watched Rob Bennett last night. He didn't euthanize Kiara. He tranquilized her and loaded her onto a truck instead. I would have had photographs, except . . ." I pulled the film from my bag, the film Houdina had yanked from the camera.

"You must be mistaken," Yolanda replied.

"I know what I saw and heard. I'm telling you he

loaded her onto a truck about ten last night and drove off."

"Of course." She sighed. "Whenever we have a corpse, animal control comes by overnight, picks it up and takes it away to an incinerator. That's the truck you saw."

"What about the injection I saw him give Kiara? It was clear liquid, not blue juice. He simply tranquilized her."

"Naturally, he tranquilized her. That's what they give an animal to put it to sleep—an overdose of tranquilizer." She sighed. "You know, Miles told me to keep after you. He said that you find any and every excuse not to work on that mural. I see what he meant." She turned her back on me. "Now, please leave my office. I have work to do. And so do you."

No matter what Yolanda said, I knew Kiara was alive—maybe not well, but alive.

I waited anxiously to hear from Jake. I called home every hour, but there was nothing on my machine. I hadn't heard from Ellen or Barb, either. I didn't know how to begin to explain Kiara's disappearance to the local police, but when I tried, they just left me on hold. When I called the O'Hare Airport office of the U.S. Fish and Wildlife Service, they would only tell me Jake was on assignment, probably out of town. Of course, wasn't everyone?

I slipped my painting smock over the same clothes I'd worn the night before, and for the rest of the day I painted. By evening I was getting sloppy, not just in my appearance, but in both my painting and my movements on the scaffolds. I decided the best thing to do was to go home, where I'd be close to the phone.

The house was dark, and it felt like a steam bath inside. The phone was ringing. The bad news is I stumbled on the kitchen stairs. The good news is I managed to grab the phone on my way down. The bonus: it was at least twenty degrees cooler at ground zero.

"Caroline, I don't have much time."

I removed a strand of yarn from around my ankle. It was the only cat toy I could come up with on short notice, but the kitten hadn't thought much of it. "Jake! Where've you—"

"I'm about fifty miles north of Jackson, Mississippi. I've been following a truck that left the zoo last night."

"Kiara's in that truck," I shouted. "And so is Rob Bennett."

"I know. But I had a flat and lost it, and I'm beyond the range of the tracking device I planted on the truck. By now it's gone through or around Jackson. That's why I'm calling. Have you seen anything more in the mural besides Texas? Anything that might tell me where it's heading? Due west to Dallas or Fort Worth? Or maybe farther south and then west to Houston?"

"The tiger was in the Panhandle in the mural," I said.

"We're already way south of the Panhandle." The despair was evident in his voice.

I reached up in a daze and turned on the kitchen light. My purse had thrown up all over the kitchen floor. I started to stuff the contents back into the leather pouch. "Jeez, Jake, you told me not to worry—that you had it all under control." My eye found the envelope on the floor, the one sent by Ellen.

"I should have nailed Bennett as soon as he crossed the state line, but I wanted both ends of the connection," Jake said. "Not just the origin, but the destination, too. Now I've lost them for good. Damn!" He pounded something.

I bent and picked up the envelope. Tony's handwritten memo was scrawled across its reverse side. "Jake, what day is it?"

"Friday."

"No, no, I mean today's the fourteenth, isn't it?" I did my best to decipher Tony's writing.

"Yeah, so?"

"I heard Rob say he had to deliver on the fifteenth. Is it possible the truck's going to San Antonio?"

"It's damn possible. Why?"

"I think that's what Tony wrote on this envelope." I stared down at the words I had initially thought to be: *Taxes—September 15th. See Antoinetta.*

"So what does it say?" Jake said impatiently.

"Texas—September 15th. San Antonio."

"You're beautiful! Look, don't mention this to anybody, you hear? Not anybody. Oh, yeah, here's something else for you to think about. Did you notice the truck?"

"It was dark. What about it?"

"It's turquoise."

Turquoise. Vince Chirico's corporate color.

Kiara was on her way to Texas in one of Vince's trucks. I hoped the truck was stolen. During the phone call, Rob had agreed to meet someone. Vince? Why hadn't I thought to mention that to Jake?

I worked Saturday on the mural, still avoiding any decisions as to how I would complete the missing part of the painting below me. I hadn't found any further sketches or notes regarding it, but it was increasingly becoming the least of my problems.

Overhead the painted cat with the strange green eyes continued to taunt me whenever I looked at it. I was no closer to figuring out what it was or what it meant. I considered repainting the eyes that were so disturbing. But it would have meant climbing to the topmost level of the scaffolds, with no railings to keep me from falling. Besides, Tony had painted them that way. But why he had, I hadn't a clue.

While I was eating lunch, a docent hurried over to my table. She said the zoo operator had an urgent call for me, and she'd put it through on the commissary phone.

"Good to hear your voice, honey."

"What?" I didn't realize my relationship with Jake had progressed to that stage.

"I miss you. Look, I'm on a pay phone, but I'm almost

out of change." He sounded calm, too casual. "Here's my number. Can you call me back, sweetie?"

Had an alien from Mom's Heather Valley taken over his body? I wrote down the number he gave me.

"Don't call me from the zoo, though, honey. It's long distance and I wouldn't want the zoo to have to pay for it. Call me quick, okay? It's important."

I grabbed my wallet and ran past the zoo gates. In the park outside was a pay phone. Jake probably didn't want what he had to tell me going over open phone lines. Probably a good idea considering the zoo grapevine, courtesy of the switchboard operator.

He answered on the first ring.

"Caroline, I want you to catch a flight tonight for San Antonio," he said. "Bring your sketchbook—the one with the drawings of Kiara."

35

THE CAB PULLED OFF THE ROAD ONTO A GRAVEL STRIP IN the middle of nowhere. The headlights circled the lot as the cab turned back toward the road. "No vacancy" blinked on and off, illuminating the meter that told me we were about thirty dollars away from San Antonio's airport. I gave the driver thirty-five and jammed my shoulder against the dented door to open it.

"Enjoy your stay at . . ." He looked up at the neon sign. ". . . the Mustang Motel," he said with a sneer. "Don't fergit all that luggage, ya hear?"

I grabbed my purse. Though I was hardly dressed for

anything illicit, I read his thoughts. Instead of the requisite miniskirt and stiletto heels, however, I had on jeans, a modest blouse and running shoes. I had traded my Sox cap for a Stetson at the airport.

Humid, sticky air accompanied me as I crossed through the darkness to the staggered row of cabins. Air conditioners hummed. The window of the motel office was dark, except for the flickering blue light of a TV. The cabin number Jake had given me, 34-B had been easy to remember. It was my bra size.

The cabin was in back. I knocked twice sharply.

The door opened, and warm light flooded out into the darkness. Jake's face came into focus. "Nice of you to drop by," he said. "Just in the neighborhood?" He wore a denim shirt and Levi's with a silver-buckled belt that only Wayne Newton would find conservative.

"Just let me in," I said. "It's giving me the creeps roaming around out here."

"Did you bring your sketchbook?"

"Of course," I said, crossing the threshold. The cabin was surprisingly homey on the inside. "How's Kiara? Where is she?"

He popped the lid on a can of Moosehead and handed it to me. "Next door."

I nearly choked on my beer. "In the next room?"

"Not here," he said. "Next door to the motel. We're sitting on the edge of a 3,500-acre ranch. She's there."

"And you're sure she's okay?"

"For the time being." He sprawled on the bed. "Why don't you take off your hat?"

I started to, then remembered why I had it on.

"What's the matter? You hiding a gun under there?" he said with a smile.

I recalled the night I'd caught him concealing a gun under his sport coat. "I like this hat," I said, adjusting it to make sure it still covered my hair. "So bring me up to date."

"On Thursday night after I got your message, I parked in back of the zoo hospital outside the gates. Saw you go inside. I wanted to get a message to you, but I couldn't without blowing my cover. When the truck pulled away, I followed it. Bennett drove straight through, except for pit stops. I knew if the clue in the painting meant anything he'd head for Texas, but it threw me when he didn't take the most direct route. Probably wanted to stick to back roads."

"I think he was meeting someone," I said. "Did he pick anyone up?"

"Not that I saw, but I kept my distance. Who knows what he did after I had the flat. I caught up with him again near Houston, thanks to you, and tracked him until he drove onto the cattle ranch next door."

"Cattle ranch?"

"Seems people aren't eating as much beef as they used to. So some ranchers have found a more lucrative use of their land. Canned hunts. If your wallet's fat enough you can shoot at water buffalo, lions, bears, all kinds of exotic deer. Guaranteed. If you don't bag anything, you don't pay. This ranch has taken it one step further. Exotic trophy weekends, the rarer the animal, the better. This weekend, guess who's the star attraction? Hunters from all over the country, members of an exclusive club, are here for a shot at Kiara."

"That's disgusting. Thank God you can stop it." When he glanced up at me, I added, "You can, can't you?"

"Yesterday I showed a local judge snapshots of Kiara I'd taken from the ridge above the ranch with a telephoto lens. I thought it would be enough. But it seems the ranch is owned by a big wheel in this county. Judge is afraid of making waves."

"But they're violating the Endangered Species Act."

"I'm afraid they're not. The ESA was written to protect animals born in the wild, not captive bred. And Kiara was born in a zoo. These hunting ranches—and there's probably a thousand in Texas alone, maybe ten thousand throughout the country—often buy former zoo animals at auctions. The larger ranches buy them for breeding stock to keep a steady supply for hunters. I'm afraid the wildlife on these ranches have very little legal protection. The only reason Fish & Wildlife is involved is when there's a violation of the Lacey Act—illegal transport of animals across state lines."

"If your photos weren't enough to convince the judge, how do my drawings help?"

"Tigers have unique markings, just like fingerprints. If we can match my photos to your drawings and you're willing to swear that you drew those at the zoo, maybe we can convince a judge that the white tiger on the ranch is the same tiger from Fox Valley."

"That's our best shot?" I prayed I had been as faithful to Kiara's stripe pattern as I had been to the oak leaves I'd drawn as a kid. I pulled the sketchbook from my canvas bag and turned to the sketches. Jake lay the eight by ten prints of Kiara out on the bed. He stood closely behind me as we compared photos to drawings. When we'd matched several, I felt a surge of pride in my work that I'd rarely felt before, just as I began to feel a bond with Jake that I had never experienced. Together we were going to rescue Kiara.

"The judge will take a lot of convincing to go after a big taxpayer," Jake said. "This might not be concrete proof, but it should work, unless . . ."

I didn't like the qualification. "Unless what?"

"Unless the owner of the ranch can produce proper USDA permits and bills of sale."

"The USDA? Aren't they the meat inspectors?"

"They're also responsible for inspecting all public exhibitions of live animals." He shook his head. "But that's where it gets tricky. Game ranches, unlike zoos, aren't considered public. They're private, and as long as they aren't open to the general public, the animals on them are considered private property. Agriculture has no obligation or right to inspect these ranches. It would be like them coming into your house to inspect your pet's living quarters. You'd consider it an invasion of your privacy."

I couldn't believe my ears. "You mean, I've been outraged that poachers in India are exterminating tigers left and right, and the whole time something like this is going on here in Texas?"

"Closer to home than that. You don't have to go any farther than McHenry County back home."

"You're kidding. What happens if this ranch can produce the proper papers?"

He shrugged. "Then officially my hands are tied."

"How can that be?"

Jake's arms enfolded me. "Take it easy. It'll be fine. Trust me."

I felt his warm breath on my neck. "So Kiara is safe?" I remembered the beautiful creature I had drawn, her piercing blue crossed eyes and huge white paws.

"Her stripes are safe for tonight." He rocked me gently, then turned me around to face him. He pulled off my hat before I could stop him. His eyes roamed over my two-tone hair. "Hmmm. I kind of like your stripes, too."

I had to smile. "I got them in the line of duty."

"You know, I could get used to having you this close," he said, pulling me closer still.

The scent of Polo made me a little dizzy. He looked steadily into my eyes, the way that always made me a little nervous with a guy.

"Isn't there something we should be doing?" I said, as his lips grazed across mine.

"Definitely." His hands fumbled with the buttons on my blouse.

My hands caught his. "I'm really too worried about Kiara."

With a hand on either side of my face, he gently brought our lips together.

I felt I was floating, but at the same time feeling very safe in Jake's arms. I wanted Kiara to be this safe.

Jake guided my head to his chest. "What if I just hold you for a while?"

"Mmmm," was all I could mange. My body conformed to his as we kissed again. He lowered me to the bed and buried his face in my neck. The stubble on his face bristled against my neck. I relaxed into the strength of his arms, as his leg slipped between mine.

I loved how he seemed to care about the same things I did, but at the moment I was thinking more about the glorious differences between us. An annoying buzzing sound went off somewhere near my left ear. Jake kissed me once more lightly, then gently reached over my head for the phone. I lay in a dream state across the bed, until he hung up the receiver.

"Let's take a ride," he whispered.

A cold shower might have been more appropriate. I sat up, my face burning from the roughness of his unshaven face.

"That was Agriculture," he said. "I was right. They have no record of Kiara's sale." With his back to me he picked up the sketchbook from the bed.

I got up and straightened my clothes. "Where are we going?"

"You're about to see a real ferocious animal." He looked at his watch. "We've got a judge to wake up."

36

JAKE PULLED UP AND PARKED A FEW DOORS DOWN FROM a large white frame house on the outskirts of San Antonio. "Here's what I want you to do. Go up to the front door, ring the bell and ask to see the judge."

I swiveled to face him, but he avoided eye contact. "You want me to . . . I thought you talked to this judge already."

"Not at three in the morning."

"And I have more experience in wake-up calls?"

"I didn't exactly hit it off with this judge. You're a woman. Maybe the old buzzard will think you're in distress and open the door. The important thing is we get in. We're racing the clock now." He checked his watch. "The hunt'll probably start at daybreak."

I shoved open the Blazer's door, stepped down, then turned around and put my head through the window. "What do I say?"

"Just ask for the judge. Then look sincere as hell till I get there. Don't worry. I'll be right behind you." He stuck my sketchbook through the window. "And don't forget this."

Passing an antler-adorned mailbox, I hurried up the front walk. Crickets orchestrated the soundtrack as fireflies directed me to the broad porch running the full width of the house. I pressed the button that glowed on the door frame. Chimes rang inside the house. I peered through the crocheted curtain covering the window in the door. In the corner of the pane of glass was an NRA decal. A light went on, illuminating a stairwell to the second floor. A stocky figure descended the stairs. The porch light went on. The lace curtain parted, and a woman with short silver hair peered out over the top of her half-glasses.

I smiled. "I need help," I shouted through the glass.

She looked to either side of me, then studied my face. Her eyes surveyed my hair.

I'd forgotten my hat. I smiled sincerely. "Please."

The bolt turned and the door opened a crack. A musty smell came through the gap.

"What's wrong?" the woman asked.

"I need to see your husband."

Her eyes narrowed. "What for?"

"I need to see him on a legal matter. It can't wait." I turned toward the Blazer and gave Jake a bent neck signal, meaning "get over here." I faced the woman. "It's life or death."

"Must be death, then. Bernie's been six feet under for ten years."

"The judge?"

"Hell, no, I'm the judge. Judge Maybelline Ryder. And I don't take to having my sleep disturbed."

I could kill Jake. Why didn't he say the judge was a woman? She started to close the door.

"Judge Ryder, I'm sorry. I misunderstood. Please hear me out."

The door hesitated. Her eyes went to the bruises on my arms from my recent fall from the ladder. "Your husband beating on you? Are you wantin' a restraining order?"

She gave me an in. "Yes, but not for a husband." I glanced back at the Blazer. Why wasn't Jake hurrying?

"Who're you signaling to there?"

Behind me a car door slammed. I waved a moth away, one of many having a convention on the porch light. "You need to stop an illegal hunt."

"Hunting in these parts isn't illegal."

I shoved my foot against the closing door, but it slid along the wooden floor. "If I can just come in, I can explain." Behind me Jake ambled up the sidewalk. He had my Stetson pulled low over his face.

The short woman craned her neck to see past me. "You can't fool me with that sorry disguise. I recognize you and I told you before, boy, you're one egg short of a dozen."

The door began to close. I pushed my shoulder against it.

The patter of Jake's boots speeded up. "I brought evidence, Your Honor. Caroline, show her your sketchbook."

I whipped open the pages to the studies of Kiara and thrust it in the judge's face.

Jake pulled out the color prints he'd taken of Kiara in a cage on the ranch. "See the markings? It's the same tiger."

"And you consider this proof?" Her forehead rippled into rows of speed bumps.

I braced my shoulder against the door. "I drew these just a few days ago at a zoo in Illinois. See? I've even dated them. And now Kiara is here, about to be shot, by some gun-crazed—" Out of the corner of my eye, a piece of metal glimmered. A rifle stood propped against the wall beside the door.

The judge's eyes turned to slits behind her glasses. "I happen to like hunting. Go every chance I get."

Jake leaned into the doorway. "We're not talking about legitimate hunting, Your Honor. My hunch is the rancher won't be able to produce the proper documentation."

"Don't instruct me on the law, sonny. You need more'n a hunch."

"But these photos—" I said.

The judge eyed me over her the top of her frames. "And I gotta wonder just how you come by those photos. You weren't trespassing, were you? Either get yourself some real proof and present it to me tomorrow in court, or get your sorry selves out of my face."

"Your Honor, tomorrow morning will be too late," Jake said.

"You'll operate through a proper court of law like anybody else."

"Judge, I'm trying to show due cause for a search and seize."

"Well, you haven't done it. Now I'm goin' back to bed." She shoved the door closed.

I struggled to keep it ajar.

"I'll call the sheriff if you don't cease and desist," she shouted through the gap.

"I've shown due cause, Your Honor," Jake shouted.

"And I'm showing you due process," she said.

The door shut, the bolt was thrown, and the light went out. Through the delicate lacy curtains the judge's form receded up the stairs. The moths flitted around us for a few moments more, but we weren't exactly glowing, so they flew off.

"You sure got off on the wrong side of her." Jake turned and walked down the steps.

"I did! Why didn't you tell me the judge was a woman?" I followed in Jake's trail. "I looked like a . . . a . . . sexist."

"And that's the worst thing in the world?"

"The worst is, I didn't do a thing to help Kiara. What do we do now?"

His arms, wrist to wrist, went up in the air. "My hands are tied."

I stomped after him. "We're not giving up!"

Jake got in the front seat. I crawled in on the passenger side.

Jake shook his head. "I thought you'd use a little charm on the old bird. Show her your sincerity and compassion for animals. Win her over, you know? Instead all you do is show her your ignorance of the law."

"Well, excuse me for going to art school instead of law school."

"I should have known I'd need professional backup," He pounded the steering wheel.

I tensed and stared through the windshield, then let my shoulders slump. "We can sit here all night and blame each other, or we can do something."

"Great. What do you suggest?"

"Can't you call your superiors? Surely they can pull some federal strings."

He leaned his forehead against the steering wheel. "While you were up on the porch insulting the judge, I got a call over the radio." He nodded toward the gear below the dashboard. "Officially I've been taken off this case."

"What?"

"The DEA—" He must have realized who he was talking to, so he spelled it out completely. "The Drug Enforcement Agency has our ranch under surveillance.

Illegal animals coming in, illegal drugs going out. Their case takes priority over ours."

"Please tell me they've scheduled a drug bust before daybreak."

He shook his head. "I have no idea. I've just been ordered not to screw up their sting."

We sat in silence, staring ahead at a road leading nowhere.

"Wait a minute," I said. A glimmer of hope made my head turn toward Jake. "Judge Ryder mentioned a sheriff. Maybe he'll help us."

"Yeah, right. Like maybe he's not part of the good-ole-boy network. Not everybody loves animals, Caroline. Besides, like I told you, I'm off the case."

"Let's try the sheriff. Drive."

37

SPRINGS SQUEALED AS THE SHERIFF LEANED FORWARD IN the steno chair behind his desk. He didn't look happy to have company on Saturday night. He quickly slipped the paperback he was reading into a desk drawer. But not so quick I didn't see it. It was a romance novel.

He listened to our story, then sat back and put his feet up on his desk. "So what you're saying is, you want me to ride shotgun for you."

"We need to get onto the ranch and stop this hunt before it's too late," I said.

Jake sat slumped in a folding chair. He had let me do most of the talking. He seemed reluctant to even be here. It was probably a male thing. One man having to ask another man's help. Either that or he'd just plain given up.

The sheriff stared at the ceiling, his hands behind his head. "Well, now, I have to think about that." About thirty, he had a receding hairline. But he also had a barrel chest that looked like it could withstand a battering ram. His biceps bulged under the rolled sleeves of his shirt. He reached over and took a swig from a bottle of pineapple-banana juice as he compared the drawings in my sketchbook with the photos of Kiara. "That is one beautiful cat. You say this drawin' is . . . anatomically correct?"

I nodded. "You can see that the stripe pattern in the photos and the drawings is identical."

"Yeah, you're quite the artist." He tossed my sketchbook down on his desk. "Speaking of anatomically correct, Clayton Hendrick's got a bull you wouldn't believe. That'd be worth a sketch or two, I can tell ya."

I pinched the smile from my lips. "So can you help us, Sheriff?"

He scratched his cheek. "You say some pretty heavy hitters are going to this hunt?"

"From all over the country, isn't that right, Jake?"

He stared at the floor. "That's right."

I fingered the nameplate on the desk: Sheriff Otis Paxton.

"I'm more interested in the local talent," Otis said. The chair groaned as he leaned forward. "I can't go in there without the benefit of a court order."

With the cuff of my blouse, I polished the fingerprints off his bronze nameplate. "We need someone with the guts to take action, Sheriff. To do the right thing." I remembered the paperback in his drawer. "I guess you could say we need a hero."

His lips curved into a smile. "You wouldn't be trying to flatter me now, would'ja?"

"I can only go by my instinct, Sheriff. You strike me as a man of strong . . . principle." I made sure he saw the admiration on my face as my eyes rested on his biceps. Was I really stooping to these tactics?

Otis stroked his chin. "So ole Maybelline didn't seem moved by your case."

"She's a hard woman, Sheriff. No compassion."

"See now, that was your first mistake. If you lived in this here county, you'd know that Maybelline Ryder loves to hunt. You'd also know she ain't about to go after Ray Don Austin. Not with her comin' up for re-election this November."

"You're our only hope," I said. I saw Jake roll his eyes.

Otis swiveled his chair around and studied the calendar on the wall. It pictured a herd of wild horses, their manes swept by the wind. "Say, do you do paintin's on saws?" He spun around, his dark eyes locked on mine.

"You mean a . . ." I made a back-and-forth cutting action with my hand. ". . . saw?"

"Yeah, you know, a paintin' on the blade that you hang up on the wall. You do that kinda thing?"

"No . . . no . . . I haven't, but . . ."

He turned back to the photo of wild horses. "Maybe you could do one of those for me. One with a Mustang on it. Yeah, I'd like that real fine."

"Well . . . I could try. Sounds like you love animals." I made a face at Jake.

Otis's chair squealed as he turned back to me. "Yessiree, had me one years back. I'd fly across the hills with that little Mustang."

"Like one of those?" I pointed to the wall calendar featuring wild horses. "The sorrel?"

"Sorrel? Hell, no. She was fire-engine red. '65 convertible. When they still gave a car an engine. Now I ride around in a Taw-rus. What kinda name's that? County bought it. But I sure do miss that little Mustang." He sat back with his hands behind his head and stared once again at the ceiling.

Jake made a face back at me. I sagged in my chair.

The sheriff picked up his rifle and sighted down the

barrel. "But if there's one thing that gives me more pleasure than cars, it's hunting politicians. Hunting 'em down and nailing 'em. Wouldn't supprahze me a-tall if ole Maybelline was planning on doing a little hunting in the morning herself."

He picked up the phone and dialed. "Harv, sorry to wake you, this is Paxton. Think I found a way for you to squirrel that judicial seat away from Maybelline."

38

BY 5 A.M. THE BLAZER WAS PASSING THROUGH TEXAS hill country, headed for the ranch. The taillights of the sheriff's car ahead glowed in the predawn darkness.

"I could sure use a cup of coffee," I said.

Jake sat hunched over the wheel. "If you'd gone back to the motel like I'd asked, you could have gotten a cup. This could be dangerous."

"I've come too far to miss this."

The headlights of a large van behind us flooded the inside of our car. The San Antonio Zoo had provided a vehicle with steel-reinforced sides. A zookeeper and a vet sat in its front seat. A deputy's car brought up the rear.

"Everything's going to go okay, isn't it?" I said. "I mean, we're going to get Kiara?"

"That's the plan."

"Guess my charm worked on the sheriff after all?"

"If you'd laid it on any thicker, I would've had to get my hip boots out of the back."

"We're here, aren't we?"

"Don't kid yourself. Sheriff Otis Paxton has his own reasons for being here."

"Sounds like he and Maybelline have gone a few rounds before."

His face was grim. "Let's just hope his agenda doesn't interfere with ours."

The Blazer bounced as we turned off the main road. "Turn Back Now" broke up the monotony of the "No Trespassing" signs nailed on every other fence post. Gravel crunched under the Blazer's tires.

"Lousy road," Jake said.

"Sheriff Paxton said he knew the best way to go in."

"Maybe. I just hadn't planned on eating his dust all the way."

So that's why Jake had acquired the attitude. The Jake Gavin Show had become the Otis Paxton Special.

"I know you're putting your job on the line," I said, "going against orders. But everyone will be very grateful."

"Not Rob Bennett."

In all my concern for Kiara, I hadn't thought much about the apprehension of Rob Bennett. Now it struck home. Rob was also Tony's murderer.

The cortege came to an abrupt halt. I leaned out the window, straining to see what had stopped us. A heavy wooden fence and gate about six feet tall, topped with spirals of barbed wire, crossed the rutted road ahead.

Jake jumped out of the Blazer and strode to the barricade, where the sheriff waited. "I thought you said we were going in the back door."

"This here is the back. FBI's got the north and west gates staked out. This access road is via the adjoining ranch." Next to Jake, Otis was short. He had looked taller sitting down.

The two men surveyed the barrier. Technology had caught up with the Old West. On the gate, instead of a padlock, was a telephone keypad and instructions.

"Lookahere. Enter security code," the sheriff read out

loud. "Hell! Stand back." He pulled his gun. I covered my ears as he entered his code in two blasts. Sparks lit up the faintly lightening sky. The gate's computerized lock mechanism whined twice before it hit the dust.

A deputy opened both sides of the gate, while the sheriff holstered his gun, tipped his hat at me, and swaggered back to the lead car.

Jake returned to the Blazer, slamming the door. "Show-off," he muttered.

One by one the entourage crossed into the forbidden zone. We waited as the deputy in the last car closed the gate behind us.

"I'll watch for Kiara," I said.

"I doubt she's out strolling around. It's called a canned hunt for a reason. The animals aren't released until the hunters have them in their sights. Sometimes they're shot before they even leave the cage."

I shuddered in the morning chill. "Where do you think Kiara is?"

"When I took the photos from the ridge above the highway, she was in a pen on the northwest side of the ranch."

Along the sides of the road, the silhouettes of scraggly bushes took shape as the first glimmer of daylight sneaked over our shoulders. It caught the little blond hairs on Jake's fingers gripping the top of the steering wheel. A four-legged something darted across the road.

I jerked to attention. "Was that an addax antelope?" The animal bounded over a hill and out of sight. "That didn't look canned to me."

"They're called Texotics. Home-grown exotic wildlife." He motioned to my right. "What's that? Binoculars are under the seat."

I groped under the seat, unwound the strap from the glasses, and held them up. "Looks like an axis deer," I said, sighting its huge velvety antlers and the flecks of white, like snow flakes, on its back. "This place is crawling with endangered species. There's an oryx and an aoudad sheep too." I lowered the binoculars.

"I'm impressed," Jake said. "You know a lot about animals."

"I know what they look like," I said. "That's the extent of my knowledge."

"There. Food troughs." Jake pointed past me. "All the hunters have to do is wait until a hungry deer comes along. My dad took me hunting as a kid, but at least it was a fair fight."

"Until deer carry rifles, you'll forgive me if I fail to see how it's ever a fair fight."

"If you were hungry enough, you'd understand."

"I'll never understand how someone can enjoy killing another living creature."

"I don't see you eating just bunny food."

He'd hit a sore point. "I don't eat as much meat as I used to. But I haven't been able to stick to being a vegetarian. Someday."

"Yeah, right. About the time you give up leather shoes."

I brandished my canvas sneaker in the air.

"You were wearing leather pumps the day I met you and don't deny it. I'm all for protecting endangered species or I wouldn't have this job. But if it's a choice between man and beast, man's gotta come first."

I crossed my arms. "Just drive." Maybe we weren't as perfect for each other as I had thought back in that motel room.

We turned a bend in the road. I squinted at another yellow sign. Bullet holes had turned it into Swiss cheese, but I made out the words: "Private—Keep Away." The sign echoed the state of our relationship. We knew enough about each other to be attracted, but now as familiarity increased, so would awareness of each other's faults. I glanced at Jake, his lips clamped shut. I sat with arms crossed. We didn't need a sign. Our body language said it all. Keep away.

I flicked on the radio, and ran through the stations. I stopped on Patty Loveless singing "You Don't Even Know Who I Am." A deafening thunderclap ripped the air. The Blazer's back window crackled. Something whizzed past my cheek with a rush of air. The radio erupted in a flurry of sparks as the object embedded itself in the dashboard.

Jake hit the brakes and pulled me across the front seat, covering me with his own body. "Damn it! This is exactly why I didn't want to bring you."

His weight knocked the wind out of me. Two more shots rang out.

"Jesus Christ!" the sheriff yelled from the car ahead.

My sentiments exactly. A scratching noise like a cat digging in a litter box told me someone was crawling across gravel. A car door slammed, followed by an amplified voice.

"This here's the county sheriff. Throw down your rifle. Come out with your hands on your head."

Jake eased the door open and slid out. He motioned for me to stay down.

A voice came from a distance. "Sorry, Sheriff. I thought you was a bird. Saw something moving and I fired."

I assumed it was safe to sit up. A young guy in camouflage-colored clothes emerged from the bushes and wove toward us with his arms up in the air. A bottle leaned out of his pocket. A deputy ran to retrieve the man's rifle.

"You gotta brain smaller'n a bug's asshole!" the sheriff shouted, gun drawn. The lawman's hat was conspicuously missing, his black hair plastered to his sweaty, tanned forehead. "You could'a killed someone."

"Nah, I never hit nothing."

The sheriff pulled the whiskey from the man's pocket and hooked his gun under the man's chin. "Anybody ever teach you it ain't real smart to use a sheriff's hat for target practice? Specially if'n the sheriff's head's still in it?"

Fear was apparent on the man's face. His left inner pant leg darkened with moisture from his thigh to his shoe. "Christ, Sheriff, I swear I was aimin' at—"

"It's lucky you *was* aimin' or you just mighta killed me." He twisted the cap off the booze and poured it down the guy's dry leg. "Now at least your pants legs match."

The deputies hooted, but I was more nervous than amused. Had the hunt for Kiara already started?

I stepped forward. "How much farther's the main house?"

"Just up the road," the man answered.

A deputy handed the sheriff his hat.

"Lookahere. Ruined. Brand-new hat. Any more hot-shots out here?"

"Don't know 'bout anybody else. I'm an early bird."

"Yeah, Wild Turkey!" The sheriff drop-kicked the empty liquor bottle into the rapidly lightening sky. "Well, you tell your friends Sheriff Otis Paxton has offi-cially closed huntin' season. Understand?" He dragged the man over to a tree and handcuffed him to a limb. "When your britches dry out, we'll be back for you. You're gonna buy me a new hat."

The lawmen snickered as they returned to their cars. Among them were two civilians I hadn't noticed before. One had a camera, the other had a notebook. Reporters. Jake got in and slammed the door of the Blazer. Motors ground. The procession of cars moved on. Just when I thought the drive would never end, I saw the house. We parked in front of the steps of the sprawling frame structure. The smell of coffee, steak and eggs drifted across the yard. Anxious faces peeked through the cur-tains of what must have been the dining room.

A tall man of average build, except for his protruding abdomen, descended the weathered steps. Over one eye he wore a patch. I had seen him before. I ran faces through the catalog in my mind, trying to pinpoint the surroundings in which I'd seen him. Tony's funeral.

"Come to join us for breakfast, Sheriff?" he asked. "No need to break in the back door."

Otis hooked his thumbs in his belt loops. "I hate to seem unneighborly, but this here fella says something lower'n a rattlesnake's belly is going on here. And knowin' you, Ray . . ." Otis spat on the ground. ". . . I hadda believe the fella."

Several men and a couple of women dressed in camouflage gathered on the porch. With the rising sun behind the house, they stood in shadow. South American revolutions have been started with fewer munitions than I saw lined up on the porch. Some looked like machine guns. Deer hides hung over the railing. I identified the various species from their unique color markings. A chill went up my spine, like I was at a morgue to ID a friend.

Jake stepped forward. "You the owner?"

"Ray Don Austin. Didn't catch your name."

Jake flashed his badge. "Special Agent Gavin, Fish and Wildlife. We have reason to believe you are in illegal possession of a zoo animal." He looked around.

"I got a lot of animals here, and every one is my private property."

"After you show us where the tiger is, I'm gonna do you the favor of checking every last animal on this ranch. None of them better have zoo numbers or markings on them. While I'm doing that, the sheriff can be checking the legality of all these firearms."

"Sheriff, are you going to let this outsider harass me this way? Aren't you coming up for reelection this fall?"

Sheriff Paxton strode over. "As I recall, Ray, you supported my opponent last election. But I won anyhoo, didn't I?"

Enough of this male posturing. I poked Jake. "Let's find Kiara."

Jake was in the rancher's face. "Where's the tiger?"

"Tiger? I don't know what you're talking about. You have a warrant, Agent What'sit?"

Otis stepped forward. "He has *me*, Ray. I got the warrant."

"Sheriff, you know we only have legal hunts here. I've got nothing to hide."

"Then you won't mind if we take a look around," Jake said.

"We've got special guests here this weekend, sheriff. You'd be imposing."

"Would we now?" The sheriff wandered toward the ranch house and put a shiny boot on the porch. He peered into the window. "Well now, if it ain't May-belline Ryder. My, my, my. Don't be shy." He motioned for the reporter to step forward. "Come on out from behind that curtain, Maybelline, and have your picture taken. In fact, let's get us a group picture with Senator Plainfield there standing next to ya."

39

"WELL I'LL BE DAMNED." THE SHERIFF SPAT ON THE ground.

"Like I told you, we aren't holding any tiger." Ray Don stood in front of the animal enclosure where Jake had last seen Kiara. The large pen—a makeshift corral with chain link fencing stretched across the top—sat conspicuously empty.

"What's this then?" I pointed at the bite marks and scratches on the feeble plywood sides of the enclosure indicating Kiara hadn't liked her accommodations. Blood congealed on the dusty earth inside the pen.

My pulse quickened. Was Kiara injured? Jake had said hunters sometimes shot the animals before they left their cages.

Jake kicked a piece of wood aside. "You had some-body come out here to turn her loose, didn't you?"

Ray Don's back stiffened. "You seem to know so much, you tell me."

"Where is she?" My wobbly voice betrayed my fears. "We're wasting time. Kiara could be injured!"

Ray Don's mouth wore a smirk. "You take orders from a girl, Agent?"

A vein throbbed on Jake's forehead. "Cut the crap, Austin. Up to now you'll probably only be slapped with a fine for violating the Lacey Act and lack of proper USDA permits. But if that loose tiger kills anyone, we're talking manslaughter."

"Awright, awright. I can show you a map back at the house," he said reluctantly.

"Here's a pencil, you *draw* me a map. Caroline, give him your sketchbook." The vein on Jake's forehead started doing the rumba.

I handed my sketchbook to the rancher. His one good eye stared at the blank page like I'd just handed him a pop quiz he hadn't studied for.

"Draw," Jake said, as though facing off in a gunfight.

The rancher used his belly as a drawing table, laying the sketchbook across it. The pencil scratched across the paper. When it was completed, Jake and the sheriff agreed to split up. The sheriff would take the southern route. The deputy would cover the west. Since we'd already covered much of the ranch's eastern side, Jake and I would search the northern edge of the ranch, bounded by the San Marcos River. The zoo men would wait for our radio call.

Jake turned the key in the ignition and the engine growled.

"I've seen Ray Don before," I said. "At the Chirico home after Tony's funeral. He was talking to Miles Crandall. Could Miles be involved in something this ugly?"

"Wouldn't surprise me. Miles is pretty mercenary. It'll all come out now."

My thoughts returned to the problem at hand. "What if Kiara's been shot?"

Jake was silent. Although the morning had turned into a bright and sunny day, gloom descended on me. I hoped we wouldn't be too late.

"Trees over that way," I said, pointing northwest. "Let's try there." I had no idea which way Kiara might have headed, but had it been me, I would have looked for cover.

Our car rumbled over the hilly terrain, the wheels kicking up dust. I searched for any sign of her, the field glasses hitting my face with every bump, but came up with nothing. Abruptly the road smoothed out. I lowered the binoculars. "What's this?"

"Appears to be an airstrip," Jake answered. At the end of the runway, bordered by trees, several Lear jets waited. "Perfect setup for drug running. Easy in, easy out."

I raised the binoculars again. Among the trees, live deer stood frozen like mannequins. "Still no sight of her." According to Ray Don's map, the river lay just over the rise ahead. "Let's try the river next."

"One thing's for sure. With all the game, at least she won't have starved to death."

"Kiara's never had to hunt," I said.

"Her instincts may still be there." Jake gunned the motor. Leaving the pavement, the wheels dug in. He skirted the trees and guided the Blazer up the incline. As we reached the top of the hill, the expanse of water below came into view. The river widened into a small lake. I spotted Kiara through the glasses. "There she is! With—" About fifty feet away from us Kiara guarded a lumpy tan hide protruding partly from the lake's edge nearest us. My voice dropped. "—with a deer." The predator/prey relationship might be a fundamental fact of nature, but I still couldn't watch those parts of the National Geographic specials.

Jake grabbed the radio to contact the men from the zoo. Through the field glasses I studied Kiara, poised and motionless over her kill. Her mouth hung open, lower incisors exposed. I scanned the length of her. Blood streaked her flank. "I think she may be hurt."

"Give me the glasses," Jake said.

I handed them over. Without binoculars my perspective widened. The white tiger's proud silhouette, magnified on the ground in the long shadows of early morning, stood against a backdrop that could only have been painted by Monet. Dewy coral and white flowers, nestled atop lily pads, dotted the water. Sunlight glittered across its surface, bringing out pink, green, and purple highlights among the blue. In a grove of trees to the east, birds called to one another, flitting from tree to tree. For a moment the beauty of the scene almost made me forget the awful path that had led us here.

Kiara had not moved. Rather than appearing alert and wary of us, she seemed almost lethargic. I heard the zoo van pull up behind us. The two men hurried up the rise to where Jake and I waited. They reminded me of Abbott and Costello, except the tall thin guy was black.

The shorter, plump man readied his rifle. "We need to nail her in one shot."

"Why's that?" I asked.

"Chemical restraint is tricky with white tigers. Weak livers," the tall man said. "They can't always metabolize the anesthetic. Could go into shock."

The short man steadied his rifle by resting it on the Blazer's hood. "She may panic if she spots the gun." He took time to line up his target carefully.

Kiara took several steps backward, then turned around, like she might make a break for it. Before he could get the shot off, a blast of gunfire ripped through the silence. Birds' wings beat the air. A divot of earth at Kiara's feet exploded into her face. She plunged into the lake and headed for the far bank.

From a clump of trees a man's voice shouted, "No way, José." A second shot thundered through the atmosphere.

I pivoted toward the trees. Another explosion sent me running toward the thicket.

Behind me Jake's voice split the air. "Caroline, don't be crazy!"

"You maniac!" I shouted. "Shoot that tiger and I'll—" What was I going to do?

Another blast tore off a tree limb. Its leaves fluttered in the air until it thudded lifelessly to the ground.

My feet pounded across the dry earth. "Stop it, you idiot!" I turned to make sure Kiara was okay. She had crossed the river and was bounding up the other bank. With my eyes locked on Kiara I ripped into the stand of trees. My foot caught on some underbrush. I landed on my chin, sending my lower incisors into my upper lip. I tasted blood on my teeth. The hunter's derisive laugh sent me flying back to my feet.

If I hadn't tripped over the fallen limb, it might not have occurred to me to pick it up. I struggled with its weight. In the tree above me the hunter, dressed more for combat than sport, straddled an equally large limb. With his rifle cradled in a forked branch, he eyed the telescopic sight. I jabbed the tree limb at him, catching him in the thigh.

"Hey!" He kicked back at me. "What the hell's the matter with you?" The man's lower jaw jutted out as he shouted. His face was scarlet behind his glasses. "Want her for yourself, huh? Well, you and your friends aren't gonna rob me of my kill!" Shouts filled the air. I heard the Blazer's engine and a splash of water. The hunter shifted until he found a sight line through the trees. "I didn't fork out good money to bag a chipmunk." He raised the rifle.

I rammed the jagged edge of the tree limb upward, throwing my full weight behind it. I shunted the rifle from his hands, but not before it exploded again. The gun careened sideways, then came to rest in another tree, forming a bridge between two branches. I glanced away to check Kiara, but the trees were too thick.

A brand new hunting boot kicked out at me. "Wait'll I get ahold of my gun!"

I stabbed him again, harder this time. The man swore and tried to grab hold of the limb. I swung it away. I caught his pant leg with the broken side of the limb and scraped its serrated edge up this calf. He howled like a coyote. Blood appeared on his shin. My arms ached under the weight of the huge chunk of wood. I was losing control of the branch. He reached down and grabbed the limb. The rough bark shredded my palms as he pulled the heavy branch from my hands and threw it at me. I slipped on the cartridge cases covering the ground and fell to my knees. The limb sailed over my head.

"I'm gonna blow your fuckin' head off!" With both hands he gripped his leg in agony.

I had to get to the rifle before he did. I scrambled to my feet. The middle-aged man groaned as he lifted his battered leg over the branch he straddled. It was just long enough for me to dash to the other tree where the gun rested. I hadn't climbed a tree since the summer my father died, but it had to be like riding a bicycle. *I can do this.*

I leaped for the first branch. My scraped palms stung as I pulled myself up. The hunter, now on the ground, breathed heavily as he crashed through the undergrowth. I swung myself up into a standing position on the branch. A thick, liver-spotted hand grabbed for my ankle. I started to slip, then found a foothold. I glanced over my shoulder. My foot was firmly planted on his forehead. I pushed off, using every muscle to pull myself up to the next higher branch. My tennis shoe came off in his hand. I stretched forward. The rifle was within inches of my grasp. He jumped up and clawed the flesh on my bare ankle. I kicked backward and struck him on the side of the head as he simultaneously—and quite considerately—leaped up at me.

Swearing, he clawed at the ground in search of his glasses.

I grabbed the rifle and turned it on him. "Back off, slimeball!"

He squinted at me. "You don't know how to shoot that," he sneered.

"Oh, yeah? Well . . . I grew up in Wisconsin. My father took me hunting all the time. But at least we ate the deer and it was a fair fight!" The dialogue came easy. I had heard it from Jake's lips less than an hour ago. I slapped the rifle butt. "Course I haven't used one of these babies lately, and I'd hate for it to just go off in my hands. You know what I mean?"

He tried to read my eyes, but he wasn't reading anything without his glasses.

I pictured the Rambo poster with my face superimposed over Stallone's. "Now back off while I get down."

He backed slowly. I sat on the branch and lowered myself to the next limb. The stocky man shifted his weight.

"Don't even think about it!" I growled. "Turn around and start walking out."

Like a gymnast, I jumped down from the lowest limb. A sharp pain stabbed my ankle as it twisted under me.

The man looked over his shoulder at me.

"Get moving or you're dead meat." I picked up my tennis shoe and limped out of the clump of trees behind him. I heard shouts from the the river. My eyes searched for Kiara. Then I saw her, zigzagging back and forth across the riverbank.

Jake used the Blazer to steer Kiara back toward the river, so the zookeeper could get off a shot. The transmission groaned as he whipped back and forth, blocking her escape. She appeared to be tiring. Finally she headed back to the river's edge. The keeper raised his tranquilizer gun and fired.

Kiara crossed the water again, heading for the spot where we'd first seen her. She stumbled through the lily pads and fell across her prey's lumpy tan hide.

Sure that she had been mortally wounded, I screamed. Abandoning my prisoner of war, I ran as fast as I could toward the riverbank, wincing in pain with each step. Ahead of me, the zoo men approached Kiara warily. As they neared her body, they motioned rapidly for Jake to join them. From twenty feet I could see Kiara's sides heaving, so I knew she wasn't dead. Using the rifle as a crutch, I hobbled as quickly as I could down to the riverbank.

While the zoo men concentrated on Kiara, Jake appeared to be more interested in the deer she'd killed. Maybe it was another zoo animal, and he was checking for the number tattoo.

I approached Kiara's recumbent form. The tan hide beneath her came into sharper focus. Kiara's catch wasn't a deer at all, but wore a pair of khaki pants and a wild Hawaiian shirt.

40

I STARED DOWN THROUGH THE SHALLOW WATER AT THE bloody chest of Rob Bennett, D.D.V.M.—Deceased Doctor of Veterinary Medicine. His upper torso lay submerged, the neck at an odd angle to his body. Kiara lay across his legs. Like a surreal painting, red water swirled around bluish flesh.

"Too late to help him." The tall black man attending to Kiara wiped his sleeve across his brow. "But you two can give us a hand with her. We have fifteen, twenty minutes tops."

Jake and I helped the men move Kiara off the body and onto a huge stretcher. Her eyes were fixed, and her tongue dangled from her mouth.

"Are you sure she's okay?" I asked. "Her eyes are open."

"She's fine. The cornea will stay moist," the man said. "No problem."

I knelt next to her on the ground and ran my hand gently along her heaving side. "It's okay, Kiara. You're safe."

The tall African-American man readied a needle, squirting the tip.

"What's that?" I asked.

"Atropine. Controls the drooling, protects her heart."

"I don't like the way she's breathing, Doc," the short man said.

"Better get the doxapram out of the truck, and have the oxygen unit ready."

"What's wrong?" I asked.

"I gave her a minimum dose of the tranquilizer," the vet said, "but she's not breathing right. Might have been too much for her."

Kiara's labored breathing continued. Stroking her side, I inhaled and exhaled in time with her. "Hang in there, Kiara, please." Her coat felt more like that of a large dog—bristly and coarse—than that of a feline.

When the stocky man returned from the van, the vet quickly filled another syringe and injected it into Kiara's foreleg. "This'll give her breathing a kick in the pants."

I continued to pet her. She soon began to breath regularly again. So did I. "You'll be okay now." I stroked her head. Her ear flicked.

"We'll watch her. If I need to, I can give her something to boost her circulation, too, which'll help her breathing even more." The vet smiled encouragingly at me.

I felt confident Kiara was at last in capable and caring hands.

Trailing a wake of dust, the sheriff's car tore across the landscape and came to an abrupt halt beside us. Otis sprang out. "You'll never guess what I found!"

Kneeling beside me, Jake said, "You'll never guess what we found." He directed Otis's view to the corpse at the river's edge.

The sheriff slammed the car door and approached the body. "Holy shit! How come nobody radioed me? I heard the gunfire, but I was on the other side of the river. He dead?" Careful not to get his hand-tooled boots wet, Otis squatted and felt Rob's neck for a pulse.

Even I could tell there was no blood coursing beneath that blue flesh, once so tan and healthy-looking. The vibrant colors of Rob's shirt—now in shreds—had faded together into a swirl of Day-Glo watercolor.

Jake got up and joined the sheriff beside the body. I stayed at Kiara's side, but listened as they talked.

"This that guy you told me about? Bennett?" Otis asked.

Jake nodded.

With a pencil the sheriff parted the ripped panels of Rob's shirt. He gave a two-note whistle. "Messy. His chest is shredded." Otis stood and shined the top of each boot on the opposite pant leg. "That tiger got him good, huh?"

"Looks that way." Jake stood up and dusted his hands.

"I better call it in. Get the coroner out here." Otis turned toward his car. His eyes locked on the rifle on the ground next to me. He walked over to me and picked it up. "Where'd this come from?"

"I took it away from that guy." I nodded over my shoulder to the general area I'd left the hunter.

"What guy?"

I stood up and turned around. He was long gone.

Otis hitched up his pants and strode back to his car. Leaning through the window, he stood on tiptoe to reach the radio. He told the dispatcher to send out the coroner right away and then returned to us. "Found his truck. It was loaded with industrial pipe packed full of crack. Seems like Bennett here was gonna take a load of cocaine back to the Windy City with him. Yessir, this place is gonna be crawling with Feds any minute. The FBI's madder 'n hell. Seems I stole their smoke." He chuckled. "You see, Ray Don knew the ranch was under surveillance and that the Feds were gonna bust him tonight, so he moved up his schedule. Two plane loads landed early this morning on that airstrip. By this evening all that crack would'a been gone, on its way to points north. Wouldn't have been for us, they would have given the Feds the slip." He slapped his leg. "Hell, I knew what was going on long before those dudes entered the picture. Only right I get credit for the bust."

The zoo men were anxious to load Kiara while she was still sedated. All five of us pitched in to lift the stretcher. We carried Kiara to the reinforced van and lay her on the straw-covered floor. One of the men closed the doors and slipped the locking bar into place.

Jake reached into his car and handed me my Stetson. "You ride back to the zoo with them. You can take a cab from there to the airport. I'll be back in a few days."

The sun was beating down on my head, so I put the hat on. "You'll let me know what happens here?" I knew I had to get back to work.

"Of course. But, uh," he glanced under the brim, "keep it under your hat, okay? The authorities back home will pick up the investigation on that end. Talk to them only. If anybody else asks, you don't know anything, okay?" He touched my arm. "Look, I'm sorry if I've been rude. I was caught between a rock and a hard place. I didn't mean to take it out on you. Thanks for the help."

Wondering if Jake would lose his job over disobeying orders, I crawled into the van between the two zoo men. On the ride back we finally introduced ourselves. The vet's name was Tom. The marksman behind the wheel was Howie.

"We'll keep Kiara under observation at San Antonio Zoo, don't worry," Tom said.

"Until she's strong enough to make the trip home," I said.

Howie looked at Tom.

Tom looked at me. "Don't count on that."

"Why not?"

"If she's killed a human, she won't be welcome in any zoo."

41

THE LATE NEWS REPORTS SIZZLED WITH THE SCANDAL. They were calling me a hero, but hearing my name uttered on television made me feel more like a criminal. I'd disconnected my phone after the first reporter contacted me after I walked in the door about 8 P.M.

On one station, protesters from CCATZ and other activists marched around the gates of Fox Valley Zoo. Vince Chirico, it was reported, had been taken in for questioning. File footage of Kiara followed. Slumped in my chair, I flipped to another channel. Claudia Baxter, spokesperson for the zoo's board of directors, was properly indignant at what had happened and said the board would "initiate a full internal investigation up to and including the highest administrative level." Yolanda Ramirez reassured the public that this unfortunate event was "a wake-up call to zoos everywhere" and would "happily result in a system wide reevaluation of surplus animal policies." Marcia Wilhelm called for the immediate resignation of Miles Crandall, who was, for once in his life, unavailable for comment.

My body wanted desperately to sleep, but my mind wouldn't shut off. I lay inert in bed, flipping channels, watching TV but seeing nothing. I channel-surfed until I felt the first waves of motion sickness.

I reconnected the phone to try to reach my mother. This was national news, and she might be worried. There was no answer. Probably out roller blading with Roberto. I had reached my grandmother earlier and assured her I was okay. I longed to call Barb or Ellen, but I had promised Jake I'd keep my mouth shut. Besides, they'd probably disconnected their phones, too. At midnight I turned out the lights and listened to Elvis records with the kitten. She especially liked the "caught in a trap" refrain of "Suspicious Minds." She jumped onto my chest and purred contentedly while I stroked her silky white fur.

I related the events of the last twenty-four hours. Her green eyes glowed as I began the tale of Kiara's rescue. But soon she yawned with boredom, apparently uninterested in anything beyond the scope of her private kingdom. Just as we were both dozing off, the phone rang. I'd forgotten to disconnect it again after trying to reach my mother. Needle-like claws dug into my flesh, and Spooks, as I'd begun to call her, launched herself off my chest.

I answered the phone. It was Jake, still in Texas.

"I've got good news and bad news," he said.

I propped myself up in bed. "Good news first."

"The zoo vets here have examined Kiara. Found her dehydrated, but otherwise in excellent condition. No sign of a liver problem. Looks like Rob Bennett falsified test results."

"Great! When will she be coming back to Fox Valley?"

"That's the bad news."

"What do you mean? Kiara didn't kill Rob, did she?"

"No. Rob died of a gunshot wound, approximately thirty minutes before we found him. Kiara must have ripped open his chest after he died. Lab tests identified human flesh on her claws. Strange thing is, the bloody pulp on her teeth was from a horse, not a human."

"A horse? We didn't see any dead horses."

"Maybe Rob had just fed her."

"Just before she was to be killed?"

"Maybe to make her lethargic, put up less of a fight."

"Who do they think shot Rob?"

"Drug runners aren't nice people. Rob Bennett could have been the weak link in the chain and they decided to eliminate him. Our friend Ray Don is in federal custody."

"So when will Kiara be returned?"

"She may not be coming back."

42

"I'M JUST SO GRATEFUL TO YOU." BARB SAID, HUGGING me.

The chants of protesters outside the zoo gates filtered through the window in her office. Animal rights people were going nuts. They'd gotten a temporary injunction to keep the San Antonio Zoo from returning Kiara to Fox Valley.

"I tried to reach you in New Orleans," I said, "when all this started."

She motioned for me to sit on the beige couch as she stood behind her desk. "I know. I feel awful about not being here to prevent what happened." She bent a paper clip back and forth. "When I heard that Kiara was euthanized, I was horrified. And now to find out that there was nothing seriously wrong with her in the first place . . . I shudder to think how many other animals . . ." The paper clip snapped in two.

"Some people will do terrible things for money." Some people will just take a job they hate.

"I knew Rob was in debt, but I never suspected . . ."

How could I be so wrong? Not only did he kill animals, but Uncle Tony, Gino. And now Vince is in custody."

"Well, one of his trucks was involved in the transport."

"It had to be stolen. Vince couldn't be involved." Worry lines popped out again all over her face. "He's brought in so much support for the zoo through his business contacts."

"Like the ones in Texas? The more money the zoo has, the more it can spend on construction."

She shook her head. "Vince wouldn't be involved in drug running."

"How could all this happen, Barb?"

She slowly lowered herself to her chair. "I blame myself. I believed Kiara was suffering and that her condition was terminal." Her hands met in a praying position. "How could I be so stupid?"

"You were lied to." I had never seen Barb this insecure. "It's not your fault. Miles signed the euthanization papers, not you. As I recall, he said he'd take full responsibility."

Barb shook her head. "Miles did what he thought best. As much as I dislike him, he's not a monster."

"At Tony's funeral Miles was talking to some men. Remember? I recognized one as the owner of that game ranch. Miles has a lot to answer for."

"You don't understand. The tests Rob showed us were very convincing."

I remembered the taped conversation I'd heard in Marcia Wilhelm's van. "But you weren't convinced. You ordered new tests." Fortunately she didn't ask me how I knew. "Where are those results?"

"Destroyed, I'm afraid, while I was away. That's the first thing I looked for when I got back. Whatever is left I've turned over to the authorities. The worst part of all this is Rob may have sold dozens of animals without our knowledge. My God, do you realize he wasn't even licensed to practice in Illinois? And that no one checked? We've been asleep at the wheel."

"But it's not up to you."

"No. It's up to the board. They're meeting down the hall right now. If they ask for my resignation—"

"You've worked too hard to give it all up."

She sighed. "I've spent the last ten years trying to establish Fox Valley as a reputable zoo. And now the rug's been pulled out from under me. But I have only myself to blame." The phone rang. "Sorry, but I better deal with this call." She pushed the lit button, and I waved good-bye.

The narrow hallway of the administration building was choked with people. The zoo board must be taking a recess. I spotted Claudia Baxter's platinum hair in their midst. She waded toward me, a coffee cup in her jeweled porcelain hand.

"How nice to see you," she said in a tone that indicated it was anything but. "I guess we owe all this to you! Is it true you figured it all out from clues Tony left in the mural?" Her disdainful eyes surveyed my hair.

"It was a lucky break."

"You're far too modest," she said. "Enjoy your fifteen minutes of fame while you can."

"It wasn't me all over the newscasts last night, making speeches and posturing. But you looked very photogenic."

She touched the side of her lacquered hair. "As chairwoman of the zoo board I had no choice. We're meeting now to discuss appropriate measures. And we've hired a new veterinarian—"

"Like you hired the last one?"

Her eyes narrowed. "—after thoroughly inspecting her credentials."

"What's going to happen to Miles and Barb?"

"Dr. Crandall has been censured. But unless official charges are brought against him, we have to honor our contract with him. Barbara DiGenova, on the other hand, is on salary. We may have to let her go."

"The perfect scapegoat."

"That's nonsense."

"Is it? With Barb out of the way, you could really run this zoo into the ground."

"You don't know what you're talking about." She turned away from me.

"You wouldn't have some personal stake in seeing this zoo shut down, would you? Like maybe some tidy little trust fund might revert to you?" She kept her back to me. "And where's Ben? Drawing up papers to avoid taxes on all that lovely money that would come your way?"

She spun around. "As a matter of fact, Ben is in Texas right now, working with a local attorney to try to reverse an injunction and allow us to bring Kiara home again. It's thanks to you she's in this predicament. We could have dealt with all this quietly."

"You're right. It would have been so much better if she had just been put to sleep and we had just shoved all this under the carpet."

She glanced at her watch.

"That's right. Hurry back to your meeting and make some more important decisions."

She turned stiffly.

"Oh, and Claud?"

She stopped in her tracks.

"Get a new hairdo."

At the end of the hallway beside the conference room door, I saw Ellen and grabbed the opportunity to talk with her. "I just heard Kiara may be home soon."

Ellen's blank face revealed not an ounce of joy. Through tight lips she said, "I'm glad she's okay, but as far as her return is concerned, I'm hoping San Antonio will just keep her."

"What? I thought you of all people would—"

"I don't want her here. And that's what I'm going to recommend when I go in there."

"But I thought you loved Kiara."

"I love her enough to realize this isn't the best place for her."

My mouth hung open. Was I hearing right? "You don't want Kiara back?"

"No. The way I feel now I'd like to see this zoo completely shut down. I'm sickened by what's gone on here."

"Rob's gone. It's over. People like you can make this place better."

Her face tightened. "You're just like Tony. Assuming you know what's best when you don't know anything. What gives you the right to make decisions about somebody else's life?" And then she was gone.

The conference room door closed in my face.

43

MURAL PAINTING OCCUPIED ME COMPLETELY FOR THE next few weeks. Everything else was put on hold, as I struggled to make up for lost time. Days had shortened with the approach of autumn, and with no artificial lighting in the exhibit, the hours in which I had to work were severely limited.

During painting breaks I tried to talk to Ellen, but she remained cool and distant, and I hesitated to invade her privacy further. Besides, my own problems were on the increase.

While the fire marshal conceded Rob's likely connection to my studio fire, the insurance company wrangled with me over compensation.

The Chirico family repeatedly threatened to fight the disposition of the estate. But Ben Rudolph assured me they had little grounds on which to base a claim. Nevertheless, I left everything in Tony's studio untouched. I didn't have time to deal with it, anyway.

With no further word from Jake, my only sources of new information were the zoo's grapevine and news reports.

Vince Chirico had admitted doing business at one time with Ray Don Austin, the owner of the ranch. But he said it concerned office building construction in Texas in the early eighties. He swore he knew nothing of the animal or drug sales. As to the truck, he claimed he had only loaned it to Rob, though why was unclear.

Miles Crandall contended he didn't meet Ray Don until being introduced at Tony's funeral. He saw the rancher as a hot prospect for contributions and nothing more. He claimed he had no idea that zoo animals had ended up at the game ranch. Furthermore, he said, the very idea of killing animals for pleasure appalled him. Remembering the huge pink fish carcass I'd seen mounted on his office wall, I couldn't help but question his sincerity. Although news editorials called for his resignation, he remained zoo director.

Barb was put on probation. The staff, quickly missing her steady hand, protested the decision so vehemently that the zoo board finally backed down. Nevertheless, Barb confided to me that she was preparing her résumé.

How Tony had found out about Rob and the Texas connection I'd never know. Claudia Baxter was at least right about Tony's passive-aggressive behavior. Instead of confronting Rob or going to the authorities directly, he'd decided to expose the scheme through the mural. The clues were all there—the tiger, the vet, the Texas hunting ranch.

Morale among the zoo staff remained low. I kept my spirits up by telling myself Kiara would be coming home soon, but as yet there was no confirmation. Further tests had revealed she did have a liver problem, but that her condition was due more to dietary than genetic factors. It seemed likely Rob had been responsible for her symptoms. She appeared to be doing well at the San Antonio Zoo, and her prognosis was good.

In her absence a male Siberian tiger named Yana arrived at Fox Valley in preparation for the opening. His chuffs, echoing from the holding area behind the wall on which I worked, both urged me on and kept me alert. How the zoo would explain the presence of a Siberian tiger in India I didn't know, but I was sure Miles or Yolanda would come up with an answer.

With the opening drawing near, exhibit designers and craftsmen worked feverishly around me. Men inspected last-minute modifications to the plumbing that sent a cascade of water over the gunite rocks along the walls to a deep trench that snaked through the exhibit's floor. I felt someone's eyes on my back and turned around. A pudgy man wearing a hard hat stared up at the mural from the floor.

I laid down my brushes. "Ben! I didn't even hear you come in."

"They t-t-told me I'd find you here."

"So what's up?" I unhitched my safety belt and walked over to the ladder.

"I've gotten the injunction overturned. K-K-Kiara's coming home as soon as transport can be arranged."

"That's great." I started to descend the ladder.

"Also, with all that's happened, the police reopened their investigation of Tony's death. You were right. They did f-f-find arsenic in him."

I missed the next step, grabbed the sides of the ladder and stared down at Ben.

"Not enough to kill him, mind you, but enough to make him dizzy. Looks like Rob Bennett saw the clues in the m-m-mural like you did and decided to get rid of Tony by mixing rat poison in with his paint. Just wanted you to know."

I continued my descent more carefully. We were both silent until my feet touched the ground.

"Then Rob must have known Tony pretty well," I said, walking over to him.

"Why's that?"

"He had to know Tony would ingest that paint by running his brush through his lips."

Ben shrugged. "He could have watched Tony paint."

"Maybe." I tapped my lips.

He took my arm and led me to a log. We both sat down. "I'm worried about you, Caroline. You've got to stop seeing conspiracies everywhere. It's over."

"Then why are there still so many unanswered questions?"

"Investigations take time, that's all. It'll all come out. Let the police do their job."

"I understand you represented Vince when the police questioned him."

"That's right. Why wouldn't I? He's the son of one of my very oldest f-f-friends."

"Why did Vince loan a truck to Rob if he wasn't involved?"

"As a favor."

"Come on. I'm not stupid."

"Well, it's going to come out, anyway. Rob was blackmailing him. Small potatoes. Seems he found out Vince was having an affair. The girl hung all over Vince when he came out here to do site inspections. Apparently Rob saw them, put two and two together, and saw how he could use it to his own advantage."

I remembered the glimpse of blond hair in Vince's car the day we'd argued. I also remembered Vince's unstable wife. "So Vince was afraid if Beth found out about the affair, it would be the end of his marriage?"

Ben nodded. "Vince never forgave Tony for ruining their family life by flaunting his affairs. Guess he didn't want to follow in his father's footsteps. Lending Rob a truck was a small enough price to pay to keep his own family intact." Ben got up from the log. "Now, when are you going to come by and sign those trust papers?"

"What if I don't want to continue doing murals?"

"The day you don't is the day you lose the inheritance."

"And it reverts to Ellen Riggs?"

Ben bit his lower lip.

"Come on, Ben. I know all about Ellen. She was Tony's first beneficiary, wasn't she?"

He sighed. "She declined it."

"And if I decline it?"

"You're certifiably insane and I have you committed." He laughed.

"I'm serious."

"If you decline the inheritance, Tony stipulated it goes into a newly established trust fund—the purpose of which would be agreed upon by both you and Ellen." He patted my shoulder. "Don't be foolish. You've earned the money."

"That's the problem. I'll have to continue to earn it by doing something I hate."

"We all do things we hate." He checked his watch. "I have a m-m-meeting with the zoo board about the Worthington-Bentley trust. They want to get started on Phase Two of the renovation, but I can't release any new f-f-funds until Phase One is officially complete."

"Seems like you have a few conflicts of interest, Ben."

"I must say, I'm surprised and a little hurt that you w-w-would think that."

"All right. Prove me wrong. Who's the secondary beneficiary of the Worthington-Bentley trust? Claudia?"

"I expected more from you, Caroline." He turned on his heel.

I had always thought of Ben as a straight arrow, putting his clients' interests first. But he was human. If the zoo lost the trust fund and if Claudia Baxter inherited it, Ben would soon be a very wealthy husband.

44

MY BRUSHES MOVED WITH GREATER PURPOSE NOW THAT I knew I'd see Kiara again soon. But deep down I wondered if Ellen was right. If the zoo couldn't provide basic security for the animals, maybe it didn't deserve to stay open. Still, was it fair to blame the institution for the actions of one man? Barb had reminded me of the likely fate of the animals if the zoo were forced to close. And it wasn't a pretty picture.

Eager to clear the air with Ellen, I looked for an opening. But she continued to avoid me each time I approached. I decided to be patient.

The day Kiara returned I hurried back to the keeper's area behind the mural. Kneeling next to Kiara's holding cage, Ellen sang softly to the tiger. My heart jumped when I saw them together. Kiara rubbed her massive head against the bars of the holding cage.

"I knew you'd change your mind once she came back," I said.

Startled, Ellen looked up at me. Then some of the warmth returned to her eyes, but they also contained the alert sense of threat that I'd painted in the sambars' eyes in the mural. She picked up a bag marked "feline food" and poured some into a large tub containing what I'd come to recognize as horsemeat. "I suppose I should thank you at least for saving her life," she said.

I shrugged and moved toward the cage. "Hi, Kiara." I longed to reach out and pet her like I had when she was anesthetized. I recognized a familiar odor in the air. "Are you making popcorn?" I asked Ellen.

She smiled. "I suppose you could describe it as burnt popcorn. Yana has been spraying his new quarters."

A heavy pounding on the door to the Siberian tiger's outside enclosure distracted us. The steel door bearing the sign "Have you checked your locks?" trembled under the male tiger's weight.

"He knows Kiara's in estrus," Ellen said, "but we haven't introduced them yet."

"So you'll mate them?"

"I doubt it."

"Why not? Then you'd have a family." That was a poor choice of words.

Ellen's eyes darkened. "Did you want something back here?" She bent over the tub and began kneading the ingredients together. I noticed the ground horsemeat was just that—bits of bone and hair were evident in the mixture. I remembered that horsemeat had been detected on Kiara's teeth by the lab tests in San Antonio.

"Just wanted to talk to you, Ellen. We're going to have to talk sooner or later—especially if I turn down the inheritance like you did."

She froze, but said nothing.

"Why didn't you tell me you were his daughter? I thought we were friends."

"You'll forgive me if I fail to see how that entitles you to my life history." She turned away abruptly.

I caught her shoulder. "Did you know the only reason Tony took this commission was to get close to you again?"

She faced me. "It was a little too late. Thirty years late to be exact."

"How did he find you after all that time?"

"His lawyer kept track of me after my adoption." Her smoky eyes darkened even more. "He thought money could pay me back for all those years apart."

"So you turned down the inheritance just to spite him?"

"He had the arrogance to stipulate that I change my name to Chirico. It would have been like slapping my adopted parents in the face. I love them too much for that. They're my real parents, not him."

"But three million dollars—"

She lifted her red, greasy hands out of the tub of horsemeat. "If it was so important that I bear his name, why didn't he marry my mother? Or at the very least raise me as his own child? But he abandoned me."

"Abandoned you? He brought you back from Italy to live with his family."

"Only after my mother committed suicide. He wouldn't make a commitment to her. He ruined her life, and then he tried to ruin mine."

"Ruin it?" I lowered my voice. "Ellen, did you have a happy childhood?"

"Of course I did," she snapped. "Why do you think I love my adoptive parents so?"

"Do you honestly think you would have been happy living with the Chiricos? Have you met Antoinetta, Tony's ex-wife?"

Ellen nodded, her voice calmer. "I went to the funeral." She raised her imperfect hand. "Antoinetta recognized me immediately."

I remembered that day and the dark-haired figure that had scurried from the chapel to the accompaniment of Antoinetta's screeching. "Then you know she would have hated you—the very fact of you—every day of your life. Tony knew that, too."

Ellen wiped her hands on a towel, stood up and faced me. She was about twenty pounds heavier than I, but we were about the same height and had the same dark brown hair.

I touched her arm. "Tony told me once I reminded him of someone—someone he cared about. I think that's why he took me under his wing. I think I reminded him of you." I recalled my last run-in with Antoinetta. "After the funeral, Antoinetta mistook me for you, came at me with a knife! Tony only did what he thought was best for you. He gave you up so you would have a better chance for a happy life."

"No matter how much my adoptive parents tried to compensate, no matter how much I love them, I'll always live with the feeling that my birth parents didn't want me. I'll never forgive him," she whispered.

"Maybe not, but can you try to understand him?"

She looked at me. "Why should I?"

"When I told you Kiara would be coming back to Fox Valley Zoo, you said it would be better if she went to another, a better zoo. You wanted what was best for her, even though it broke your heart to lose her. You put her needs before your own. Can't you understand how Tony might have felt the same way? He brought you back from Italy. He wanted to make you part of his family. He even painted you in a family portrait I can give you. But he realized he couldn't let you grow up in that hateful atmosphere. It would destroy you. He wanted a better life for you—just like you want for Kiara."

She turned and walked away.

45

THE SCAFFOLD'S HIGHEST PLATFORMS HAD BEEN REmoved, leaving only two levels. I was fast approaching the part of the mural that remained a mystery. I wondered what Tony intended to paint. Maybe it didn't matter. I decided I'd paint a white tiger emerging from the elephant grass in the foreground.

With my sketches of Kiara as reference, I found myself reveling in this opportunity for self-expression. I had felt I owed it to Tony to complete the mural in his style and was pleased that I had been faithful in doing so. But I had struggled with his technique. Tony's animals were far more static than mine. After leaving his studio, I had fallen under other art influences. I was captivated by the wildlife paintings of the German painter Manfred Schatz. Like him, I chose to suggest animals in motion by blurring wings and legs. I didn't detail every hair, every whisker, but painted impressionistically. As my brush found a sense of freedom, I also felt a surge of momentary sadness when it occurred to me that I was leaving Tony behind. I had developed my own style. I needed to say good-bye to him. Maybe now I was finally ready.

With a sense of relief that I was closing in on the finish, I settled on what had become my favorite bench outside Asia World. Yolanda Ramirez found me there, munching on a Chicago-style hot dog.

We hadn't spoken much since the flare-up in her office, but today she seemed cheerful enough. "The invitations for the formal opening have all gone out, Caroline. Here's yours." Her pencil-thin arm handed me a thick envelope. "Go ahead, take a look at it."

I tore open the envelope as she wheeled closer to me.

"Well, what do you think? Pretty creative, huh? It was my idea."

I stared down at a printed section of the mural, mounted on an irregular-shaped piece of cardboard. "What's this?" I asked, turning it over. On the back was a formal printed invitation to the grand opening.

"I took Mr. Chirico's original color sketch and had it enlarged into a giant jigsaw puzzle. Each one of our major contributors will be sent a piece of the mural puzzle in the mail, you know, as a teaser to come see the completed version. When they arrive they will each add a different piece to the puzzle, which will be displayed on an easel. Clever, huh?"

"You mean you had a color version of the full mural all this time?" My voice was shrill. "Tony's original painting?"

"Well, sure. We couldn't wait for you to finish the mural, then photograph it. We never would have met our printing deadline."

"Did you know I've been looking for this for the last two months? Of course you did," I said answering my own question. "You were at our first meeting when I mentioned I needed to find Tony's sketches."

"I didn't realize you meant this," she said defensively. "I didn't consider this a sketch."

"It's a preliminary painting, a sketch, same thing." I closed my eyes and counted. "Where's the original?"

"It's on my desk. The printer just sent it back."

I lost no time getting to the administration building. I ran up the steps and into Yolanda's office. A large manila envelope with a printer's label lay on top of her desk. The flap was open. The envelope was empty except for the cardboard stiffener.

I grabbed the phone on the desk and called the printer at the number on the label. The head of production said the color separated film had been returned with the original artwork. I inquired about the printing plates. He told me they were rarely saved, destroyed at the end of the print run. I demanded to see a chromalin, progressive proofs, rejects, anything.

"Who is this?" he asked. "Are you responsible for payment of this job?"

When I said no, he hung up.

It was clear anyone at the zoo could have slipped into Yolanda's office and removed the original color rendering and the film negs from the envelope, but I got blank stares all around when I asked. The invitations printed on the individual pieces of the puzzle were already in the mail, so there was no way to piece together the puzzle until they all would come together once again on opening night.

46

THE SCAFFOLDING HAD BEEN REMOVED THE DAY BEFORE, so I stood on an extension ladder, putting the finishing touches to the mural. Resting my hand on a maulstick for steadiness I added "clicks"—highlights—here and there.

Asia World would open tomorrow. Nearly everything was in place—all except for a faulty six-foot section of bamboo railing, weakened by moisture from exposure to the waterfall that cascaded next to it. It would be replaced by a specially treated length.

Landscapers spread a thick layer of wood chips over the cement floor of the tiger enclosure, while others watered the plants. Artificial leaves had been added to the uppermost limbs of the huge gunite banyan tree behind me. The foliage filtered the daylight streaming through the glass ceiling without blocking the visitor's view. A dappled light pattern blanketed the floor. For a moment I imagined I really was in an Indian forest.

A sense of celebration pervaded the zoo. With the return of Kiara, morale had risen. The future looked brighter than ever for the zoo and its residents. For the moment, even Marcia Wilhelm and CCATZ had packed up and gone home.

Descending the ladder propped against the wall, I stared up with satisfaction at the mural. It was complete. A moment of sheer relief washed over me. I had survived and had met the deadline without a day to spare.

And at that moment I made the decision.

I'd never do another.

47

THE GALA OPENING OF ASIA WORLD WAS SET FOR THREE o'clock Sunday, the last day of October, by invitation only.

An Indian summer sun beat down on my back as I left the house and walked to the car. Out on the street, children crisscrossed front lawns in their Halloween costumes. My simple sundress, navy with a few bright flower bursts, was perhaps too summery for the season, but temperatures had been in the eighties all week.

Before I pulled out of the driveway, I glanced at myself in the rearview mirror. My Claudia B bob had grown out into more of a shag. I tugged on the ends as though that might make the strands longer. I had tried several dark rinses the night before, but I'd only succeeded in adding more colors to the palette. I looked like a badly colorized version of myself. But then, people expect artists to look eccentric.

The sunlit leaves, just past peak color, drew my eyes from the highway heading west. As I crossed the Fox River and exited the tollway, the fog rolled in. The sudden change was typical of Chicago area weather. I drove on through a thick gray cloud to the zoo, the Camaro's wipers clearing beads of perspiration from the windshield.

The zoo gates had closed early to the general public for the members-only preview. Cars crawled through the foggy parking lot like the ghosts of lumbering beasts, their glowing eyes casting light rays through the mist. As I curved around a line of limousines to park, a woman swept from the back seat of a stretch limo. I slammed on the brakes. She passed serenely in front of me, oblivious to the near fatality. Her ivory gown had broken out in a terminal case of pearls, and an immodest tiara sat atop her upswept hair.

I glanced again in the mirror. You're out of your league, I told myself. I considered leaving, but I had one last question to be answered. And though I didn't look it—in fact hadn't even touched a penny—this was my last day as a millionaire. I intended to tell Ben of my decision to turn down the inheritance on Monday.

I walked to the entrance, my arms crossed to keep warm. Jake had offered to be my escort for the evening, but said he had an errand to run first and would meet me at the gate. My bag held our passport to Asia World—the invitation printed on the back of the mural puzzle piece. It was the real reason I wasn't turning back. I was eager to put it in position with the adjoining pieces, eager to finally know what Tony had planned for the full mural, but also a little afraid, of what I couldn't say. I shivered and hurried through the fog.

A man in a navy blue suit with his hand in his pocket waited at the revolving gate. At first I didn't recognize him. He looked so different than when I'd left him in Texas. Jake's features sharpened as the mist between us lessened. I liked the look on his face when he saw me, then it occurred to me it was the first time he'd seen me in a dress.

"You look great." His blue eyes sparkled. "And I really like the, uh . . ." His index finger made circles by his hair.

"Fright wig?" I laughed and kissed his cheek. "Thanks. You look good, too."

He stepped back to look at me fully, then put his lips to my ear. "Pretty seductive," he whispered.

"Don't be fooled. This could be my evil twin."

"The more evil, the better." He pulled me toward the

bushes surrounding the entrance to the zoo. Either the bushes were prickly or an electric charge went up my half-bare back. He kissed me for a good minute. How could it be a bad minute? Running his warm hands up my goose-bumped arms, he said, "You're as cold as ice."

"Is that an observation or a criticism?" I leaned forward and initiated the next kiss.

He grinned, wrapped me in his arms and whispered, "I'm all yours till tomorrow morning."

"Come on." I kissed him on the cheek and led him back to the zoo entrance. I found the invitation inside my small black bag and presented the puzzle piece to the security guard.

The guard looked at it, handed it back, and opened the gate. "Just follow the path."

A red carpet led from the gate to Asia World. The zoo was eerily quiet. Following several other couples up the ramp, we passed a dozen scattered smokers. The vapor they exhaled was swallowed up by the fog, as though their smoking were responsible for the cloud that billowed around us.

Inside the metal outer doors a woman with a cobra face mask handed me a giant panda mask and Jake a tiger mask. "These are great." I slipped the elastic band over my head.

"Being an animal comes naturally to you, doesn't it?" Jake said.

I arched an eyebrow at him, then adjusted the paper mask into place.

"I've never met a human who tries to see the world through an animal's eyes as much as you do." He inched his fingers along the side of his tiger mask, but didn't put it on. "Even in your artwork, you paint from the animal's viewpoint. A low horizon line for a rabbit, an aerial perspective for an eagle. It gives me the feeling I'm not a man looking at a painting of a tiger, but another tiger looking at a tiger." He shook his head. "I'm not saying this well."

"You're doing fine, but I think you're giving me far

too much credit." The edges of the mask had cut down my peripheral vision. I only had eyes for him. "Something tells me, Mr. Gavin, that you like animals just as much as I do."

"Of course, I like animals. But, like I told you, I was raised on a farm—"

"You said you grew up in Wisconsin, nothing about a farm."

"If I didn't mention it, it was just an oversight." He caught my eye as though checking to see if I bought that explanation, but it hadn't occurred to me to doubt it until just then. "Anyway," he continued, "when animals are your livelihood, you don't get sentimental and emotional over them."

"Animals are my livelihood, and emotions have everything to do with it. Emotions aren't necessarily a negative thing."

Jake shrugged and opened the interior door to Asia World. We left it at that. As we passed under the Japanese pagoda, the tinkle of Oriental music and the thunder of falling water competed with the sounds of conversation throughout the building. It was somewhat disconcerting to see gazelles and orangutans talking freely with tigers and rhinos beneath twinkling Japanese lanterns.

I turned to Jake. "Aren't you going to put that on?" I motioned to his mask.

"I'd feel silly. Besides, people who wear masks generally have something to hide." He thrust his chin toward my mask. "What are you hiding?"

I wasn't sure if he was just flirting or if he was serious. Before I could pursue it, a tuxedo-clad Miles Crandall took center stage. Ironically, he wore the mask of the smallest species of bear. With the sun bear mask pushed back on his forehead, he stood inside the door surrounded by Minicams. He raised his hands in front of him like the four-legged beast balancing on two. "Ladies and gentlemen, the dedication ceremony will begin in an hour on the far side of the building in India, Land of the Tiger. Be sure to place your puzzle pieces before then. In the meantime, feel free to tour Asia World at your leisure. And remember, we need your support for Africa World, our next project."

I held up the puzzle piece for Jake to see. "I'd like to put this in place."

"Caroline Canfield!" Miles pushed his way toward me through the crowd. "Keep it rolling on me," he said over his shoulder. A man with a Minicam and a woman with a microphone trailed behind him. He pumped my hand. "The expeditious artist who met our deadline," he explained to the camera. Let other painters be remembered for being great or even merely good. I'd be known for being fast.

The reporter sidestepped past Miles. "Miss Canfield, how do you feel about being the person to uncover the message of the mural?"

"Well, I—"

The woman yelped and bent over. I noticed Miles's foot planted firmly on her instep. The snow monkeys mimicked the woman's scream and echoed it through the room.

"Oh look, the Governor!" Like the head of a wagon train, Miles waved the cameraman to follow. His other arm shot up vertically into the air. "Jim-bo!"

After Miles moved on, I brandished the puzzle piece once more before Jake's eyes.

"What's the hurry?" Jake asked.

"These were printed from Tony's original color comp—the only one that's left."

"Don't tell me you think there's something else in the mural," he said.

"I just want to be sure, that's all." I remembered Claudia's word. "Closure."

As we waded through the crowd, I glanced up into the steely eyes of Vince Chirico. Like Jake, he wore no mask. He raised a champagne glass to me.

"How are you, Vince?" I asked.

The corner of his mouth curled. "Couldn't be better.

My next two projects have been canceled, my wife threw me out, the cops are still hounding me, not to mention my creditors, and with no money from my father, I don't have a pot to pee in. Life's great! Have I forgotten to say thank you?" He tossed back the full glass of champagne, then grabbed another from the tray of a passing waiter.

Jake pulled me forward before I could reply, but what would I have said? It's your own fault, Vince? What was the point? We crossed through Japan to Indonesia and then to China. Jake kissed me in every country. I was beginning to really love the Asian continent and considered just crossing borders for the rest of the evening, but when I looked it was getting close to four o'clock. We hurried past the red pandas, the komodo dragon and the elephants to the most crowded room of all. The noise level was deafening in India. Jake and I inched our way forward past a white-turbaned man playing a sitar.

Jake stopped to read a factoid silk-screened on a board. "Listen to this," he said, reading from the sign. "Since tigers typically take their prey from behind, Malaysian villagers began wearing masks on the backs of their heads so they wouldn't be attacked. They believe a verse from the Koran is inscribed on each man's forehead and the tiger cannot face that message—proving that if you stay calm and face them, tigers will respect you."

"Yeah, I'd hate to get eaten alive without a little respect first," I said. "Come on, I want to get up front near the puzzle."

"You go ahead. I'll get us some champagne." Jake and I went off in opposite directions.

"Caroline!" A tall redhead wearing a two-piece mask—black face mask with red-capped exotic bird's headdress—worked her way in my direction through the crowd. A gathered burst of red silk over the left breast was the only color accent on the slinky, off-the-shoulder black gown. Even I recognized a sarus crane in a designer original when I saw one.

I fingered the fabric. "Barb, not this old rag."

Her lips pursed momentarily. "This happens to be an original François Oudinot," she said. "Very *au courant*. Not that that means anything to you."

I smiled, glancing down at my sundress. "This just happens to be an original J.C.—excuse me, Jean Claude Penn-ee." We both laughed. She eyed my hair.

"Say one word, and you're Kiara's dinner."

"Don't be silly," she said. "It's quite . . . arty."

Jake returned with two plastic glasses of champagne. "I thought you were heading for the puzzle display."

"I was rudely interrupted—very rudely." I introduced him to Barb.

Jake handed me a tulip glass and offered the other to Barb.

"No thanks, I'm sticking with Perrier tonight." Her eyes studied him. "So, you're Jake. I've heard good things about you." She took his arm and led him away from me. Over her shoulder she said so I could hear, "However, I can't say I admire your taste in women."

I laughed, but I wondered if I looked half as striking on Jake's arm as she did. I caught up with them. "I really want to place this puzzle piece." I headed off through the crowd down the walkway. Barb and Jake followed. We made our way to the easel holding the giant puzzle at the far end of Tiger Forest. Approximately nine feet by three feet, it was only half complete. I put my magnetized puzzle piece in position. It stood alone in the lower right corner of the frame, the adjacent spaces still vacant.

Two hands gripped my upper arms from behind. I turned around.

Ben Rudolph hugged me. "Caroline, the m-m-mural is wonderful," he said gesturing toward the wall. Ben wore a hat, not a mask. The long skinny bill of the hat mimicked the snout of a gavial, a skinny-nosed alligator.

I easily recognized the woman beside Ben. Behind the black face mask with white streaks over the eye slits, Claudia Baxter's eyes darted over me, evaluating my look, or lack thereof. In her shimmery turquoise gown, Claudia reminded me of a blond Nancy Reagan.

She placed a red-fingernailed hand on Ben's arm. "Would you get me more champagne, dear?"

Ben patted her hand and headed for the refreshment table.

In addition to the black face mask with white streaks, Claudia wore a peacock headdress. She saw me examining it. "I know what you're thinking. It's the male bird, but the female is so drab." Her eyes scanned me up and down. "However, you're quite colorful."

"Like it? I owe this tri-tone look entirely to the Claudia B salon," I said as I tugged on the uneven, multicolored strands of my hair. "And don't worry, I give your salon full credit whenever anyone asks." I was pleased to see her lips purse. I shifted my attention to the tiger exhibit and leaned toward Barb, who'd been chatting with someone else. "Where's Kiara?"

"She won't be out until the special presentation at four o'clock," Barb said.

"What about Yana?"

"He won't be shown at all today. When he's on exhibit, he's taken to spraying the tiger you painted in the lower right corner."

Claudia chortled. "He may not know art, but he knows what he likes."

Barb patted my back. "Don't take it personally. Yana's only marking his territory, just like you sign a painting, or a mural." Barb and Claudia scanned the mural, as Ben returned with a glass of champagne for his fiancée.

"Don't bother looking for my signature. I didn't sign it," I admitted. "It's really Tony's painting. I just finished it."

"Well, in my humble opinion," Ben said, "your painting surpasses even Tony's. The landscape is breathtaking, but it's the animal portraits that make it come alive. You'll have no problem getting more mural commissions."

"I need to talk to you about that on Monday, Ben," I said.

A body leaned over my shoulder. Vince's voice broke in. "You don't actually think she'll go on working, do you? She's a millionairess now, haven't you heard?"

Jake shoved him away. "Why don't you go sober up somewhere?"

Vince swung at Jake, missing him completely, but managing to put his fist into the easel. The puzzle tumbled to the floor of the walkway.

"Vince, don't make a scene." Barb took her cousin by the arm and started to escort him away.

"Leave me alone, Bebe." He shook her off and merged into the crowd.

Behind Barb, several guests righted the easel and backboard and replaced the pieces that had fallen off. I tilted my head past Barb to see if any new pieces had been added. Two more were now adjacent to mine, but Barb's shoulder blocked my view.

She sighed. "Please forgive Vince. He's upset that the zoo board has eliminated his bids on the next building phase. They had no choice, what with the scandal."

"Let's have no more talk of that." Miles loomed over us. "Only good things ahead. Isn't that right, Mr. Rudolph?" Miles slapped Ben on the back. "Our trust fund is secure."

Ben smiled and drew Claudia closer as she whispered gently in his ear. Engagement seemed to agree with them. Maybe they really were in love. The lawyer cleared his throat. "My beautiful fiancée has just drawn my attention to something, Dr. Crandall. Part of the exhibit is cordoned off, as though it's still under construction."

We all directed our vision to the walkway that diverged from the main path and ran behind the waterfall nearest the painted wall. The entrance and exit to this secondary pathway were blocked by sawhorses.

Ben cleared his throat. "If the exhibit is incomplete, the trust fund clearly states—"

"Nonsense." Miles straightened his back and glared down at the lawyer. "Of course, it's complete."

"Then why does it appear that work is ongoing in that area?"

"Mere precaution. The bamboo railing's faulty, and the spray from the waterfall makes the walkway slippery. But that's considered a repair. Postcompletion repair. If you care to see it, I have a work order as proof." Miles's eyes traveled the room, then his arm shot up in the air. "Senator!" He marched off.

Out of the corner of my eye I saw Yolanda Ramirez in a silvery cocktail dress. Wearing a snow monkey mask, she spoke with a woman wearing a slimming cobalt blue dress with the russet mask of a red panda. The woman's long dark braid identified her. Ellen Riggs studied the mural intently, especially Tony's work closest to the top. When she turned and saw me watching them, I waved, but she didn't respond.

Yolanda wheeled her chair over to our group. "I have to compliment you on the mural. It's indescribably beautiful. You must feel very—" She searched for a word.

"Tired," I said. "In fact, if you think this panda has dark circles around its eyes . . ." I pointed to the mask I wore. ". . . you should see the real ones underneath." Everyone laughed.

"Really, it's practically perfect," she said.

"Practically?" Barb threw her arm around me. "If my friend did it, it couldn't be anything but perfect!"

"I just meant—never mind, it's such a small thing, really."

"Wildlife artists live in dread of making a mistake. What did I do wrong?" I said.

"Not wrong, really." Yolanda pointed at the coppery-colored tiger standing on the ruins of the Indian temple, the one Tony had painted. "It's just those eyes. They're so . . . green. They're unnatural."

"You're right," I said. "I noticed the poor color choice, too, but Tony painted that tiger, and, well, I was reluctant to change his work."

"You told me he hated painting wildlife," Jake said. "I suppose he just made a mistake, huh?"

"Well, I see nothing wrong with the eyes," Barb said, squinting.

I appreciated her support, but I knew she couldn't see them from where we stood. And now that Yolanda had mentioned the anomaly, the bilious green eyes were all I could see. "Tell you what, all my equipment is still in the back. I'll fix the eyes tomorrow."

In another Nancy Reaganesque gesture, Claudia poked Ben.

He stepped forward. "Uh, legally today's the d-d-deadline for completion. As I told Dr. Crandall, if the m-m-mural isn't done, I'm afraid the zoo loses the trust." He checked his diamond-studded watch. It wasn't Ben's taste. It had to be gift from Claudia. "There's still eight hours, however, before time's up."

I looked for a glimmer of fun in Ben's eyes. He crossed his arms.

"What do you expect me to do, Ben?" I asked. "Climb up in heels on a ladder now? The mural's done. This is just a repair," I said, stealing Miles's argument.

Claudia leaned over and whispered to Ben again.

He raised his head. "I could accept that, but for one thing. You've told us yourself the mural isn't signed. Isn't a signature the true mark of completion of an artist's work?"

I glared at him. "Fine. Who's got something I can write with?"

Jake reached into his suit coat and extracted a felt-tip pen. "Will this do?"

I grabbed it from his hand. "There's no law that says I have to sign it in the lower right-hand corner. I can do it from the walkway, right there."

The group followed me. Pushing the sawhorse aside, I strode up to the wall.

"Are you crazy?" Barb rushed forward. "There's a reason that's roped off."

I reached over the railing, but my arm was about six

inches short of the mural. I glanced down. The cementlike fingers of the banyan tree stretched upward, as though pointing me away. I tested the sturdiness of the railing. It seemed secure enough to hold me.

"Don't even think it," Barb said.

"I'm not going to lose the money for the zoo now." I pulled off my mask. "Hold this," I said to Barb, as I rested one foot on the bottom rail of bamboo.

Jake grabbed my arm. "Don't be nuts."

"I can do it. Just hold onto me."

I heard the whir of Yolanda's wheelchair behind me. Three sets of arms enfolded me as I bent forward and leaned into the railing. The crowd had hushed. Their eyes were riveted on me. The waterfall crashed beside me as I strained to reach the wall.

Miles pounded over. "Stop her! If she falls, our liability insurance won't cover it." You could count on Miles to have his priorities in order. Barb explained to him Ben's position on the terms of the trust.

Miles did an about-face and made a stirrup out of his hands. "Leg up?"

I slipped off my heels, lodged my right foot between his beefy palms and leaned forward once more. My left hand made contact with the wall and braced me, as my thighs hugged the bamboo railing for support. With my right hand I scribbled my name like any respectable graffiti artist. But going back to dot the "i"s was my mistake. I wobbled forward. I wobbled backward. The gasp that ran through the crowd panicked me and sent me teetering beyond the edge. Miles let go of my foot and grabbed my arm. He lurched forward. His full weight slammed into the railing. Snap.

The rotted wood broke loose from its bolts to the floor. It bellied out like a gate from the adjoining section, but the bolts to the wall kept it from fully dislodging. Miles flailed over the edge of the pit, still gripping my arm. If he fell he'd take us all with him. "Help him," I shouted. My companions' arms abandoned me as they stretched out to rescue the zoo director. Miles's grip on my upper arm loosened as my friends pulled him back.

With no one holding me, I toppled forward. My panty-hosed foot slid across the middle rung of the railing, wet from the spray of the waterfall. I tried desperately to regain my balance. Primate screams—human and other-wise—erupted around the hall. Just as I felt myself slip-ping into the pit below, strong arms wrapped around my legs and tugged me backward. I fell into a sitting position right into the lap of my rescuer—Yolanda Ramirez. Though her arms were spindly, I was awfully glad to have been wrong about their strength.

48

THE AFTERNOON LIGHT HAD GIVEN WAY TO EARLY evening. With only a dreary gray sky visible through the skylights, incandescent torches attached to the top of bamboo staves brightened the inside of the tiger exhibit. The artificial torches flickered like the real thing, sending shadows of figures dancing around the room, as in some ancient ceremonial rite.

On the landing nearest the mural, our group nestled close together like birds clustering in a tree at nightfall. We awaited the start of the dedication ceremony. My knees were still a little wobbly from the near fall, but it was a condition I was used to. I was grateful to still find Yolanda like a sentinel at my side.

Duct tape had been used to secure the damaged rail-ing section to its neighbor, and sawhorses again guarded the entry and exit to the damaged area. Miles tapped the microphone. It screeched back at him as though in horror. Under his wrathful eye, technicians scurried to unravel the mike's cord. As we waited, my eyes drifted back to the puzzle display to my right.

Standing behind me, Jake must have noticed the turn of my head. "Looks like a few more pieces have been slipped into place," he said.

"Don't say slip," I said. "Don't ever say slip."

I studied the painting on the easel. The rest of the tree with the snake coiled around it was now visible. The barrel of a hunting rifle emerged from behind the tree just as in the drawings I'd seen before, but something was different from the tissue drawings I remembered. Something about the rifle itself. It wasn't like any hunting rifle I'd ever seen. But I wasn't familiar enough with guns to say why I got that impression.

"There's something odd about this gun," I whispered to Jake.

"Rifle. It's clear to me it represents the hunting ranch."

"It's partially in the section of the wall where the grid drawing was smeared." I circled the area with my finger.

He shrugged. "So? Rob Bennett smeared it before anyone else could see it."

"Why wouldn't he have destroyed the other clues then," I asked, "the snake wrapped around the tree and the 'V' carved into the trunk—the symbol for veterinarian? That was far more incriminating to him directly."

Jake shrugged. "He probably didn't notice all the clues. I didn't until you pointed them out."

Once again taking the podium, Miles began with his usual self-aggrandizing comments, including how he had singlehandedly rescued me moments earlier. He got a laugh when he introduced me, the artist, as "the fastest draw in the Midwest." The governor spoke briefly, as did Claudia Baxter, head of the zoo board.

Then the torches along the wallway dimmed. Like

magic, the skylights turned opaque black. The electricians had told me it was done with an electric charge.

The soundtrack opening of the computerized audio show began. "Like all cats, the tiger is a creature of the night." A hologram of a tiger appeared in the dark corner of the exhibit. Gasps of surprise came from the crowd as the three-dimensional tiger moved across the exhibit.

"State of the art." The whole room heard Miles's poor imitation of a whisper.

The narrator continued. "The big cats are nature's most efficient carnivores, with fluid muscles of crushing force, powerful jaws and teeth designed to rip through flesh, and a short digestive tract designed for a meat eater. The tiger first immobilizes a victim by grabbing it with its claws and then tearing the life from it." Sambars sounded their alarms in the distance as the voice-over continued. A rustling in the artificial foliage and an imitation moonbeam from the ceiling revealed a robotic deer moving cautiously through the brush. Another motor whirred. "Stealthily stalking its prey, the tiger zeroes in on the likeliest victim, the weakest of the herd, who is unaware that death has come for her."

"Oh, no! Run, you sweet thing!" a woman shouted. "I can't watch this!"

"Shhhh!" came a hiss from the crowd. "It's not real!"

Another motor whirred. The tiger hologram disappeared. The deer was propelled diagonally across the exhibit below us. The faceless voice said, "As the sambar takes flight, the tiger leaps for its prey!"

The crowd waited breathlessly. Nothing happened. Then slowly a big white paw emerged from the underground ramp. Hardly leaping, Kiara appeared, sniffed at the stuffed sambar, yawned, and lay down with her back to it.

Groans filled the room. Torchlights brightened. Miles hurried to the microphone. He cleared his voice. "I'm afraid Kiara is already well-fed for tonight, but she will soon learn to recognize the mechanical sambar as a source of food. It contains a vitamin-enhanced protein mixture inside the shell. We call this . . ." He glanced at his notes. ". . . behavior enrichment."

"If Kiara's behavior gets any more enriched," someone said, "she'll be comatose."

Miles chuckled in embarrassment. "Indeed." His beefy palm smothered the mike as he turned toward Barb. The grin turned into a glower. "Who fed that cat? I want an explanation immediately."

I didn't envy Barb's having to huddle with Miles.

As the torchlights came up further, the woman who ran the zoo switchboard—almost as efficiently as she ran the zoo grapevine—said hello to me, then turned to Jake. "You're Jake Gavin, aren't you?"

"That's right."

"I had a message for you just before I closed down the board." She fumbled through her purse. "I wrote it down. It's here somewhere."

Jake's face was hard to read. "You can give it to me later."

"Oh, but I promised her I'd give you the message."

"Later, when you find it." He began to steer me away.

"Well, I basically remember it." Her eyes scanned the ceiling as though the message were written there. "Your wife said to tell you her flight was canceled because of the fog. She said she'd catch a cab back home from O'Hare."

Jake went white. When she saw his face, the woman went red. I don't know what color my face was, but my mood turned black.

I shook off Jake's hand. "Wife?" Like a startled, insecure animal, I bolted.

He pushed through the crowd after me. "Caroline, let me explain."

I wheeled around. "It's just one lie after another with you, isn't it?"

"You don't understand."

"I understand 'your wife' perfectly. Your wife: the woman you are married to."

"We're getting a divorce—"

"Oh, please." I pushed on.

Jake grabbed my arm. "Stop overreacting!"

"Good night, Mr. Gavin, Mr. Statler, whoever the hell you are! Now I see why you didn't put on that mask. Why should you? You wear one every day of your life."

"Just let me—"

"I don't want to hear one more word from you." A finger in my face never fails to irritate me, so I made sure to point mine in his. "And I don't ever want to see you again."

He looked at his shoes. That boyish look wasn't going to work on me this time.

I yanked my arm away and got lost in the crowd. I must have walked a complete circle, because in ten minutes I found myself back in front of the puzzle display. Most of the guests had already left for the dinner that followed at the local Hilton. A few feet away Barbara explained to a man that I was the muralist. I knew she was leading up to introducing me. I stiffened my shoulders and turned my back on them. Calm down, I told myself. Finish what you have to do here first. Then just go home and crash.

Barb studied my face, shook the man's hand and came over to me. "Okay, what's wrong? You haven't looked this angry since—"

"I want to fix the tiger's eyes. And then I want to get out of here."

"No way. The mural's done. You've signed it. *Finis.*"

Maybe I looked like I couldn't handle sentences with more than three words.

Maybe I couldn't. "The mural's wrong. I'll fix it!"

"I won't have you getting up on a ladder that high. Come on, we're all going to the Hilton."

"Not me."

"Don't be silly." She glanced around. "Where's Prince Charming?"

"He turned back into a frog." My eyes were fixed on the mural. "Don't worry. You go on to the banquet. Is Kiara off exhibit?"

"Ellen's just putting her in her holding cage for the night. Promise me you'll make sure all the gates are locked before you go in. I'd check them myself before I go, but I've got to leave."

A thought had just occurred to me. Maybe the eyes weren't Tony's mistake. "It's like the roses and wildflowers," I said.

"What?" Her nose practically touching mine, Barb peered into my eyes. "Hello. Are you in there? Are you okay?"

"You go ahead. I'll be fine."

My friend gave me a squeeze, then turned and glided away.

Out of the corner of my eye I saw Claudia and Ben standing nearby. The lawyer eyed me with concern and walked over.

"Did I hear you say you're going to fix the m-m-mural tonight?" He fiddled with the stem of his watch. Maybe he was setting an alarm.

"Don't worry. I'll have it done before midnight."

"I suppose I'll have to take your word on that."

"Worried Claudia might lose out on her aunt's money?"

"If the zoo loses this trust fund, the money simply goes to another charity. If you made the effort to get to know Claudia, you'd see her for the philanthropist she is." He shook his head. "But you'd rather let your suspicions ruin long relationships. Haven't you lost enough f-f-friends?" He took Claudia by the arm and steered her away.

Since August I had lost a lot of friends. And some potential ones. All because of this mural. And now I had one more lead it was asking me to follow. I walked back to the puzzle, which was almost complete now except for a few missing pieces. I picked up one that had fallen to the floor. The puzzle piece with the rifle behind the tree. Despite what Jake had said, I knew this was no ordinary hunting rifle. It resembled the one I vaguely remembered the Rifleman used to carry on the old TV series. It had the same pump-action trigger. Where had I seen that gun before?

49

THE MEMORY SHOT THROUGH MY HEAD LIKE LIGHTNING. I recalled the picture on the wall of the Chirico house, the day of Tony's funeral. Vince standing in the snow, proudly aiming his new air rifle at the camera. He was the one who had smeared the panel in the mural drawing, who had stolen the section from the tissue drawings. And just as he had crudely painted roses to hide Ellen's presence in the family portrait, he had painted over the tiger's eyes in the mural.

My heart pounded like it would burst. Tony had often defined the artist's job as one of organization—setting visual priorities. I needed to do that now with my thoughts. I'd go to the police as soon as I'd assembled all the pieces into a coherent story, just like the pieces of the puzzle.

But what could be behind the tiger's eyes that would confirm Vince's involvement in the whole scheme? What clue was he trying to hide? There was only one way to find out.

I heard a shoe scuff the concrete and spun around. Ellen stood on the walkway.

"Still here?" she asked. "I thought everyone had left."

I glanced around. The deserted exhibit hall was dark except for the incandescent torches twinkling along the pathway. How long had I been standing in front of the puzzle?

"I was just about to look for you," I stammered. "Is Kiara in her holding cage?"

"Why?" She walked toward me.

"I intend to fix the tiger's eyes."

"You're going to a lot of trouble for such a small thing."

"I'm compulsive that way." I laughed nervously. "That tiger has bothered me since I first saw it. Its proportions, even the coloring of its stripes are wrong. It looks more like a—" I cut off my sentence, but I couldn't stop the thought. Baby tiger or a kitten.

Ellen leaned forward and touched my arm. "Caroline?"

I couldn't let on that anything was different—not until I had time to think it all through. I had to be sure. "It won't take long," I said.

"Why don't I stay and keep you company?" She stared uncertainly into my eyes. "We have some things to sort out, you and I, and you shouldn't be here alone."

"No!" I said a little too vehemently. "I mean, I don't want to ruin your evening."

"Miles already did that." Her fingers ran along the edge of the puzzle on the easel. "He ripped my head off for feeding Kiara. But it was Yana's day to fast, not Kiara's. I wasn't about to change their feeding schedule just for his silly show."

An angry growl echoed from the holding area. "Owoom!"

I jerked to attention.

"Yana's been uncontrollable since Kiara came into estrus," Ellen explained. "I've switched their holding cages rather than resort to a tranquilizer or a sedative. The smaller cage might calm him down. If you hear him acting up, don't worry."

"So it's okay to go into the exhibit?"

"You're safe. I've checked the doors." Ellen's eyes studied me. "You seem preoccupied. I don't feel right leaving you here alone."

"Go on," I said. "It'll all be over soon."

"That's an odd thing to say."

"I just meant I'll be done and out of here quickly," I said. *And on my way to the police.*

Ellen started to leave, then pivoted around. "I'm sorry for the way I've acted. You don't really think I wanted Tony dead."

My pulse raced like I'd just downed two pots of coffee. I spoke with as little emotion as possible. "I don't think that."

I spoke again as she turned to leave. "Ellen?"

She turned back to me.

"He called you Kitten, didn't he? His little Kitten."

"How did you know that?"

"It doesn't matter," I said. Now was no time to tell her where I'd found her cat pin.

She sighed. "Well, don't stay too late. There's only a skeleton crew on. Even security's short. Everybody's at the party. The outer doors are already locked. Just be sure to lock up the back exit as usual when you leave."

"I won't forget," I said.

She shrugged. "Okay. You're on your own."

"I don't ever forget that."

Although I heard them stir once or twice in their cages, even Yana and Kiara had settled down for the night. They could afford to sleep. They couldn't imagine what I knew.

In the holding area, I pulled off my dress and slipped on a long-sleeved, full-length smock. As I buttoned it, I glanced down at my feet. High heels. Great. At least I could count on them to keep me alert.

I needed only one tool. My X-Acto knife fit easily into the pocket of my smock. I also threw in a packet of fresh blades, knowing the sharp edge would dull quickly as I scraped. I hoisted the extension ladder into position directly beneath the painted tiger, then stepped back to be sure the ladder was positioned correctly.

Behind me loomed the large gunite banyan tree. Shadows of its stony fingers, which stretched to the glass ceiling, played across the mural. My shoulders tight with tension, I twisted my neck back and forth to relax the muscles. With only the electric torchlights to guide my steps, I started the climb. About ten feet up the ladder I realized the heels I wore were asking for trouble. I stood on one rung, lifted first one foot, then the other, and slipped off my shoes. I jammed each into corresponding pockets of my smock and continued up the ladder.

When I reached the top, my eyes were level with the tiger's. At close range the color appeared even more unnatural. Permanent green light. Color straight out of the tube. Something no realist painter I knew ever did, certainly not Tony. Vince must have chosen a green at random and painted over the eyes. And the intense black of the pupils of the eyes. Mars black. Another color choice Tony wouldn't have made. But Vince had, and then disposed of the evidence in the Dumpster next to the zoo hospital. How could he guess that Houdina would pull the tube of black paint from the Dumpster?

I pulled the X-Acto knife out of my pocket. Unlike the top layer of flowers in the family portrait in oil, acrylic paint couldn't be dissolved with turpentine or paint thinner. And although acrylic was thinned with water, it was impermeable to water once it dried. It had all the characteristics of plastic. I'd have to scrape and peel the top layer away carefully so as not to remove more than just the top layer of paint.

The blade had little effect on the hardened surface at first. I applied a little more pressure and held it steady as the blade scratched across the iris. I soon developed a rhythm to the tedious work. My eyes strayed to the body of the painted tiger and traveled its length.

Why was the overall color of the cat so odd, as well as the proportions of the limbs and head? Had Vince painted over the whole tiger? No, the shading was too masterful. Tony had meant to paint the tiger this way, to look more like a kitten.

I turned my attention back to the eyes. Mechanically my hand had continued to vacillate, scraping at the paint. The green I exposed underneath was truer to the color of the tiger's eye. My hand speeded up. The blade tore through the paint to the gessoed wall behind. Damn! I had pressed too hard and cut through both layers of paint.

I'd have to be more careful. With the same precision that a surgeon might use to remove a cataract, I delicately began scraping the surface of the tiger's other eye. This time I wouldn't be distracted. I concentrated fully on the intricacy of my work. I noticed black points at the pupil's top and bottom edges as I scraped the top layer away. I used my left hand to steady the right and restrain it from the excitement that I felt. I scratched away a little more residue top and bottom. And then I saw the real difference in the cat's eyes. Not the color green, but the shape of the pupils. The one on top that I had scraped away had been perfectly round, but the pupil underneath—the one Tony had painted—was a slit, the pupil of a domestic cat. Unlike a tiger's eyes, whose pupils stay round whether dilated or retracted, the pupils of a domestic cat's eyes will be round when dilated, but turn to slits when retracted.

Tony hadn't painted a wild cat, he'd painted a pet cat.

The cat was in profile except for its head, which faced the viewer. But given the sideview perspective of the body, a tail should logically be visible. This cat clearly had none.

The memory hit me so hard I had to catch my balance. Tony's rendering of this cat hadn't been a mistake. He knew exactly what he was doing. And now so did I. He was pointing to Rob Bennett's accomplice. Someone I'd had doubts about but would have trusted without question, perhaps as little as a half-hour ago.

It all fit together, but I didn't want to believe it. My God, I had nearly accused the wrong person. The tailless tiger's eyes. The gun. Even the drawing pencil. All clues to the identity of the murderer. It would be up to the police to prove where the clues led, but I had the paths for them to follow, because Tony had left us a road map.

I raised my hand to cover my eyes. I felt light-headed, maybe from the champagne I'd drunk earlier, but more likely from the shocking knowledge that slashed through my brain. I knew the secret of the mural at last. And worst of all, in spite of closed eyes, I saw the face of a murderer.

50

THE FLICKERING TORCHES AT MY BACK CAST OMINOUS shadows on the wall. I glanced behind me as though something were hovering there. A vibration shook the ladder as a motor whirred. I glanced down. The metal door leading to the holding cages underground rolled open.

"Hey, what's going on? I'm in here." My voice bounced off the walls unanswered. A gut-wrenching feeling sliced through me that I had signaled my suspicions earlier.

I zeroed in on the gaping black tunnel, the tiger's entrance. Empty so far. The keeper's door in the wall offered escape. But was there time? I dropped the knife into my pocket and raced down the ladder. Just as the sole of my foot hit the wood-chipped floor, the torches dimmed and went out. In the darkness I'd never find my way across the uneven landscape.

At the base of the ladder lay the panda mask. It must

have fallen into the pit during my scuffle earlier by the railing. I'm not sure what made me reach down to pick it up. Maybe it was the need to confirm reality, the hope that this was all just a dream. Unfortunately, the paper mask felt very real in my hands.

"Hello!" I called out. The whirring sound again. A wheelchair? Yolanda Ramirez come to rescue me a second time that evening?

A spotlight flashed its beam from the corner of the exhibit to the concrete wall. Blinded momentarily, I froze.

"Who's there?" I shouted, squinting into the light. A security guard?

The light beam flickered, then went off. My eyes, trying to readjust to the darkness, were drawn back to the tiger's ramp. But all I could see was the big black blob burned into my vision by the spotlight. I searched my memory for what logs, trees or trenches stood between me and the keeper's door if I made a run for it.

An escalating growl surged from the tunnel. The ladder vibrated against the wall. My knees buckled. I grabbed the rails of the ladder. Another rumbling bellow sent a shiver from my head to my toes. I climbed the rungs as fast as I could. The panda mask slid down my arm, its elastic headband resting in the crook of my elbow. Footsteps pounded above me on the walkway.

"Close that gate!" I shouted, struggling to turn around without losing my balance. Behind me a figure stood shrouded in shadows. "Don't just stand there—help me!"

The dark form glided forward on the walkway. "Why would I do that, Caroline?"

I didn't have to see her to know who it was.

She moved closer until she stood on the walkway to my left.

"Why?" The word left my lips like a prayer.

"Why? My life is at stake," Barb answered. "Everything I've worked for. My reputation and respect as a genetic specialist in the zoo community. That's why."

Her voice was harsh and raspy. She flashed a light on the cat in the mural. Its mutilated eyes accused her. "I knew you couldn't leave well enough alone." She flashed the light in my eyes.

"The Manx kittens," I said. "You killed them, didn't you? You took them from me and you killed them." I remembered their sweet copper-colored faces and their rust-colored, striped warm bodies, just as Tony had painted them. I shielded my eyes from the glare of the flashlight. "Is that when all this started? Your playing God?"

"I did the humane thing," she snapped. "They were deformed. Manx cats are bred as an oddity—to be tailless. Never mind that in the process the poor things end up with weak spines. It wouldn't have been long before problems manifested themselves. As soon as you showed them to me I knew what I had to do." Her voice echoed through the concrete expanse. "Manx kittens, white tigers, it's all the same. Man tinkering with nature for his amusement."

I needed time to think. "Barbara, whatever has gone on here—"

"Can be fixed?" She threw her head back and laughed. "Can all those animals that were sold without my knowledge, can they be helped? Don't talk to me like I'm a child," she said through clenched teeth. "And what about this place, where animals perform? The money from the trust should be spent on genetic research, not on this circus. And when I'm in charge, that's how it will be spent. But first I have a little more house-cleaning to do."

"Is that what you call it?"

"First you, then Kiara."

"Why Kiara? She can't turn you in."

"Haven't you been listening?" Barb's shrill voice filled the unlit hall. "There's only fifteen hundred places for big cats in zoos. That includes lions, tigers, snow leopards, panthers, jaguars, and all their subspecies. No space for genetic trash. That's why the cheetahs were the first to go. Beyond help . . . no point . . . a lost species. Lions were next. No genetic records for the captive population. But tigers still have a slim chance. I have to protect them—give them the best chance for survival. Don't you see that? One weak animal giving up its place in the ark for the survival of the rest. Just like you have to go, so I can finish my work." Barbara stooped, picked up something in her fist and threw it into the exhibit. "Yana, come!" The ball of meat landed on the ramp leading to the holding cages below ground.

"What are you doing?" I edged further up the ladder, glancing back over my shoulder. Through the semidarkness, the tiger emerged from the black tunnel and scarfed up the meat.

"We call it behavior enrichment, Caroline. Weren't you listening to Miles?" Her voice was frighteningly calm. She threw another meatball closer to the ladder. I heard the splat as it hit the concrete floor.

Yana bounded over and inhaled it.

"Today was Yana's day to fast," Barb said. "Unlike Kiara, I'm sure he's ravenous."

A full moon glowed eerily through the fog hovering outside the glass-paneled ceiling. Yana paced restlessly below in the moon glow.

My mind reeled. I needed a plan of escape. Keep her talking. "How could you go along with Rob Bennett? It was against everything you believe in."

"Get something straight. He went along with *me*. It was my plan. Rob had agreed to fake Kiara's disease along with the rest of the genetic trash filling this zoo. He'd create phony health records, then euthanize the animals and file phony necropsy results."

As she spoke, I inventoried my arsenal. One X-Acto knife, with extra blades, and two high heels. Great. "But instead he sold them behind your back."

"He betrayed me."

"Like you betrayed animals that weren't really sick."

"Not sick enough to die quickly. So I just hastened their end."

"Like you hastened Tony's?" I glanced down. For the moment Yana was preoccupied with exploring the floor.

"Tony was going to destroy me with that mural." Barbara's voice cut through the darkness. "He had to be stopped."

"Stopped from painting the truth?"

"Why didn't he just tell me the whole truth? About the Texas connection and the hunting ranch. I would have stopped Rob if I'd known. But Tony had to be cryptic about it, hiding clues in the mural. If only I'd seen all of them, I'd have known the whole story."

"But you only saw the things that pointed to you," I said. "Like the BB gun aimed at the tiger. Vince told me the story—why Tony nicknamed you Bebe. But it wasn't until I recognized that the tiger was really a Manx kitten that I figured it out."

"You're the only one left who could."

"Look, Barb, if you turn yourself in—"

"Do you think I'm a fool?" She leaned forward, straining to see me. "Seems those hunters can walk away with their hands slapped for killing helpless animals, but when you kill *people*, it's different. I'll lose my position here, my credibility in the zoo community." Did she really believe that was all she stood to lose?

Even through the darkness I could feel her nearsighted eyes squinting at me in hatred. "How is your nearsightedness any different than Kiara's crossed eyes? That's all that's wrong with her, isn't it, Bebe? Yet no one decided you were unfit to live because of your defect."

My neck ached as I half turned to see Barbara. She threw another glob of meat at the base of the ladder. I tried to recall how high tigers could leap. Twelve, fifteen feet? Now I saw how she had led Kiara to Rob's body on the ranch. Yana charged and bumped the ladder.

I hung on. "What about Gino? He knew what you were doing, didn't he?"

"Gino was easy," Barb sneered. "I told him if he gave me the mural drawings I'd sponsor his American citizenship. Then the fool got greedy. Like I could afford to let him live." Squinting, she leaned over the railing and flipped another meatball to the ladder. "Yana!"

"You didn't find out about Rob until I turned up with those safari park photos," I said. "The liger with the deformed ear. You recognized it." If I could draw her closer I might have a shot at hitting her in the head with the spiked heel. It was all I had.

Mirroring Yana's actions, Barbara began to pace along the walkway. "I thought that liger had been euthanized. I realized then that Rob had lied to me all along. That he wouldn't euthanize Kiara, but was going to sell her like all the rest."

"So while Miles and Ellen gave me the grand tour that first day, you stole the photo from my portfolio and confronted him," I said.

"He said if he went down, he'd take me with him. So I pretended to go along."

"And waited for the opportunity to kill him, too." I shuddered and cradled the shoe in my hand. I needed to lure her closer. And then do what? Even if I stunned her by hurling the shoe, how was I going to escape from Yana?

"I actually enjoyed killing Rob." She laughed. "When I got your message that Kiara was to be euthanized, I called Rob from New Orleans. I wanted to get rid of Kiara so badly I said I'd go along with him after all. I told him I'd met a lot of people at the convention who might want to do similar business with him. That got his juices flowing."

I remembered the phone call Rob took while Houdina and I eavesdropped. "You told him to pick you up on the way to the ranch."

"Truck stop near Baton Rouge, as a matter of fact. Congratulations, Caroline. You've been paying attention. I would've killed Rob right then and there and euthanized Kiara myself in the back of the truck, but I realized we were being followed. I had no choice but to go on to the ranch with Rob."

"Where you could find a secluded spot to kill them both," I said. "The drug raid was a perfect cover. You shot Rob, then made it look like the drug runners killed him to silence him. Kiara escaped from her cage before you could kill her, too, but you figured one of the hunters would pick her off. So you took off in the truck. Only the cops had a roadblock up, so you abandoned the truck and went over the fence at an unobserved point on foot."

"And that concludes our program for this evening," Barbara said in a smarmy voice. She appeared to be wiping her hands on a towel, then tossed a bundle of cloth over the railing onto the lower rungs of the ladder—my sundress smeared with horsemeat. "Yana, eat."

At the base of the ladder Yana sniffed and clawed the dress, getting my scent. He raised his massive head and scanned the exhibit, as though looking for something. I knew that something was me. I leaned into the shadows as I clung to the ladder like a lifeline.

A large form rose up before me. The ladder shuddered. Yana rested his huge forepaws on what I guessed to be the tenth rung as he licked another rung clean. He let out a roar. "Ow-oom!"

My arms hugged the ladder.

"Yana, food. *Ce que tu manges, ce que tue es,*" Barb shouted.

"What?"

"You are what you eat." Barb rubbed her forehead. "No, that's not what I want to say. I want to say, you are what eats you. Oh, well." She laughed in an unfunny way. "It's believed that when a tiger eats a human, the person's spirit enters the tiger's body for eternity. That's why the tiger walks with his head low. He carries the weight of all his victims. But it's not such a bad end for someone like you."

She seemed to be slipping in and out of reason. Maybe I could use that to my advantage.

"Yana, food." A meatball hit my back, bounced off me and hit the floor. "Damn!"

Yana pushed off the ladder to retrieve it. The ladder bent, swayed and rocked under me like I was on a trampoline. I gripped its sides. If I could coax Barb down the walkway closer to the wall, maybe I'd have a clear shot at her, but I'd have to get her past the sawhorse.

In the shadows I pulled one of my shoes from the pocket of my smock. "You can't see a thing from there. You'll have to get closer, Barb."

"I know what you're up to," Barb said. "But you won't rattle my cage that easily." She marched forward. Leaning over the railing, she was seven feet away from me at most.

The shoe tightened in my hand. In the darkness interrupted only by moon glow, I aimed. With all my might, I whipped the heel at her face. The shiny shoe glimmered as it passed through a moonbeam. Unaware of my actions, Barb bent down as though to pick something up. The shoe hit the railing and bounced off, falling to the exhibit floor.

With a look of surprise Barb stood up and glanced into the pit. Her laugh filled the room. "You clumsy oaf. You're hopeless."

My efforts hadn't gone completely unappreciated. Yana reared up. A giant paw batted at me. A claw sliced through my pantyhose and ripped through my calf. I clamped my eyes shut with pain. Blood trickled down my shin. Gritting my teeth, I pulled my legs higher, until my knees rested on a rung. Drops of blood landed on the big cat's nose. His tongue lapped them up.

Placing his massive front paws on the ladder, Yana began to climb. His irises glowed in the darkness, reflecting the ghostly light of the moon filtering through the fog outside the glass-paneled ceiling. The aluminum ladder buckled under the cat's weight. At the rung where his front paws rested, the ladder's angle to the wall changed from 30 degrees to 0 degrees. The top half where I perched slammed into the wall, jarring my fingers loose. My feet slipped out from under me, legs flailing in the air.

"Get her!" Barbara cheered the big cat on.

My hands made a desperate stab for the rung above me. I slipped two rungs lower before I caught hold again. The ladder shuddered as Yana lashed out at me. I felt the cool air current on my injured leg as his paw swept the air. With my back to him I was in the worst possible position. I knew I couldn't turn around and face him without falling. I remembered the mask still hanging loosely from my arm. It was worth a try.

With one hand I slipped the mask over my head and twisted it until the face of it sat snugly on the back of my skull. I could picture the big black eyes of the giant panda staring down Yana. Barb and I might have trouble seeing in the darkness, but the tiger had great night vision. I prayed he wouldn't attack from what he perceived to be my front.

The wild cat was quiet. I waited. Were these my last moments before being torn to shreds? The ladder flexed violently as I felt the big cat push off, nearly toppling me in the process. I glanced cautiously behind and below me.

Yana stood with his back to me, his tail erect. He sprayed me. The scent alone nearly knocked me off the ladder. Seemingly content with marking me, Yana resumed pacing. I wiped my face with the sleeve of the smock.

"You may think you've won round one, Caroline, but in fact, you've just raised the stakes. I see now the true nature of our relationship. Never friends, but two animals in competition. And only one of us can survive."

I saw now what Barbara had stooped to pick up. She raised and pointed a long narrow tube in my direction. I recognized the blowgun. "You can't get away with this," I shouted.

"I'll simply blame it on Ellen's carelessness in not locking the holding cage—and in attempting to tranquilize Yana, I shot you by accident. You fell from the ladder. I was only trying to save your life," she said innocently.

Rolling into a ball like an opossum, I made myself as small a target as possible. I could barely stand the gamy tiger scent all over me.

"Just do what you do best, damn you. Fall!" Barbara shouted.

A projectile whizzed past me. I didn't for a second doubt that the dart contained blue juice. I jerked away and nearly lost my balance. Yana leapt up. His massive paw batted the ladder backward away from the wall. I grabbed the rails and threw my weight inward, willing the ladder back to the wall. But the ladder had a mind of its own. I gripped the rung over my head as tightly as I could, but my sweaty palms were not cooperating. I glanced behind at the cement tree limbs below me as I fell backward with the ladder. Something told me it was all over. My last sight would be of concrete trees. Barbara—the stronger, the fitter—would win.

The hell she would! I raised my legs to my chest and stuck them through the ladder's steps. The backs of my knees hooked over a rung, while my hands gripped the rung overhead. My neck snapped back as the ladder slammed into the concrete tree. Pain shot up my spine at the jolt. I shook my head to clear the stars from my eyes. At a backward forty-five degree angle, the ladder rested in the saving embrace of the stony banyan tree. I hung by my knees upside-down from an upper rung.

"Shit!" I heard Barbara spit out.

I wouldn't give her the satisfaction of knowing I damn near did. The potent odor of the tiger was getting to me. My eyes began to tear. With much effort I unhooked my legs from the ladder and with arms extended gripped the trunk of the tree. I lowered myself—headfirst like a serpent—to the limbs, slithering through the intertwining branches. My clawed leg ached so badly I had to grit my teeth to keep from screaming. I grabbed hold of a tree limb and let my legs continue to slide along the trunk until they were once again below me and planted firmly on another limb.

Yana leaped up at me, his claws tracing the length of

the banyan's trunk. An artificial crack of thunder roared through the exhibit hall. Yana's actions had triggered the wind machine and water sprinklers overhead. He deserted his post to seek shelter. I leaned back against the trunk. Monsoon-force rain whipped around me. The twisted limbs of the banyan blocked Barb from getting a clear shot at me. She'd have to move the sawhorse and come around to the side.

"You'll fall sooner or later . . . You always do," Barb shouted through the raging simulated storm. She struggled to hold both the blowgun and the flashlight. I crouched farther into the shadows, as I shifted onto another branch in a clockwise direction and struggled to keep the trunk of the tree between us. She strained to see me in the shadows as she edged down the walkway. Another whooshing sound. The dart ricocheted off the tree.

I needed to lure her closer to the railing. "You're so blind, you'll never hit me with those darts, Bebe."

She laughed and moved aside the sawhorse that blocked the pathway containing the faulty bamboo section, then shouted at me above the storm. "You're the clumsy one, not me."

I craned my neck around the trunk of the tree to observe Barb's movements. Raising the tube yet again, she leaned over the railing to see me, but the tree lay in the shadows. The long tube projecting over the railing was whipped left and right by the wind swirling through the exhibit. Barb aimed and fired. The dart nicked my shoulder and fell to the floor.

"Damn you!" She launched the blowgun at me as though it were a javelin. The long skinny tube landed in the branches above me. "All right, have it your way," she shouted.

After a moment I turned and scanned the walkway. Barb was nowhere in sight. But I was sure she had not just given up and gone home. She had gone too far, admitted too much to me. She'd be back for the final kill.

I pulled the X-Acto knife out of my pocket and loaded a fresh blade into its tip. Just as quickly as the storm had begun it stopped. The only sound was the steady drip of water trickling from the sprinklers mounted in the rock formation on the walls. I noticed that the walkway where Barb had been standing glistened in the moonlight. Wet, it was wet. Hadn't someone—was it Miles?—mentioned that the walkway was slippery when it was wet?

My hair was plastered to my head, and the soggy smock clung tightly to me. I reached upward and dislodged the blowgun from the branches above. I slipped the handle of the knife into the barrel of the gun, but it fit too loosely to stay there. Ripping a pocket from my smock, I wrapped it around the handle of the knife and stuffed it back into the end of the blow gun, the blade projecting outward. I climbed a few limbs higher into the tree until I was level with the walkway. Extending the blowgun to its full length, I was just able to reach the damaged railing. With the blade I sawed through the duct tape holding the railing together.

The room started to spin. What was happening to me? Though the last dart had just nicked me, some of the tranquilizer must have entered my bloodstream. My eyelids felt like an elephant was sitting on them. I giggled at the mental picture. If I could just rest, then I could think what to do next. My chin hit my chest. I heard the clink of metal as the dart gun hit the floor. I jerked awake.

I felt another presence in the room and glanced below. It was clear now where Barbara had gone. Kiara had joined Yana in the exhibit. They circled and sniffed warily at each other. The damp wood chips below gave off a refreshing woodsy scent that revived me.

I realized I didn't have much time before Barb would be back. Now that I had dropped my only weapon, the only chance I had was to disorient Barb. If I moved far enough away, she wouldn't be able to see me. But moving away from her would also take me farther from the walkway and any means of escape. I glanced down at the two tigers roaming the ground floor. There was only one direction to go. I began to climb toward the ceiling, one limb at a time. As the floor and the tigers receded below, I chanted to myself. It's only the old oak tree I used to sit in. Just the old oak tree.

Barb appeared again sooner than I had hoped. She glided down the walkway to her last position, emerging into a light beam cast by the moon that glowed through the glass ceiling. She held a raised pistol in her hands. When she didn't find me where she'd left me, she scanned the exhibit. Her neck craned left and right, inhumanly, like a robot. "I don't have time for this. Where are you? Give it up, Caroline."

Her eyes squinted into the darkness where she'd last seen me. Kiara chuffed a warning to me, as though she sensed that what was about to happen was no more fair play than the hunt she was almost the victim of.

Barb surveyed the terrain below her. I stood on a limb just to Barb's right and above her in the tree, a closer target than I'd been before. But like a dog chasing birds from a back yard, it hadn't occurred to her to look up.

"All right. It doesn't matter what order I do this in." Barbara leaned well over the railing. I followed the direction of her gaze. Kiara and Yana warily circled each other. Yana's growls echoed up the walls. Kiara swiped out at him. They bared their teeth and growled at each other. Yana tried to mount Kiara.

Barb held the pistol unsteadily in one hand and the flashlight in the other. She took aim. Kiara was too large a target for even Barb to miss. I'd sacrifice my hiding place by doing it, but there was no question what I had to do. I pulled the shoe from my remaining pocket and whipped it at her outstretched weapon. The heel struck her hand and bounced off. Obviously startled, she reeled in my direction. In the same moment she fired wildly into the air. The tigers bolted and disappeared into the tunnel leading to their holding cages.

"You can't stop me!" Barb's screams of rage filled the

air, as loud as any ferocious animal's. Clearly out of control, she fired indiscriminately overhead again and again. The glass ceiling above us shattered. The sky rained glass. I tucked my head under my arms. My arms and legs stung with the nicks inflicted by the thick glass shards that showered down on us.

Given an opening in the glass ceiling, fog began to sift down into the exhibit hall. Like a huge gray vulture with an enormous wingspan, it slowly descended through the shattered skylight. It swirled around me, and for a moment I had the sensation that the cloud was motionless and I was rising through it. Like a soul on its way to heaven. Was this what it felt like to die? My head spun and my vision dimmed. I staggered backward on the limb on which I stood. I grabbed the branches on either side of me and lowered myself into a sitting position, my back pressed up against the trunk.

My head drooped. Through the wisps of fog I saw Barbara. She staggered on the walkway as though drunk, her arms extended in front of her, trying to feel her way like a blind person. The thick dense limbs of the banyan tree had shielded me from the worst of the falling debris. Barb hadn't been as lucky. A large sliver of glass protruded from her right eye.

Any normal person would be screaming in pain, but crying out would have been a sign of weakness for Barbara. Not even an insult crossed her lips. I felt strangely detached. My head hung lower on my chest. Through the swirling haze I saw Barbara slip on the west walkway, tumbling forward, her arms outstretched, searching for something to grasp on to as her world fell apart. Her body language screamed for help in a way her lips never could. The rumble of Kiara's roar bellowed up from the bowels of the exhibit hall like a death wail. I heard the snap of cracking wood and saw a black bundle plunge through the mist. Mercifully, the fog filtered out the rest.

51

*ALL ELSE PASSES. ART ALONE ENDURES. ALL ELSE PASSES.
Art alone endures!*

Why was that dominating my thoughts? I rocked my head back and forth across some hard surface, but I couldn't open my eyes. Make the nightmare stop! Bars dug into my back and thighs. I have to get a new mattress, I thought. I ran a hand across my pounding forehead. "My head!" My eyes creaked open. The room was a low-key watercolor awash in the darkest values of Payne's gray. Where was I? One beacon of light drew my glazed-over eyes.

With only the moon above lighting the room, I raised my head to orient myself. Pain shot through my neck. At first I thought I was in a smoke-filled room, but then I remembered the fog. It was thinner now, in the first stages of lifting. I lay back on the tree, my spine against the trunk. Gritting my teeth, I turned my head and glanced down.

A black blob in the treetops below me. A vulture? Then I remembered. Barbara's body. Impaled on the gunite trees. One of its unyielding limbs had passed completely through her chest. Tigers. I remembered tigers. Yana. Where was Yana? And Kiara?

I struggled to sit up. Every muscle in my body screamed NO. An irritated growl sent me upright in spite of the pain. The floor, covered with glass shards, sparkled below me. Off in the corner Yana mounted

Kiara's back, his teeth gripping the ruff of her neck. Something told me they wouldn't mind if I left.

It was all I could do to lift myself into an upright position. My head ached worse than the worst hangover. But I was alive.

I mentally traced a path of escape for myself. From the top of the tree I could reach the open skylight. But where would I go once I reached the roof? I shuddered to think.

Plan two was to follow the limbs of the banyan tree in a circular path until I made contact with the man-made rocks protruding from the wall behind the waterfall. That route would lead me to the walkway.

My fists tightened around a tree branch. I took a deep breath and somehow found the same lack of fear I'd known as a child. I lunged for a higher branch and grabbed on. I clung to the limb, feet dangling high above the tigers' heads. But they were preoccupied, uninterested in me.

My legs flailed as I shimmied along the branch, but I kept a firm grip. I swung my right leg up and hooked onto another stony arm. My arms and legs ached like they hadn't ached since doing the bird's nest on the rings during gym class—right before I fell to the mat on my stomach. I blocked the memory quickly.

I stretched my legs from the tree to the rocky ledge against the wall. It was still wet and slippery from the waterfall. When I felt my feet were firm on the ledge, I pushed off from the tree. I rested until I got my breath back, then edged along the wall. My cheek scraped against the wet, rough rock. My fingernails scratched for a hold in the concrete surface of the man-made rocks. Finally I reached a series of steplike ledges with ferns growing from them. I braced myself against the gunite rocks and started to climb. If I could just get up several more feet, I'd be able to reach the walkway. I worked my way up three steps and took a deep breath.

Using one of the hemp vines that dangled from the rocks, I pulled my body past the damaged bamboo railing. I stood safely at last on the walkway.

52

IT WAS THE SUNDAY BEFORE CHRISTMAS, BUT NOT enough time had passed for me to come to terms with the events of last autumn. I still wore a whiplash collar and a back brace and on bad days my leg ached unrelentingly. Most of the factual questions had been answered: the hows, the whens, the wheres. But the whys still troubled me. Maybe they always would.

The insurance company had come through with compensation for my studio. I planned to rebuild in the spring. There was no rush. I hadn't even touched my paints since Barbara's death.

Work had always been my salvation, my rescuer, but not this time. There were too many memories attached. Memories of Tony, as well as Barbara, haunted me. I considered other occupations, a job with a predetermined destination in mind. Bus driver? Cabbie? Maybe I'd replace that slimeball George and take over his job as elevator operator. Except the building was no longer mine.

The Chirico family had dropped their objections to the settlement of the estate, but I doubted if Vince and I would ever reconcile. The terms of Tony's trust called for too big a sacrifice, so I turned the money down like Ellen had. People told me I was crazy, and maybe they were right. Maybe Ellen and I were both a little too independent for our own good. But I wouldn't spend my life doing what I hated—not even for three million dollars. And Ellen wouldn't change her name to Chirico.

But Tony had left us a third option that made our decisions easier to live with. When Ben Rudolph returned from his honeymoon, he helped us set up a trust fund similar to the Worthington-Bentley trust but on a smaller scale. Ellen and I were joint trustees. The interest from the trust would be made available at our discretion in the form of grants to further the study and preservation of endangered species.

The future of Fox Valley Zoo remained questionable. Legally the Worthington-Bentley trust could not be denied them. Public opinion and that of the zoo community was another thing. So they had funding if not much else. A committee was organized and chaired by Ellen on how to prevent what had happened from recurring, and she had lectured before other zoo societies on the topic. Miles Crandall had been fired, and a nationwide search for a new director was in progress. Ellen was reconsidering the job of curator of mammals, but she wanted to stay in a "hands-on" position with the animals.

As for the residents of Fox Valley Zoo, the sad truth was that other zoos didn't want them. They just didn't have the room to spare at the expense of better specimens. Barb had been right about that. So at the very least, keeping the zoo open gave them a place to live out their lives, relatively well cared for. There was no way Fox Valley would become an accredited zoo anytime soon. But if enough people cared and got involved, they might be able to turn it around. Even Marcia Wilhelm had stepped forward with some reasonable suggestions.

And Kiara? Well, the thing that Barb had most wanted to prevent had actually happened because of her actions that night. Kiara was pregnant and would give birth to two cubs in the new year. The gene for whiteness would continue. But it remained undetermined whether Kiara would produce a white cub herself.

And since Yana was a healthy Siberian—Barb had seen to that when she acquired him—the infusion of fresh blood at least increased the probability that the hybrid cubs would be healthy, if not genetically pure. Barb's intentions had been good, and probably right, but the way she'd gone about it—and the lives she'd taken in the process, both animal and human—had been so wrong.

Blowing snow across the sidewalks, the wind whipped outside the arched church windows. The snowflakes, though tiny, were starting to accumulate. But I didn't care. I had nowhere to go.

I opened a bottle of Chardonnay, ignited the gas fireplace, and turned on the FM station. Elvis sang "Blue Christmas." Spooky—the name I'd given the white kitten—settled on the footstool in front of me as we admired the tree Ellen had helped me put up the day before. Not many residences could accommodate a fifteen-foot tree. The reflections of multicolored Christmas bulbs danced in the fish-eye lenses of Spooky's eyes. I was just dozing off when the phone rang.

"How you feeling?" the male voice asked.

"Sleepy." I sipped the wine. Life was basically good, as long as animals, wine and toasty fireplaces existed. "Where are you?"

"Getting ready to leave. Just wanted to say good-bye. I was afraid you wouldn't talk to me."

"Life's too short to carry grudges," I said.

"Look, I know I blew it. I wanted to tell you the truth, but I also didn't want to lose you. I am getting a divorce."

"It doesn't matter now, Jake."

"I know, I just—" He sighed. "I'm taking a leave of absence from the agency. At their suggestion, in fact. The FBI and the DEA claimed we could have really messed up their sting."

"So you're taking the flak."

"Aw, hell, it'll die down. The end result is what counts. The ranch has been shut down permanently. The government confiscated the land. The law may not always be perfect, Caroline, but it's all we've got."

"So where are you going?"

"I don't know. I just gassed up the old Blazer."

"Blizzard's comin' in from the west." The subject of weather is a relationship barometer. When the two of you are reduced to talking forecasts, it's clear a cold winter lays ahead in more ways than one.

"Guess I'll head east then, and try to stay ahead of it. Can I call you?"

"I'd rather you didn't." My throat was tightening, but I knew a clean break was best.

"If I do get my act together, do you think sometime in the future—"

"I don't plan more than a day ahead anymore, Jake. Let's leave it at that."

"The last thing I wanted to do was hurt you," he whispered.

God save me from men who don't want to hurt me. They're the ones that have almost destroyed me. Almost. "You better get started, or you'll get caught in the thick of it," I said, not knowing myself if I was referring to snow or emotions.

"At least I learned one thing," he said. "Next time I meet a woman I like, I'll be square with her from day one."

"I learned something, too," I said.

"What's that?"

"Not to pick up strange men in funeral homes." I laughed weakly, but my voice cracked.

We said so long, and I hung up the phone. One more good-bye. One more loss. I squeezed back the tears, then, realizing there was no one there to see them, I just let them come.

*   *   *

Crying has one benefit at least. It tires you so badly, you finally pass out.

I must have fallen asleep, because when I woke up the snow appeared to be about knee-deep. The sky had that eerie lightness about it that tells you there's still a lot more where that came from. I looked at the clock. It was two in the morning.

I felt rested and, for the first time in months, almost invigorated. I punched the CD player, and the soundtrack from *Dances with Wolves* began. Turning toward the west, I took note of friends I'd ignored for too long. After the fire I had relocated all my salvageable equipment to the opposite end of the house. I crossed the room, passed the communion rail and went up three steps. I had set up my drawing board and easel in the center of the chancel, where the altar had once stood. If that location couldn't inspire me to paint again, no place could.

Out of the corner of my eye sat a jar stuffed with paintbrushes. They looked neglected and worn. Next to them, propped against the wall, leaned a clean stretched canvas. Its pasty white face accused me. *So this is what you gave up three million dollars for,* it said. *For the right to ignore us. Haven't you felt sorry for yourself long enough?*

I crawled over to the art materials on all fours. I pulled a fat round brush out of the jar and ran its bristles across the palm of my hand. The brush had plenty of spring left in it. My eyes reverted to the glaring white face of the canvas.

I closed my eyes. A smile crossed my lips as Tony's voice pounded in my mind: "Never love anything so much you can't give it up." I'd given up the money, because I couldn't give up painting what I loved best—animals. Had I followed Tony's advice or not? What did it matter? It was my decision—the right one for me.

The theme from *Dances with Wolves* resonated from the walls. I opened my eyes and reached over for the blank canvas. I held it at arm's length as I imagined my next painting.

"Yeah, wolves," I said out loud. "That'll work. They're just wild dogs. How dangerous could that be?"

All else passes. Art alone endures.

I grabbed the paintbrushes in my fist and set the canvas on my easel.